\

Henry Romilly

The Punishment of Death

to which is appended his treatise on public responsibility and vote by ballot

Henry Romilly

The Punishment of Death
to which is appended his treatise on public responsibility and vote by ballot

ISBN/EAN: 9783337387419

Printed in Europe, USA, Canada, Australia, Japan

Cover: Foto ©Andreas Hilbeck / pixelio.de

More available books at **www.hansebooks.com**

THE

PUNISHMENT OF DEATH

TO WHICH IS PREFIXED HIS TREATISE ON

PUBLIC RESPONSIBILITY AND VOTE BY BALLOT

By HENRY ROMILLY, M.A.

LONDON
JOHN MURRAY, ALBEMARLE STREET
1886

PREFACE.

Henry Romilly, the author of the following treatise, was the fourth son of Sir Samuel Romilly. He was born October 21, 1805, and died December 25, 1884. His tastes and education inclined him towards the pursuit of literature or jurisprudence, but circumstances prevailed to induce him to engage in that of commerce at Liverpool, where, so long as he remained, he also occupied a seat upon the bench of magistrates.

He married, in 1850, Rosa Gardiner Morris, an American lady, a descendant of the old Quaker settlers of Pennsylvania.

He withdrew from commerce in 1858, and spent the remainder of his life, on a property belonging to him in a retired part of Hereford-

shire, in promoting the welfare of his poorer
neighbours.

His conviction on the subject treated of in
the following pages was not derived from any
authoritative opinion of his father, who—as
appears from a private letter written in 1783,
when he was twenty-six years of age, and was
called to the Bar—considered that capital punishment could not altogether be dispensed with,
but who, at a later period—while death was still
the penalty for stealing property of the value
of one shilling—may have thought the time
unsuited to a discussion whether it should
remain the appropriate punishment for murder
or treason.

It has been thought that the occasion of the
publication of this treatise might be usefully
availed of to recall attention to another, also
written by my brother, on the subject of
'Public Responsibility and the Vote by Ballot,' published in 1865, and subsequently in a
second edition, with an answer to Mr. J. S.
Mill's objections to it, in 1867.

Of this treatise, Mr. Grote, the historian,

and most able and consistent advocate of secret voting at elections for members of the House of Commons, wrote in 1865 as follows :—

'It is an admirable piece of reasoning, and I have read it with the greatest satisfaction as well as instruction. The manner in which Mill's arguments are handled is as good as can be. There are various points of view which are new even to me, much as I reflected on the question in former days.

'The one reform which I care most about is the Ballot, because that connects itself with the full liberty of private judgment, of which, indeed, it is only one exemplification, under peculiar perils and temptations.

'The importance of guarding the full liberty of individual judgment and the expression thereof against the tyranny and persecution of bystanders—often themselves conscientious— appears to me even greater in my old age than it did when I was younger. No man has gone further in upholding this right than John Mill, and that by excellent arguments in his " Essay on Liberty ;" but when I read his arguments

against the Ballot, they really disallow and even
condemn all right of private judgment on the
part of the voter. I know of no two things
more contradictory than the " Essay on Liberty "
and the reasoning against the Ballot.'

This treatise is reprinted at the end of this
volume.

FREDERICK ROMILLY.

CONTENTS.

———◦◦◦———

THE PUNISHMENT OF DEATH.

LETTER I.

You ask me whether it can be right under any conceivable circumstances that a man should be allowed deliberately to put to death a fellow-creature. As regards private persons, the question is easily answered; as regards a Government, not so easily. In regard to private persons, let me put the strongest case it is possible to put. A is doing an enormous amount of mischief in the world which there seems to be no prospect of stopping except by his death. Can B be permitted to put him to death? Clearly not; because if the permission exists in one case it must be extended to other cases, and that would put the lives of men at the absolute disposal of their neighbours, unless a tribunal were set up

B

to decide when the permission was to be granted
and when it was to be withheld. But if such
a tribunal is set up, then it is clearly best to
place the power of life and death exclusively
in the hands of the tribunal, and to withdraw it
altogether from private persons. Accordingly
Governments have, with few exceptions, assumed a power over the lives of their subjects,
and have endeavoured by adequate punishments
to prevent private persons from encroaching on
it. A Government assuming such a power must
begin by asking itself this question : What
limitations must we place upon the exercise of
the power of life and death ? If there were no
limitation, no man living in that society could
ever feel his life secure. He could scarcely be
said to be better off than if his life were at the
mercy of his fellow-subjects, for nothing could
be much worse than to be liable to be brought
before a tribunal on a general charge, not confined
within very strictly defined limits, of unfitness
longer to retain life. If a man's general course
of living were liable to be investigated with the
possibility of any such practical conclusion as

this, his life would be one of constant alarm and uncertainty. Accordingly all Governments, which have not been mere vulgar despotisms, have invariably restricted their power over the lives of their subjects to the case of strictly defined acts, to be proved by conclusive evidence. The restriction might of course be carried to the extent of entire abandonment. By a very few Governments in the history of the world the power has in fact been abandoned. Indeed, there are two fundamental objections to the depriving a human being of life which are as applicable to the case of a Government as to that of a private person ; objections so serious that the mere contemplation of them might, one would have supposed, have made Governments hesitate long before they assumed such a power.

The first of these objections is that you cannot take away the life of a criminal without in great measure depriving him of the opportunity of making good his claim to mercy at the hands of another and a higher Tribunal, that Tribunal which will decide his fate in another world. By putting him to death, you are encroaching on a Tribunal immeasurably above your own, in a matter of which you are wholly unfit to judge. I do not, of course, mean that the existence of that Superior Tribunal affords any reason against the application of a system of punishments to the maintenance and protection of civil society ; but I do mean that it is a strong reason against allowing deprivation of life to form one of the punishments under that system. The act so punished is an act which, in the belief of a Christian, would also be punished by that Superior Judge. For it is one part of the Christian creed that acts which men consider wicked in relation to their consequences in this world, will be punished in a world to come ; and it is another part of that creed, that by sorrow for a past offence, accompanied and attested by a subsequent course of virtuous action, atonement may be made for that wicked act, and its punishment by such atonement averted. Now if time is a necessary accompaniment and test of the reality of such repentance —and it is scarcely possible to conceive it to be otherwise—then by putting to a speedy death

the perpetrator of a great crime we are, so far as
we can do so, cutting off from him the opportunity of averting its punishment in another
world ; we are in intention, if not in effect,
arrogantly and cruelly interposing between that
man and his Almighty Judge.

The other fundamental objection is that
which exists to a ruler deliberately doing the
very thing which he professes to look upon
with the strongest feeling of grief, indignation,
and horror when it is done by one of his subjects. It seems to be a plain practical contradiction for a ruler, who professes it as his object
to stimulate by every means in his power the
feeling that human life is sacred, and to preserve, unimpaired, the sentiment of horror for
the act of taking away human life, to follow up
the perpetration of a first deliberate homicide
by the perpetration of a second deliberate homicide. But this is, in truth, what society does
when it sends a murderer to the scaffold. You
may reply that such a contradiction is inseparable from punishment in any shape and in any
degree ; that when you punish you inflict pain

in addition to the pain which has been already inflicted by the offence. True, the infliction of pain is inseparable from all punishment, but a ruler may make choice of the kind of pain which he will inflict. He need not make the pain of the punishment correspond in kind with the pain inflicted by the offence. He lies under no obligation of perpetrating a cruel personal outrage, by way of punishment, on the man who has been convicted of having perpetrated a cruel personal outrage. The ruler who, in his capacity of a punisher of crime, so acts, is not, of course, open to the whole of the same censure as the criminal, but he is open to the censure of encouraging by his example acts which he professes to hold in detestation and horror. When a man perpetrates a murder, he is committing several faults. 1st. He is violating one of the laws of his country. 2nd. He is violating one or more of the great moral laws, the law which forbids revenge and cruelty, or some other. 3rd. He is giving an example of indifference to human life which, if it became general, would bring men down to the level of

wild beasts. 4th. He is usurping the function
of that Being who has bestowed life upon us
as a free gift, and has done nothing to indicate
a permission to men to decide for each other the
duration of that life. Now, when a ruler sends
a criminal to the scaffold, he is not committing
the first nor the second of those faults, but he is
committing the third and the fourth of them ; and
he cannot excuse himself on the plea of necessity,
for he might have chosen a kind of punishment
not open to those grave objections. The punishment which disgraces a man, that which deprives
him of liberty and of the exciting pleasures of
his former life, that which reduces him to the
bare necessaries of existence, or which inflicts
compulsory labour upon him, these punishments
are, singly or in combination, susceptible of
almost any given degree of severity from the
lowest to the highest, and they do not, any of
them, give an indirect sanction to the acts
which they are intended to prevent. That
Governments have seldom or never been alive to
these preliminary objections to the use of capital
punishment—the second of them, indeed, an

objection to the use of all cruel punishments— is a lamentable fact, which is resolvable into that other still more general fact, that Governments have for the most part been quite blind to the important though indirect influence which their situation as leaders of public opinion gives them over the conduct and character of their subjects. It is impossible not to believe that the popular sentiment of the sanctity of human life would be greatly increased if civilised Governments generally took up the position that for no human object whatever, under no circumstances whatever, could it be right for any man, or body of men, invested or not invested with authority over their fellow-men, deliberately to deprive a human being of life.   Unfortunately Governments, so far from being in advance, are generally (through dread of change, and of the trouble and perplexity which change always more or less brings with it) grievously behind their subjects in the appreciation of this matter.   We all know how slowly and reluctantly during the first thirty years of the present century English judges and legislators were, so to speak, driven by the yearly increasing hostility of prosecutors, jurors, witnesses, and the general public to abandon a system which affixed the punishment of death to offences against private property of a very secondary degree of criminality. Even at this day in England and elsewhere it is almost impossible to get a legislator or a judge to make a fair comparison, or indeed any comparison at all, between the direct benefit arising from the supposed superior efficacy of the death punishment as compared with any other punishment in deterring from murders, and the indirect but widespread mischief arising from the public exhibition of administrators of the law perpetrating deliberate homicides. And yet it is one of the conditions of the proper determination of the question for or against the punishment of death that such a comparison should be made. If any serious doubt can be shown to exist in regard to the superior efficacy of the death punishment as compared with some other practicable punishment as a deterrent from murders, the indirect question to which I have referred

above will, of course, assume a degree of importance in exact proportion to the magnitude of
that doubt. In my letter No. IV. I shall enter
on this question, and shall say something upon
the fear of death as a deterrent from great
crimes.

LETTER II.

In reply to one of the two principal arguments of my first letter you refer me to the following passage in Mr. Mill's speech of April 21, 1868, in the House of Commons, in favour of capital punishment :—

Much has been said of the sanctity of human life and the absurdity of supposing that we can teach respect for life by ourselves destroying it. But I am surprised at the employment of this argument, for it is one which might be brought against any punishment whatever. It is not human life only, not human life as such, that ought to be sacred to us, but human feelings. The human capacity of suffering is what we should cause to be respected, not the mere capacity of existing ; and we may imagine somebody asking how we can teach people not to inflict suffering by ourselves inflicting it. But to this I should answer—all of us would answer—that to deter by suffering from inflicting suffering is not only possible, but the very purpose of penal justice. Does fining a criminal show want of respect for property, or imprisoning him, for personal freedom ? Just as unreasonable is it to think that to take the life of a man who has taken that of another is to show want of regard for human life. We show, on the contrary, most emphatically our regard for it by the adoption of a rule that he who violates that right in another forfeits it for himself, and that, while no other crime that he can commit deprives him of his right to live, this shall.

'The argument,' says Mr. Mill, 'is one which may be brought against any punishment whatever.' It certainly may, but the question is one of degree, and there are important differences between the cases put by Mr. Mill which seem to me to weaken the force of his comparison. There are overruling necessities in some cases which have no existence in others. It is a necessary condition of the maintenance of civil society that Governments should for that purpose take away private property and place restrictions upon personal freedom. Money must be raised, and the performance of certain duties must be enforced, if a country is to be defended from external aggression, or justice administered. But there is no similar necessity for putting men to death. A Government might, without endangering its existence, divest itself of that power ; and some Governments have, in fact, done so.   But if a Government should divest itself of the power of taxation, or abandon all restrictions on personal freedom, society would fall to pieces.   In all cases, without exception, it seems to be the plain duty of a Government to set an example of respect for great principles—for truth, personal freedom, the sanctity of the law, the inviolability of property, the sacredness of human life—by abstaining from all unnecessary infractions of them.   That duty, like all others, may, of course, in certain cases and to a certain extent be overruled by a superior duty, and the first and paramount duty of a Government is to maintain its own existence. No such overruling duty can be said to exist in the case of capital punishment, unless, indeed, it should be proved that without capital punishment all reasonable protection to life is impossible, protection to life being amongst the first and greatest purposes of all Governments.   Such proof would, of course, constitute an overruling necessity ; but in the absence of any such proof, when it is admitted that except as a punishment

for great crimes Governments can have no occasion to put men to death, and when it has
become a matter of controversy whether there
may not be some other and more effectual
punishment for great crimes, the argument in
favour of a Government setting the example of
an inviolable respect for human life must be
allowed to retain considerable force. The
amount of good that a Government does by
setting an example of strict adherence to a great
principle, the degree in which such adherence is
possible, and the degree of weight which attaches
to each of the various circumstances which may
tend to overrule the duty of a Government in
that respect, must of course be considered separately in the case of each of those principles, and
in the case of each particular Government and
country. The benefit of such adherence extends
over so wide a field, is so indirect, and, therefore,
so little capable of being proved by particular
instances, that it is universally underrated by
both peoples and Governments.[1] In the present

---

[1] An instance of this is to be found in the treatment of
Ireland by the Imperial Government on the first occurrence of

instance it is not so much that, as a matter of
fact, the putting criminals to death is, on the
part of the administrators of the law in Great
Britain, accompanied by any want of respect for
human life, as that the exclusion of that punish-

any symptoms of political disaffection in that country. Every
one perceives that a certain danger is imminent, and that to put
an unrestricted power of arrest and imprisonment in the hands
of the Government is the most certain and obvious mode of
meeting that danger ; above all, the easiest mode, the greatest
saving of trouble, and the least strain on the capacity of the
governors. No one thinks for a moment of the mischief of
sowing broadcast amongst the people the impression that Ireland
is not governed with that strict adherence to legality which obtains in other parts of the kingdom, that the system pursued
is more a state of warfare than of civil government, and that if
laws are set aside on one side they may be set aside on the
other. Still less does any one remember that extraordinary
measures of repression are almost sure to create in the public
mind exaggerated impressions of the extent of the disaffection,
leading each particular man to feel that his own disloyalty is
safe in proportion as it is shared by the rest of his countrymen.
Governments, both Whig and Tory alike, have been morbidly
alive to, and have therefore always (as in the case of Fenianism)
exaggerated, the particular danger, and have therefore been
almost entirely blind to the more remote and more indirect—
but not less certain—danger of that frequent deviation from its
own principles of government, and accordingly they have
always, on every occasion of disaffection, been ready to pass
Irish Coercion Bills. History is full of similar mistakes of
Governments. The events in Jamaica, in the autumn of 1866,
after the outbreak at Morant Bay, afford perhaps the most
striking and melancholy instance on record of the blindness to
great principles produced by sudden and exaggerated panic.

ment from our criminal code would extend and strengthen the respect for human life; not so much, perhaps, by preventing murders as by creating a more constant, anxious, and conscientious solicitude for the safety of men's lives amongst the very numerous class of persons engaged in occupations dangerous to life, and a stronger feeling amongst those classes of the criminality of neglect in that respect.

Nothing can be more true than Mr. Mill's observation, that ' the human capacity of suffering is what we should cause to be respected.' The great lesson, embracing within itself all other lessons, which men have to learn is to contribute all they can to the comfort and happiness, and mitigate in all they can the pains and misery, of their fellow-creatures; but I very much doubt whether it is wholesome doctrine to place the respect for human life within this universal law, and think no more about it. There are special temptations to take away life, special temptations to negligence in regard to life, passions of extreme force and suddenness threatening life, all of which require to be specially counteracted; and of the measures of counteraction at the command of rulers I believe that their solemn renunciation for themselves and their subjects of all right to take away life would not be one of the least effective.

In the last sentence of the passage I have quoted, Mr. Mill says that ' rulers show most emphatically their regard for human life by the adoption of a rule that he who violates that right in another forfeits it for himself, and that while no other crime that he can commit shall deprive him of his right to live, this—the wilfully taking away life—shall.' This seems to amount to an affirmation of the desirableness of that quality in punishment which, under various names— characteristicalness, analogy, retaliation—Bentham has described in his treatise on the ' Principles of Penal Law.' He has defined it as being ' that rule which makes an offender suffer an evil similar to that which he has wilfully inflicted; that rule which prescribes in the way of punishment the doing to a delinquent the same hurt he has done to another.' The importance attached to this quality by Bentham,

C

trifling though it be, seems to me to be over-
rated. He says that one great merit of the
law of retaliation is its simplicity, and I think
he might with truth have added, its *only* merit.
Of the other two merits ascribed to retaliatory
punishments—one that they are popular, the
other that they are in a superior degree efficacious—it may, I think, with truth be said that
the popularity, unless deserved, is an evil rather
than a good, and that of the superior efficacy
there is no proof. Bentham observes that ' no
rule will find so easy an entrance into the apprehension, sit so easy on the memory, as the
rule that every offender shall suffer an evil
similar to that which he has inflicted. The
rule,' he says, ' is at once so short and so expressive that he who has once heard it is not
likely to forget it, or ever to think of a crime .
but he must also think of its punishment.' To
this I have only to reply that the association
between a crime and its established punishment,
whatever that punishment may be, is quite
certain enough for all practical purposes, and
that the strength or vividness of the association

will very seldom be increased by making the pain of the punishment correspond with the pain inflicted by the offence. The rule that poisoners shall be hanged is as short and expressive, as likely therefore to dwell in the memory, as the rule that poisoners shall be put to death by poison. ' The idea,' says Mr. Bentham, ' of perishing by the same kind of death which he is preparing for his victim would be peculiarly frightful to the poisoner.' Why so ? The idea of the pain is not made more vivid by the preparations. The sight of a dagger does not give increased force to the idea of the pain of a stab, nor the loading of a pistol to the idea of the pain of a gunshot wound. The act of mixing up poisonous ingredients in a cup, or of putting the cup in the way of the intended victim, will not call up into the mind of the man so acting the particular pains of a death by poison more vividly than the particular pain of a death by hanging. It seems to me to be fanciful in the extreme to suppose that the hand of a sailor who is about to push one of his fellow sailors overboard is more likely to be arrested by the prospect of being himself thrown overboard than by that of being hanged from the yard-arm. Nor, unless it should be proved that death is, on the whole, the most deterrent punishment for murder, can I see any good reason for supposing that the hand of the man who is preparing to take away the life of another is more likely to be arrested by the prospect of losing his own life than by that of any other punishment. If death is more dreaded, it will of course be more deterrent than any other punishment ; but the circumstance that it will inflict upon the murderer a pain similar to that which he is himself about to inflict will not make it more dreaded. He may, besides, have reason to believe that the pain will be very different in the two cases ; he may know that to his intended victim death would be a happy release, and to himself the most terrible of all evils. Or the case may be the very reverse of this ; he may know that he has himself no fear of death, whilst the situation of his intended victim makes it probable that to him it would be a frightful calamity.

Although Bentham has stated the arguments in favour of analogy in punishment very clearly, the following passage proves that he attached but little importance to it. 'If in other respects,' he says, 'any particular mode of punishment be eligible, analogy is an additional advantage; if in other respects it be ineligible, analogy alone is not a sufficient recommendation. The value of this property amounts to very little, because even in the case of murder, other punishments may be devised the analogy of which will be sufficiently striking.' In confirmation of this view of the subject, I would observe of imprisonment for life—which would seem at first sight to have but little analogy with the crime of murder—that if it should be carried, as it ought to be, to the extent of cutting off the murderer completely and to the end of his life from all communication with the external world, including in that term even his own nearest relations, the analogy is close and striking in the very point in which—if in any—analogy may be supposed to be beneficial, and is wanting only in those points in which analogy

cannot but be injurious.   The analogy between
the sudden extinction by death of the worldly
career of the murdered man and the sudden,
forcible, complete, and permanent withdrawal of
the murderer from everything which has hitherto
constituted his worldly career by life imprisonment, is quite sufficiently obvious and striking
to produce upon the public mind any beneficial
effects which may be supposed to be derivable
from similarity between the suffering produced by
the punishment and that inflicted by the criminal. The reproduction of the horrible and revolting details of a sudden death by violence may be
calculated in a still greater degree to strike the
imagination, and may thus in a still greater degree flatter the popular fondness for retaliation,
and satisfy the popular idea of retributive justice ;
but whatever advantage—if any, which I must
be allowed to deny—there may be in this, it can
be obtained only at the expense of evils by
which it will be much more than counter-
balanced ; for it is difficult to conceive anything more hurtful to the feeling of popular
respect for legally constituted authority than

that which associates the administrators of the law with acts of extreme violence; which allows the revolting incidents of such acts to form one of the chief links whereby the criminal and the officers of justice are connected with each other in the public mind.[2]

Montesquieu—so says M. Dumont—has given the authority of his name to this doctrine of ana-logy between the offence and the punishment, but his arguments ('Esprit des Lois,' Book XII. cap. 4) are vague and weak in a degree which is really surprising. A man who commits sacri-lege, he says, should be punished by deprivation of all the advantages given by religion. But if, as is highly probable, the person committing that offence is wanting in the sense of religion, this deprivation will not only not be the most deterrent punishment, but will scarcely be de-terrent in any degree.

[2] One of the most curious and instructive facts in modern societies is the sort of moral and social blight which attaches to the executioner of criminals condemned to death by the laws of the country; for if the punishment be such as to deserve our respect and approbation, the office is in a high degree useful and honourable. No such obloquy rests upon the officer carry-ing out any other description of punishment.

It seems to me that there is only one case in which it might be useful to aim at analogy between an offence and its punishment, the case in which the offender has given proof of thoughtlessness, of want of appreciation of the fact that by his conduct he has been inflicting pain on others. Nothing tends more to cure children of cruelty than suffering of the same kind as that which, from mere thoughtlessness, they have been inflicting on others, and the same remark applies more or less to persons of all ages.

LETTER III.

BEFORE I say anything on the question of the deterrent efficacy of capital punishment, I wish to express my dissent from an opinion which has been given by many of the witnesses examined before the Capital Punishment Commission of 1864-5, to the effect that the fear of punishment generally has little or no influence in preventing great crimes. When a man is meditating the commission of a great crime, say they, the passion by which he is hurried on neutralises all other considerations. He contrives to shut out from his mind everything which could interfere with his design, and never, in fact, enters into any serious calculation of consequences. This is probably in the main a correct view of the matter. The explanation of it is that all very strong passions are, by the constitution of the human mind, absorbing. They occupy for the time the entire mind. Whilst under the influence of anger, lust, or fear, a man seems for the moment to have lost the use of his reason. This proves but little, however, against the deterrent force of the fear of punishment, which operates at times when men are *not* under the influence of strong passions, and operates exactly in the same way as other deterrent motives, not so much in preventing some particular act when a man has arrived at the point of seriously meditating the commission of that act, as in forming within him a habit of mind which prevents him from ever arriving at that point. A habit of mind may be so strengthened by the frequent recurrence of the thoughts in which it originated as to end by being perfectly effectual in preventing a man from ever finding himself face to face with an intended crime, great or small.

Suppose the case of a perfectly selfish man, one whose sole ultimate principle of conduct is his own pleasure or advantage. It may have occurred to his mind hundreds or thousands of times in the course of his life that if the whole

of the consequences—possible, probable, and certain—of a great crime, whether in the shape
of legal punishment, the fear of detection, the
trouble of keeping up contrivances to prevent
detection, the aversion of his fellow-men if he
should be suspected, the mere stings of conscience, are fairly valued and set against any
possible personal advantages to be derived from
the perpetration of the crime, these latter would
be purchased at too high a price, ' que le jeu,' to
use the French expression, ' ne vaudrait pas la
chandelle.' The effect of such thoughts occur-
ring more or less frequently at times when he is
not under the influence of any strong passion or
temptation is to produce a habit of mind which
(although the man may be altogether wanting
in moral principle, and thoroughly impervious
to any motive arising out of genuine regard for
the welfare of his fellow-creatures) may yet
carry him respectably through life, and may
make it a matter of moral impossibility that he
should ever commit a great crime. Eliminate
one of its chief elements, that of legal punishment, from this oft-repeated calculation, and

who can doubt that the safety-valve will be seriously weakened, and great crimes will increase in number. This is a matter which can only be decided *à priori*. Experience affords but slender means of estimating the efficacy of deterrents, for the world hears only of the cases in which the passion or temptation has been too strong for the habit of mind formed by the deterrents, the cases in which the crime has in fact been carried out. It hears nothing of the cases in which the deterrents have got the better of the temptation, and the perpetration of the crime has been prevented.

What does the world know of the Palmers whose hands have been arrested by feelings produced in great part by the fear of punishment? There may have been, for aught we know to the contrary, ten such men for every one who has carried out his iniquitous design.

LETTER IV.

THAT the fear of punishment is, on the whole, much more efficacious in preventing crime than the witnesses before the Commission on Capital Punishment, to whom I referred in my last letter, suppose, I have no doubt ; but that question has no very important bearing on the question to which I now propose to address myself, viz., the comparative efficacy of death and of perpetual imprisonment as deterrents from great crimes, and especially from the crime of murder.   I say *perpetual imprisonment*, because I admit that, before I go any further, I am bound to reply to the question which the advocates of capital punishment are entitled to ask as the preliminary to any discussion on their part with those who are opposed to their system.   To that question, ' If the punishment of death should be abolished, what punishment will you substitute for it?' there seems to me to be only one answer, that which is, in fact, given to it by the great majority of the advocates of abolition examined by the Commission, viz., imprisonment for the remainder of the offender's life. Imprisonment contains some valuable qualities as a punishment which no other punishment contains, and to these I shall refer hereafter, but the most important point is, that if perpetual, it contains, in an equal degree with death, the one great quality which constitutes the special deterring efficacy of that latter punishment, viz., that it cuts off entirely and for ever the *worldly*[1] career of the offender. One thing may, with scarcely an exception, be affirmed of a murderer, whether the motive of his crime has been gain, or anger, or a sexual passion, viz., that he is a man pursuing worldly interests with intense ardour ; and if at one single blow you can annihilate those interests, leaving him with not an atom of hope of their renewal, by substituting for them that monotonous, wearisome round of unexciting events

---

[1] I use the word 'worldly' in the sense of world to a man moving about freely in it.

which make up the life of the interior of a prison, you are in truth cutting off that man's worldly career, in any sense which he is disposed to attach to the word, almost as completely as if you deprived him of life.

Another quality of death as the punishment of murder which constitutes one of its chief recommendations, although it has not very often been referred to by speakers or writers on the subject, is one which is possessed in an equal degree by perpetual imprisonment—I mean the protection it affords to society against a repetition of the outrages of the individual offender. Society may justly insist upon receiving this protection ; and the point is more important than might at first be supposed, for when a man has once shown by his conduct that he is one of those who pursue their own pleasures or interests with an intensity of selfish ardour so great as to make them indifferent even to the lives of other men, there can be no sufficient security, except that of physical incapacity, that one murderous outrage will not be followed by others. One of the great evils of abolishing the punishment of death—if some punishment should be substituted for it which should, under any circumstances whatever, after any lapse of time whatever, end in the offender being again let loose upon society—is the feeling of insecurity which would thereby be produced. Against this evil, against the dread of having a Burke or a Müller moving once more freely about amongst them, cost what it may, the public must be protected, and perpetual imprisonment would be as effectual a protection as death. But the imprisonment must be perpetual in fact as well as in name.[2] No allegation however strong of altered habits, of heart-felt repentance, of amended life, should be allowed, on so vital a point, to interfere with the one great duty to society. These feelings may be, and frequently are, feigned, and when backed

[2] Mr. Bentham (in Book II. part ii. of his *Principles of Penal Law*) observes that even in the case of the most dangerous description of homicide, assassination for lucre—a crime proceeding from a disposition which puts indiscriminately the life of every man into immediate jeopardy—the danger is not so great as from madmen who are restrained by none of the considerations which influence ordinary malefactors, and yet that, in the case of madmen, confinement is found sufficient to give to society the necessary security against further mischief from the same individual.

up by frequent professions of a deep sense of
religion, they may, however insincere, be played
off upon gaolers, chaplains, and magistrates
with such skill as to baffle all the vigilance and
penetration even of a very acute mind.   Indeed,
the sincerity of the prisoner himself is no sufficient safeguard.   He may deceive himself in his
estimate of the trustworthiness of newly formed
principles and amended habits, and, leaving the
prison with a very real wish to lead a good
life in the world to which he returns, his virtuous intentions may, at the end of no very long
time, break down under the influence of temptations which, not having for a long time been
tested, he falsely believed to have lost all power
over him.

The advocates of capital punishment usually
dispose of the question by a short and simple
dilemma.   By universal consent, they say, anything short of perpetual imprisonment in substitution of death as the punishment for murder
would be insufficient, but in practice perpetual
imprisonment is an impossibility.

I have nothing to say against the first of

D

these propositions, and what I have to say against the second of them I will defer for the present, observing only in the meantime that all the greatest reforms in human affairs have been brought about by steady perseverance in the doing of old-established impossibilities.

LETTER V.

ON the question of the comparative efficacy of capital punishment and imprisonment for life in deterring from murders, there is little or nothing in the way of direct experience to guide us. Judges, advocates, gaolers, gaol chaplains, and all persons whose duties bring them into personal contact with criminals, have for the most part concluded, from their observation of the demeanour of criminals, that there is no punishment comparable to that of death in the terror which it inspires. But their experience scarcely touches the real point at issue. It is defective in both the things which have to be compared. It tells us nothing as regards one of those things, and it tells us something which we know already, but of which the knowledge is of no use to us in regard to the other. Of the terror inspired by the prospect of imprisonment for life nothing can be known from experience, because, as a practical reality, as anything more than a verbal threat not intended to be carried into execution, it has no existence in our criminal system.   Until perpetual imprisonment as the punishment of murder shall have been rigidly carried out for such a length of time as practically to exclude from the minds of persons under temptation to commit murder all hope of relaxation in their particular case, we cannot be said to have any direct experience in the matter. The evidence of judges, gaolers, gaol chaplains, &c., to the effect that death is the most terrifying of all the punishments of which they have any experience, may quite be trusted as far as it goes, but it, unfortunately, does not go far enough to throw much light on the subject of the desirableness or otherwise of capital punishment, for it is confined to the period intervening between arrest and execution ; and what we want to know is, what degree of terror is inspired by the prospect of death upon the scaffold, before a crime has been perpetrated, before it has been finally determined on, before it has suggested itself to the mind as a practical possibility. The various and striking forms in which terror exhibits itself on the deck of a sinking ship affords little or no material for judging of the degree in which the dangers of the sea deter men from sea voyages ; and the trifling difference between the wages of mining and of other kinds of coarse labour does afford proof that danger to human life when remote and uncertain is not an element of very great weight in determining human conduct. No doubt the fear of the death punishment, as of all punishment, operates more or less at *all* times, and it may be said by those who bring their personal experience to bear upon this question, that if death has more terror for a criminal than any other punishment at one time, it must have so at another ; that if it be the most terrifying of all punishments after sentence,[1]

[1] That death, after sentence, is more terrifying than imprisonment for life, after sentence, is not—in the absence of all experience of the latter punishment as a practical reality—capable of proof from direct experience ; but I have little doubt that experience, if it were not wanting, would prove it to be so. Death, to be carried out in the course of a few days or weeks, would, I believe, in nineteen cases out of twenty, be much more terrifying than life imprisonment to commence at the end of the same number of days or weeks.

it will be the most terrifying, and therefore the
most deterrent, of all punishments before the
commission of the offence, and that the difference
—be it great or small—between the fear of pain
when the pain is almost certain and near at
hand, and when it is remote or uncertain, is as
applicable to imprisonment as to death. That
if death be more dreaded than imprisonment
when the crime has been brought home to the
perpetrator, and he is about to undergo his
punishment, it will also be more dreaded than
imprisonment at the time when the idea of perpetrating the crime first enters his mind. That
this may at all events be assumed as true in the
absence of proof of its falsehood. There is little
to be said, as I have already shown, from direct
experience either in proof or in disproof of this
view of the matter. The subject is one on
which, in the absence of such experience, we
are in a great measure driven to *à priori* reasoning; but it is a great mistake to suppose that
à priori reasoning in such cases is necessarily
inconclusive. Universal observation may have
proved to us the truth of certain principles of

human nature, which may serve as the stepping-stones to a conclusion quite as certain as any which could be derived from direct experience.

Now the weak point of death as a deterrent, in all cases, is our constant familiarity with the thought that being absolutely certain sooner or later the time of its occurrence is altogether uncertain. Whatever the terrors of death may be when it seems to be near and certain, it has no terrors for men in their ordinary condition of health and occupation. Indeed, if it were otherwise, if the possibility of a death close at hand were constantly present to men's minds, not only would all the enjoyments of life be poisoned, but all its practical utility would be undermined. No human being has ever existed whose path has not been constantly beset with the risk of death in an endless variety of forms, and originating in an endless variety of causes. There is not a single moment, from the beginning of his life to the end, when something may not occur from disease, accident, or the hostility of other men which shall be the commencement of a process ending more or less rapidly in death. But the human mind has been so constituted that the absence of all power of foresight in regard to the time, the form, and the proximate cause of the event deadens all fear of the event itself, and men go about their business in life as perfectly insensible to all fear of its being brought to a sudden termination as though it had been ordained by nature that life in this world should never end, or should be of a certain minimum duration. It is one of those elements of the mental constitution implanted in us by the Almighty, for which we have most cause to be grateful ; for if we had been differently constituted, life would have been a constant torment.

A man takes a railway journey. He know that people occasionally lose their lives by railway accidents. How is it that his journey is not poisoned by the fear of any such consequence to himself ? The reason is that so many of the other actions of his life involved similar risks, and that if each particular case be taken separately the risk is very small. If he allows himself to be agitated by fear of accident on a railway, why not on board a steamboat, or in going up a ladder, or in riding or driving, or shooting, or sleeping in an inn bed of which the sheets may be damp, or in eating his dinner, which accident or malice may have made a vehicle of poison.   The number and variety of events which involve these small risks of death is so great that if in all of them he gave way to fear, he would scarcely be at peace for five minutes together during the whole of his life.   The result is that he gives way to fear in none of them, and habit soon enables him to pass through life altogether undisturbed by any fears except those of some danger of the imminence and deadliness of which he has palpable evidence.

If death by drowning were the only death which they were subject to, men would hesitate seriously before they would commit themselves to a ship ; but what is the chance of a death by drowning added to the innumerable chances of deaths from other causes which already hang over our heads?   No such hesitation accordingly is ever felt.   So the chance of losing his life upon the scaffold is only one more added to the numberless chances of deaths from other causes which hang over the criminal.

Whatever effect the fear of death generally may have upon his conduct, it will not increase it in any great degree to add death upon the scaffold to the other forms of death which already threaten him.[2]

It may be said that death upon the scaffold will present itself with force to his imagination as the direct and natural consequence of the particular act which he is meditating. But human life is full of deliberate acts of which the same thing may with equal truth be said. The sailor, the miner, the railway engine-driver, the soldier, the physician, and many others, are constantly, of their own free will, without one instant's hesitation, placing themselves in situations which are, not in a very trifling degree, dangerous to human life. I have myself seen three men embark in an open boat for a promised pecuniary reward of no great magnitude to row

---

[2] Except in so far as death upon the scaffold brings with it certain pains which would not accompany other forms of death —disgrace, more intense grief and unhappiness to relations and friends, &c.

a distance of less than a quarter of a mile with a chance which no one could better estimate than they could, certainly not exceeding one chance of life against one of death, and I saw two of those men struggling hopelessly for life within five minutes of that deliberate act of theirs. Hundreds of men, workers in a coal mine, are, as we all know, after an explosion ready to descend at a moment's notice into the bottom of the mine at the most imminent risk of their lives, if there is the smallest hope of their rescuing one single fellow-workman. It may be said that these examples only prove that the noble and generous impulse which fills the breast of good men (the physician or the minister of religion, for example, who goes into a focus of deadly infection to administer comfort to a fellow-creature) is stronger than the fear of death, and proves nothing against the reality and strength of that fear. But then it must be remembered that in this question of capital punishment it is also the relative, not the positive, strength of the fear of death which is the material consideration ; and when the case comes to be applied to the man who is meditating the commission of a great crime, it is unfortunately only too certain that the bad passions are at least as strong as the good ones ; quite as likely, therefore, to get the better of the fear of death.

Another cause detracting from the efficacy of capital punishment is this, that in the opinion of the world—the bad portion of it equally with the good—a certain disgrace attaches to the fear of death.   The man who avows that the thought of death is a frequent source of uneasiness to him is generally despised.   Such a feeling is considered a weakness.   It was so considered by the friends of Dr. Johnson, and would, I have little doubt, have been so considered by the associates of Thurtell.   A man in a violent storm at sea, or in any situation involving danger to life, knows so well that the betrayal of any striking signs of fear would lower him in the estimation of the persons by whom he is surrounded, that, from that cause alone, he will make the strongest efforts to repress any such feelings.   That the profession of being superior to the fear of death may, in some cases, be

affected, and in others may be little more than
a knack of keeping the mind hermetically sealed
to painful thoughts, is, I dare say, true, but this
does not affect my argument. The important
point is certain, viz., that all men, good or bad,
are a good deal influenced in their professions
by the expressed opinions and feelings—whether
real or affected—of other men ; and if in their
professions, then also in their conduct. There
can scarcely be habitual profession without
more or less of the reality. The habitual profession of indifference to death will tend in some
not very trifling degree to produce the reality of
that indifference. The consciousness that he is
palming off upon his associates feelings which
have no real existence within his breast is
always painful to a man ; and if the desire to
stand well with his associates leads him to
speak lightly of the prospect of death, he will
constantly, as a mere relief to himself, be making
more or less of an effort to think lightly of it,
and it is difficult to believe that those efforts
will be altogether inoperative.

From the above considerations it does not

of course absolutely follow that death may not still, on the whole, be the most deterrent of all punishments, but those considerations do make it plain that there are certain elements of weakness detracting from its efficacy as a deterrent which have no existence in other punishments. Mankind has no feeling of contempt for a man who is terrified at the prospect of imprisonment, and the association between the crime and its punishment is much closer, much more difficult to exclude from the mind when the punishment is imprisonment for life, than when it is death.   When imprisonment is the threatened punishment, the association which is formed in the mind of the criminal is between the pain of the punishment as the consequence, and his own criminal act as the one only possible cause; whereas, when the threatened punishment is death, the association is between the pain [3] of the punishment and his own criminal act, as one out of a great number and variety of possible causes, for death may fall upon a man from

---

[3] To speak with perfect accuracy, I ought to say the *principal part* of the pain.

innumerable causes wholly unconnected with his misconduct. But the efficacy of the association as a deterrent will be weakened in exact proportion to the number and variety of the circumstances which may by possibility lead to the same painful consequence. A man meditating a crime punishable with death may be supposed to reason thus with himself: ' I am constantly doing things which are dangerous to human life; why, then, should I hesitate at this thing? The world despises a man who fears death. The world admires a man who meets death with courage, admires a man who does not allow the fear of death to divert him from his purpose. If, on the one hand, it is disgraceful to be punished, on the other hand it is honourable to die with calmness and resolution. There is nothing fine or honourable to be set against the disgrace of going to a prison.'

Disgrace is no doubt common to all punishments; but when a man dies on the scaffold there is a counterpoise to the disgrace in the admiration excited by his firmness; and there is no such counterpoise when a man goes off in the prison van to be immured in a cell. It is idle to say, in reply to this, that the bravery a man exhibits on the scaffold is not deserving of admiration, and that, instead of making the fact of that admiration the foundation of an objection to the punishment of death, we ought to set ourselves to destroy that false sentiment of honour. Whether false or not, it exists, and we must deal with it. But it is not altogether false. It *is* better to meet a deserved punishment with firmness than with weakness. The firmness is a great quality which, under more favourable circumstances, might have made this delinquent a noted benefactor of his race. It is not in human nature to be insensible to an exhibition of power in the endurance of extreme pain, mental or bodily. I do not deny that the fortitude which should endure many successive years of imprisonment and its attendant hardship and privations without a murmur is more worthy of admiration than the spasmodic fortitude which enables a man, during the half-hour immediately preceding his execution, to preserve his features unmoved, his voice unaltered, and his steps unshaken ; but upon nine men out of ten the half-hour's fortitude on the scaffold will tell a thousand times more than the twenty years' fortitude within the prison walls. To admiration of the twenty years' fortitude within the prison walls minds not of the highest and rarest order would be wholly insensible. There are thousands of men who, after witnessing an execution, or even after reading a narrative of it, might say to themselves, 'This man has committed a barbarous murder, but, after all, he is a fine fellow,' and would have been utterly incapable of making any kind of moral estimate of his daily and hourly conduct during twenty consecutive years of a prison life. The idea of one man within the prison walls being different from another man within the prison walls will never enter their imagination. They will understand perfectly that the prison life would be a cutting off of all the pleasures of the present life, but as a stage for the exercise of heroism deserving the admiration of the world it will be unintelligible to them. Nor if perpetual imprisonment were rightly administered could they ever know of it.

E

LETTER VI.

I PROPOSE in the following letter to go on with the subject of the efficacy of the fear of death as compared with that of perpetual imprisonment as the punishment of great crimes. I have already referred to the opinion expressed by many of our most distinguished criminal judges that death is the most terrifying of all punishments, an opinion formed chiefly on their observation of the demeanour of great criminals when upon their trial. I have shown that the opinion, however well founded, is unfortunately not very pertinent to the question of the deterrent efficacy of capital punishment, for however great and undoubted the terror, it unfortunately comes too late to be of any use—after the commission of the offence and not before it.

No spectacle is so likely to lead to false conclusions as that of a man who is absolutely at your mercy, and who knows that you are either actually signing his death-warrant, or in a certain event which he perceives to be in a very high degree probable, will do so. The paroxysms of anxiety and fear suffered by a man in that situation afford little or no ground of inference in regard to the power of the fear of death over men placed in circumstances of a totally different kind. A man who is paralysed with fear when he lies helpless at your feet might be capable of rushing into action wholly undisturbed by such fear if he were a free agent, even though death were as probable and as near in the latter case as in the former. I do not say that this is true of all men, but innumerable examples of men voluntarily placing themselves in circumstances of danger deadly and imminent —some of which I have already cited—prove that it is true of a large proportion of mankind ; and if so, it is little likely to be false of the man meditating the commission of a great crime, whose impression in regard to death as the consequence of his act is that it is neither very near nor very probable.

A man will of course be much more violently
affected by the near prospect of a punishment of
which the entire and direct pain is to be concentrated within the space of half an hour, than
by that of a punishment of which the direct
pain is to be spread over many thousands or tens
of thousands of half hours.   The near approach
of the latter punishment is that only of the first
weeks or days of it, but the near approach
of the former is that of the punishment in its
entirety.   Let me apply to the illustration of
this point the analogous case of a reward.   Conceive, for the sake of argument, a pleasure of the
most intense kind to begin and terminate in the
course of a single day.   The near approach of
that pleasure would affect a man with a much
more exuberant joy than the near approach of
some pleasure which should be much less intense although of much greater duration.   Let
me suppose the case of a man who has rendered
some great service to his country.   Say that his
reward is to consist of a public ceremonial, in
the course of which honours are to be showered
on his head in the sight of his assembled coun-

trymen. His courage, his benevolence, or his wisdom are to be proclaimed to the world in the midst of the shouts of admiring multitudes, and of the sympathy and approval of all that is best and noblest in the country. The sensations of that man on the day preceding the one on which his public triumph is to take place will, of course, be very different from those which he would have experienced on the day preceding that on which he should have received the first half-yearly payment of a pension for life if that had been the allotted reward of his services. Any one who understands the difference between the feelings and signs of joy of two men under the influence of those two different kinds of reward will also understand the difference between the feelings and signs of grief and terror of two men, of whom one is in the course of a few days to be publicly put to death, and the other is to be conveyed to a prison, there to spend the remainder of his life. Give a man the choice between these two punishments on the day immediately preceding the proposed execution, and the probability is as ten to one that he will choose the prison. Give him the same choice twelve months before the sentences are to be carried out, and it is an even chance that he will choose the scaffold. It is the same with all cruel punishments; indeed with all punishments of which the whole of the pain is concentrated within a very short space of time. Give a man the option between receiving three years hence thirty lashes or a year's imprisonment, and he might choose the former; give him the same option, the punishment to begin immediately, and he will go to prison. The conclusion seems to me to be inevitable that the prospect of death on the scaffold is greatly more terrifying than the prospect of imprisonment for life during the short period intervening between arrest and execution, but that this affords no ground of inference whatever in regard to the comparative terrifying powers of the two punishments before the commission of the offence, where the comparison would be undisturbed by any dread of intense pain close at hand.

From what precedes I conclude that the opinion (referred to by me at p. 37) is erroneous which assumes that death on the scaffold is more terrifying than imprisonment for life in the same proportion before the commission of the offence and after arrest ; on the contrary, it seems to me certain that pain which is intense and of short duration will terrify proportionally more when near at hand, and proportionally less when remote and uncertain, than pain which is less intense but of longer duration.

LETTER VII.

I NOW come to what seems to me to be the most serious of the objections to the punishment of death as a deterrent from great crimes, and I must observe that it is an objection which in no degree applies to imprisonment for life. The objection is, that the circumstances which unavoidably attend its practical application are such as to excite the sympathy of the public in favour of the perpetrator of the crime, and thereby seriously to impair the efficacy of the punishment as an example. The administrators of the law in England, from the highest to the lowest, from the judge to the turnkey, seem to labour under a frightful consciousness that the punishment is too terrible to be carried out with that cold, unmoved inflexibility which is the proper demeanour of a magistrate and his officers when they are executing a just and

necessary law required for the protection of
society against the criminal assaults of its
enemies. It is in truth not in human nature
to be cold and unmoved when the business on
hand is the taking away the life of a fellow-
creature. The human heart rebels against it,
and relieves itself by acts of personal consideration, of kindness, of tenderness almost, for the
criminal, which, in so far as they are known to
the world outside—and to a great extent they
must be known—can operate only in one way,
that is, to excite the public sympathy in his
favour. Mr. Justice Shee, in his evidence before
the Capital Punishment Commission, amongst
other suggestions for the mitigation of the evils
of capital punishment, recommends that the
treatment of criminals under capital sentence
should be in the highest degree kind and gentle,
and avowedly directed to the end of preparing
them for death ; that it should be such as to
soften their hearts and dispose them to repentance and resignation. But certainly no such
recommendation was needed. Nothing under
our system of capital punishment can be more

kind and gentle than the treatment received by
convicted murderers under sentence of death.
As a matter of fact it is so, and it is not in
human nature that it should be otherwise. It
is attended with very injurious consequences,
but it is inevitable.   People of average humanity,
professing a religion of which one of the principal doctrines is that of a future state of rewards
and punishments, who are about to deprive of
life a man whose soul is charged with a horrible
crime, are driven, as a mere relief to their feelings, to use every possible method of persuasion
in order to draw from him such expressions of
penitence as may suffice to satisfy them that
they are not going to kill body and soul together.   But all this tenderness lavished upon
convicted murderers, and paraded before the
public—as, by the aid of the Press, it invariably
is—tends, of course, to mitigate those feelings
of disgust and abhorrence for great crimes which
it should be the endeavour of society, by every
means in its power, to stimulate.   The holding
up to us a malefactor of the very worst kind as
a proper object of compassionate interest is not

the only evil.   Another, and perhaps a greater, evil is the suggesting to us that an offence which an earthly tribunal has just pronounced to be unpardonable is, by a perfectly just and wise Judge, and by virtue of a certain number of professions of penitence, the genuineness of which there is no time to submit to any real test, likely to be pardoned.   Nothing is less to be desired than that the judge and officers of human tribunals should publicly enter upon the question of the probable fate, at the hands of the Almighty Judge, of offenders against human laws.   Their sole function is to protect society by punishing acts by which, if left unpunished, society would fall to pieces.   The question they have to try is confined to the particular act which constitutes the man's supposed crime, but by the principles of our religion, as we understand and accept it, that is only part of the question which the Almighty Judge will try in the case of His creatures.   According to the belief of a Christian that question is co-extensive with the man's entire life, from its first day to its last ; and if human judges, by putting a criminal to death, deliberately send him before that Supreme Tribunal upon a different issue from that which would have had to be tried if- his life had been allowed to run its natural course, it is impossible that they should not feel oppressed by the terrible responsibility incurred by them, and should not feel an irresistible desire to convince themselves that at least that man's case in another world has not been made worse by their interposition. A clergyman attending upon a convicted murderer under sentence of death is placed by those human judges in a very false position. It is scarcely possible that he should avoid giving some kind of assurance to the prisoner, deriving authority from his sacred office, of pardon in the next world. The words he uses never, I dare say, in their strict and literal sense, amount to that, but when we reflect upon the number of criminals who, at the last moment, express a confident expectation of pardon and happiness in the next world, it is difficult to believe that this is not the practical result on the prisoner's mind of his intercourse with his religious adviser. The ministration of the clergyman in substance, although not in direct terms, in effect, if not in intention, usually amounts to this, ' Be sorry for your fault, express that sorrow to your Maker, and you may confidently hope for pardon.' If so, the case can scarcely fail to come before the public as that of a man who, having committed a crime so bad as to render it impossible that he should be allowed longer to remain in this world, will be received as one of the blessed in a world to come ; and if a clergyman, perceiving the consequent mischief to society, sternly refuses to lend himself to the production of such an impression, he is in fact, during those last few days on earth of this wretched man, aggravating his torture in a degree of which the bare contemplation is scarcely endurable. Mr. Justice Shee goes so far as to recommend [1] that at executions a form of prayer should be read by the chaplain of the gaol, reminding the criminal of the promise of pardon to all those who truly repent. But what is to be the test of true repentance ? The man will be deprived of life in

[1] Page 629 of Capital Punishment Commission.

the course of a fortnight. What test of genuine
repentance is possible in that time ? If his life
were spared, would he cure himself of his faults
and lead an amended life ? Would sorrow for
his past wickedness, and the determination to
make such atonement as might be possible, stand
firm during the long course of his prison life ?
Who knows ? We are not going to put him to
that trial. Having refused him the opportunity
of giving any substantial proof of the reality
of his repentance, we must of necessity be
satisfied with such proof as the shortness of
his allotted time admits of. The consequence is
obvious, viz. that a few sentences uttered in
the solemn and impressive manner which is inseparable from all that a man says or does in the
last hours of life, expressive of sorrow for his
sins and of hope of the pardon of his Creator,
must be considered effectual. Neither the
clergyman nor any other of the persons attending upon him during that short but sad interval would dare to throw a doubt on that point.
The conclusion suggested to the public mind is,
that the murderer's salvation is secure. All the

intercourse with him from the day of his conviction to that of his execution tends to this conclusion.   In passing sentence, the judge urges
him to lose no time in making his peace with
God.   Within the prison the attendants upon a
man who has only three weeks to live, of course,
scrupulously abstain from making any allusion
to his crime ; the chaplain prays with him, and
repeats to him that the mercy of the Redeemer
has no limit that man can assign, and it generally ends by his going to the scaffold in the
expressed belief that he is as secure of eternal
happiness as the most virtuous man that ever
walked upon the earth.

I am not now discussing, and do not intend to discuss, the question of the efficacy of
that three weeks' repentance of a convicted
murderer, or any other purely religious question.
It would be highly culpable and arrogant, and,
so far as the subject I am engaged upon is concerned, quite useless to do so.   I am considering
religion in one point of view only, viz. in its
effects on the affairs of the world, as the great
support and foundation of pure morality amongst

men in their relation with each other. Now religion can be made to give a sanction to morality in one way only, namely, by the assumption that the actions which we look upon as constituting virtue and as a proper subject of reward, and those other actions which we look upon as constituting vice and as a proper subject of punishment, are also so looked upon by our Creator and Judge ; and it is plain that if, on the occasion of the perpetration of some act which in our estimation is one of the very highest degree of wickedness, we are to encourage the belief that such an act will be no bar to the admission of the perpetrator, in another world, amongst the ranks of the just and virtuous, we are simply repudiating our own theory, and knocking from under us the very foundation on which, by that theory, the union between religion and morality rests.   But I have endeavoured to show not only that we do in fact, under our system of capital punishment, give encouragement to that belief, but that, so long as human sympathies survive, it is inevitable that, under that system, we should do so.

The alternative is one against which all human sympathy revolts.   The   mere   instinct   of humanity repels the idea of torturing a man whom you are about to deprive of life, by throwing doubts on the efficacy in another world of the words of sorrowful supplication which he has just addressed to his Creator.

I wish to guard myself against misconception on another point.   I do not assert that there is any hypocrisy in a convicted murderer's professions of penitence ; on the contrary, I believe them to be perfectly sincere.   That a murderer, unless he has positive disbelief in a future state of reward and punishment, should be penitent, in a certain sense of the word, between sentence and execution is not only probable, but is nearly certain.   It is scarcely conceivable that a man who is leaving this world and going, as he believes, into another should not yield to the strenuous efforts made by the minister of religion in attendance upon him to turn his mind to the most effectual means for conciliating the Being on whom his fate in that future life must depend. It is not credible that there should be no reality

F

in his sorrow ; for who can fail in truth and
sincerity to lament an act which was done with
an exclusive view to objects connected with this
world when matters have so turned out that he
has not only failed in those objects, but has
brought himself into a position of terrible doubt
with regard to the only thing which is now left
to him, to his prospects, viz., in a world to come.
But what does all this prove, except the certainty
of the evil which I have pointed out as a necessary consequence of capital punishment.   The
sequence of cause and effect is sufficiently
obvious—genuine remorse for his crime on the
part of the criminal, exhortations to prayer on
the part of the minister of religion, accompanied
by représentations of the efficacy of true repentance in procuring a remission of sins in
another world ; confident anticipations of pardon and happiness hereafter on the part of the
criminal, published to the world with all that
particularity and minuteness which are sure to
attend his last words and acts ; weakening of
the motives which operate as a counterpoise to
the temptations to great crimes.   No one who

reflects upon the tenacity with which every man clings to the one remaining hope when all other hopes have been extinguished, will feel much surprise at the readiness and confidence with which criminals under sentence of death grasp at the prospect of pardon and happiness in another world. The fact is one of which the instances are numerous, one of them I will cite, because it furnishes me with an illustration of another of the evil consequences of capital punishment ; that evil, arising out of capital punishment, is the frequent union in the same man, the frequent association, therefore, in the mind of the public, of what is praiseworthy, and good, and touching, with crimes of revolting atrocity. The case I refer to is that of Bordier in 1867. He deliberately murdered the woman with whom he lived as a wife, and—but for some sudden mental reaction at the moment of the intended crime—would have murdered his children also. Attempts were made to save him on the ground of insanity, but there was no evidence of insanity which could have weighed for a moment with any man of sense. His last days, however,

between sentence and execution (a minute description of which appeared, of course, in the
newspapers) were in the highest degree edifying.
He was described as 'fondling and caressing his
children as a young mother would her infant
babe.' In a letter to his mother he speaks of
the woman whom he has killed as 'her that I
had loved even to my last sigh.' 'He prays
for the maternal benediction.' 'He dies without
a complaint.' 'He has had the happiness to
reconcile himself with his God, whom he has
known and loved.' 'Man,' he says, 'may re-
pulse and chastise me, but God, who sees in me
my profound repentance, pardons and consoles
me in my prison. I put my confidence in my
Saviour who died for me. The priest who
attends me every day has promised to write and
give you other details. Adieu,' he says, 'my
dear mother, and may we meet in a better world.'
To his sister he writes that, 'as his last hour
approaches, when he must pay to mankind the
debt for the crime he has committed, he is ready
to appear before his Creator, to render an
account for all his actions, good and bad, with

the certitude that He will pardon him.' To his shopmates he writes thanking them for all the kindness they have shown him. 'I feel pretty well,' he says to them, 'and am ready to suffer for the crime I have committed, and I hope with courage, and also to be forgiven by the blessed Lord.' At the execution he conducts himself (so says the report of the 'Star' newspaper from which this account is taken) in a most becoming manner, and exhibits great firmness without anything approaching to bravado. The marks of physical suffering arising from bad health and a painful surgical operation are described, notwithstanding which, he walked up the steps leading to the scaffold with a firm step. 'When he arrived at the top,' it is said in conclusion, 'he bowed twice to the crowd, and a good many of the persons assembled cheered and clapped their hands.' There is nothing extraordinary in all this. The same thing takes place, more or less, in the case of a large proportion of those who die on the scaffold. If there is anything which will bring out what is good in a man's character —gratitude for past kindness, sorrow for past faults, entreaties for forgiveness to those he has injured, hope of pardon in another world, founded partly on such portions of his life as he knows to have been right—it is the prospect of a sudden termination of his earthly career within a few weeks ; and it is only natural that the world should respect those who, during those last few weeks, and at the final scene of all, are able to keep down mere brute terror and open their minds—even though it be then only for a short time, and too late for any practical use in this world—to what is good and true.   But how does all this operate as a deterrent from great crimes? And, if it is desirable that what is good in the perpetrator of a cruel murder should be laid open to the public, why not, and à *fortiori*, what is good in lesser criminals? But the truth is that, neither in the case of great criminals nor of small, is it any part of the business of a Government to provide the public with occasions for passing moral judgments in complicated cases of human character.   This function may well be left to Him whose judgment is unerring.   The proper business of a Government is to deter

from crime, and it can never conduce to that
end to inflict upon the perpetrators of the
greatest and most revolting of all crimes a
punishment of such a kind that, without fault
on the part of any one concerned in the matter,
it cannot be carried into execution without
affording an opportunity for the public exhibition of the criminal under circumstances and in
a form calculated in a high degree to deaden our
horror for the crime, by exciting our sympathy,
respect, and even admiration for the man.

' But why conceal the truth,' I shall be told,
' you who are a lover of truth, in regard to what
is commendable in a criminal, and tends with
justice to detract from our bad opinion of him?
Of our bad men as of our good, of our murderers
as of our judges and statesmen, surely it is best
that we should know the true characters.' Yes,
I reply, but in the case of the murderer under
sentence of death, the commendable points of
character are *not* true. They are in the greatest
degree deceptive. They are the mere short-
lived effect of the peculiar situation of a man
who is to be removed from this world in the

course of a few days. If he were pardoned, would they continue to form part of his real character? No one believes it. It is difficult to conceive of Bordier, the destroyer of the woman whom he was morally bound to cherish and protect, that he was compassionate, tender, forgiving, patient, grateful for past kindness. His exhibition of himself in this character was not, I dare say, the mere acting of a hypocrite, but, in any sense having moral significance, it was as fictitious as that of the professional actor on the boards of a theatre. It may have been a true representation of the feelings of the man who was about to die, but not of the feelings of the man as he had lived. To the general public it was altogether misleading.

In your answer to my last letter you observe with truth that the evils pointed out by me would be removed by preventing publicity, by withholding from the public all particular information in regard to the intercourse of prisoners under sentence of death with their relations, their religious adviser, and their attendants within the prison. Already, to prevent the

special evils arising from public executions,
we have determined to execute our criminals
within the prison walls. Why not go a step
farther and, in order to prevent the perpetrators of great crimes from being paraded before
the public in colours such as to excite pity,
respect, and admiration, why not, you say, draw
an impenetrable veil over those last days of the
convicted murderer ? I entirely concur in this
view of the matter. In the interest of the public, and to prevent any weakening of the motives
which deter from great crimes, I have no doubt
that, so long as capital punishment is maintained, it would be desirable to oblige the
friends and relations to take their final leave of
the condemned prisoner within twenty-four hours
of his sentence, and from that day to withdraw
him absolutely and entirely from the observation
of the public. Any particular information in
regard to his words, acts, and demeanour during
those three weeks are more likely, I believe, to
weaken than to strengthen the deterrent effect
of his punishment on the public mind. I do
not deny that, with a view to the repression of

great crimes, it would be desirable, if possible, to bring home to the public mind the mental agony of those three weeks, for that—as I have elsewhere observed—constitutes the real pain of the death-punishment. But this is precisely what we have little or no power of doing, for the purely mental pains are not those which manifest themselves most forcibly by external signs, are not those which the persons having communication with the prisoner during those last days would be most likely to perceive, would be most disposed to dwell upon, or, if they were so, would find it easy to describe. Mere pity for the man whom they are about so soon to deprive of life makes it inevitable that they should dwell in preference on the words, feelings, and incidents which reflect credit upon him—on his religious hopes, on his expressions of sorrow at the thought of his past wickedness, on his entreaties for forgiveness at the hands of those he has injured, on his intervals of mental calm rather than on those of mental disturbance, on his resignation and hopes of future happiness rather than on his terror and despair.

'The great business of the civil ruler,' says
Fielding, 'is to raise terror and to strip it of all
pity and all admiration, and to effect this,' he
adds, 'it seems that the execution should be as
soon as possible after the commission and conviction of a crime.'   In the present day regard
for the eternal interests of the criminal will
always prevent any material shortening of the
interval between sentence and execution, but it
would in a great degree answer the same purpose (that is, it would prevent the terror in the
public mind from being weakened by pity and
admiration) to make that interval a closed book
for the public.   With all men, but more particularly with the uneducated, awe and dread are
stimulated by a certain mixture of mysterious
concealment.[2] It is the same with imprisonment

[2] Speaking of the priests 'whose politics,' he says, 'have
never been doubted,' Fielding observes that 'those of Egypt in
particular, where the sacred mysteries were first devised, well
knew the use of hiding from the eyes of the vulgar what they
intended should inspire them with the greatest awe and dread.
The mind of man is so much more capable of magnifying than
his eye, that I question whether every object is not lessened by
being looked upon, and this more especially when the passions
are concerned, for these are ever apt to fancy much more satisfaction in those objects which they affect, and much more of

for life as it is with the death punishment and
its antecedent three weeks of prison life ; both
will produce less terror in the public mind in
proportion as the real incidents are known.   Of
all spectacles the most imposing and the most
wholesome which you could present to the public eye would be the formal passage of the condemned criminal from that public court and
from the presence of that audience which has
just heard sentence pronounced upon him, into
final and complete oblivion.   This is as certain
in relation to the man who is to live out his
natural life within the walls of a prison as of
the man whose life is to be cut short on a
scaffold in the course of a few weeks.   Bring
that man again upon the public stage in any
shape or under any circumstances, and you
infallibly bring him there as an object of sympa-
thetic interest, which, if your object is example,
is the very last sentiment you can wish to associate in the public mind with the perpetrators of
great crimes.

mischief in those which they abhor, than are really to be found
in either.'—' Causes of the Increase of Robbers,' p. 464 of
vol. x. of Murphy's edition of Fielding's works.

Your suggestion, however, judicious though it be, is impracticable. The difficulty is that which meets us at every step when we go out of our proper sphere to put limits upon the duration of the life which the Author of nature has bestowed upon us. As a matter of feeling, it is intolerable to the administrators of the law, in dealing with a man whose worldly career they are going to cut off in the course of three weeks, to do anything which can aggravate his sufferings or those of his relatives during that short and sad interval. No consideration, therefore, of the public interests, no argument of any kind, will ever induce them to deprive him of intercourse with his relations up to nearly the last moment of that three weeks' life. But, if the relations are admitted to the prisoner, more or less the public is admitted to him. The relations will of course do all they can to subtract from the load of infamy which presses upon the family by making public every word or act of the prisoner which can raise him in the public estimation, and by keeping back every word or act which can have the contrary effect. The public will be told of his penitence, his prayers, his patience, his hopes of pardon in another world, his gratitude for the little kindnesses of his attendants ; but of anxiety, of terror, of despair, there will be not a word. The unaided imagination of men will form something like an adequate picture of these torments of the mind, the effect of which will only be weakened by those other details which are sure to be exaggerated by the affection of relations and friends.

LETTER VIII.

I COME now to perpetual imprisonment as a punishment for murder.   Three objections have been made to it by witnesses examined before the Capital Punishment Commission of 1864-5 : the first that it is not severe enough to be efficacious ; the second, that it is too severe to be tolerated ; and the third, that, whether too cruel or too mild, it never would or could be carried into effect.   The third of these objections must be dealt with at once, because that objection, if sound, puts an end to the controversy.   If the only punishment which would have a chance of success as a substitute for death is incapable of being applied in practice, it would be supremely idle to say another word in favour of abolition. But do these objectors mean that there are substantial difficulties in the way of carrying out perpetual imprisonment, or merely that Govern-

ments would not have firmness to carry it out ?
Both suppositions must be considered.

The only substantial difficulties I can find
stated in the evidence taken before the Commission are the following : First, it is said that a
prisoner, kept separate, never allowed to see or
even to hear from relations or friends, debarred
from all communication with the outer world,
treated, in short, as civilly dead, subjected to a
painful and wearisome routine of labour, and
fully aware that this treatment was to terminate
only with his life, would, under the pressure of that
entire deprivation of hope, become desperate ;
would either lose his reason or become unman-
ageable ; that if he did not go mad, he would
murder his warders or perpetrate other outrages,
and the situation of the gaolers would become
untenable.   Now, I will put the case as strongly
as it is possible to put it against my own view
of the matter, for I will suppose the case, not of
a single prisoner, but of a combination of all the
prisoners of a gaol—so far as combination in
such a situation is possible—to subvert all order
in the prison.   But it is clear that in a fair trial

of strength between the prisoners and the gaolers the former would have no chance, because superior force may be brought to bear upon each prisoner separated, and he may be subjected to such discipline (solitary confinement, darkness, fetters, reduction in the supply of food, &c.) as might be required to induce him to keep the peace.   A prisoner who should, nevertheless, continue to be outrageous and obstinately refuse to submit to everything required of him, could, of course, only be treated as you treat a maniac ; and as long as that outrageous conduct continued, so long would it be necessary to keep up that treatment.   The gaolers could not do otherwise ; they must either do that or give up the gaol to the prisoners and take to their heels.   It is absurd to suppose that there would be any improper cruelty in so treating a prisoner ; for either the man is really mad, in which case you cannot do better than treat him as you would a refractory patient in Bethlehem Hospital, or, if not mad, he has the remedy for his sufferings in his own hands.   No rational manager of a gaol will, in the present day, treat prisoners with more

G

severity over and above the usual and recognised routine of the gaol than is necessary to maintain discipline and prevent the establishment from being subverted. But will any one explain what conceivable motive a sane man, being a prisoner in a gaol, can have in entering upon a course of outrageous resistance to the persons who hold him in custody, and whom he knows to be able to conquer him by sheer physical force ? , If he deceives himself on the point of their superior strength, twenty-four hours' experience will set him right. The only practical result to him must be the abridgment of the few comforts he has in his present state of life.

The proposition on which the argument rests is that a man who is confined for life without hope of release will become desperate in the sense of being violent dangerously to himself or others. But supposing, for the sake of argument, that it were so, of what practical importance is it except to the man himself ? The gaolers can have no difficulty in protecting themselves. If the man's desperation goes to the extent of making life insupportable to him,

you cannot of course keep life in him in opposition to his determination to put an end to it,
because he may refuse all food.   That is an
extreme case, which admits of no remedy ; and
as nothing can be done, it is idle to discuss what
you ought to do.   The man dies, but the gaoler
is not placed in any difficulty.   In every case
short of that extreme point of desperation you
can do all that is wanted.   You can control
your prisoner as you would control a maniac,
so long as you are unable to induce him by the
ordinary motives to submit quietly to the routine
of the gaol.

The most common form in which the objection has . been put by the witnesses before the
Capital Punishment Commission is that prisoners
for life, rendered desperate by the extinction of
all hope of release, would murder their warders,
and that, inasmuch as the most severe punishment known to the law had already been inflicted
upon them, you would be rendered helpless by
inability to carry punishment any further.   The
same argument might be applied to the murderer under the present system during the period

which intervenes between his sentence and his
death on the scaffold.[3]   The argument, besides
being in the highest degree fanciful, altogether
overlooks the fact that, although the application
of punishment as a deterrent is the appropriate
mode of repressing violence amongst the people
of a country, there are other more direct and
more efficacious means at the command of the
governors of a prison, means which are indeed
applicable to all establishments which are under
the immediate direction and control of public
officers.   Of course, in the most skilfully managed
prison you are not absolutely exempt from the
risk of violence on the part of the prisoners, for

[3] At pages 100 and 101 of the evidence taken before the
Capital Punishment Commission, Mr. Hunt puts the argument
in these words : ' Supposing that capital punishment were
abolished, and that a prisoner, convicted of murder under circumstances of the greatest atrocity, were sentenced to imprisonment for life, if he murdered his warder, what would you do
to him then ? '   The answer is obvious.   ' I should do exactly
what you would do if, under the present system of capital
punishment, he had been sentenced to be hanged, and murdered his warder in the interval between the sentence and his
execution.   Neither you nor I could do anything except to prevent his committing a *third* murder, and that is to look more
closely to the discipline of the gaol.   I could not keep him in
prison for a longer term than that of his natural life, and you
could not hang him twice.'

you may be taken unawares in a case in which you did not anticipate outrage ; and such cases do from time to time occur in prisons, but they are exceedingly rare.   You can always take adequate precautions against any class of prisoners, or any individual prisoner whom you believe to be specially dangerous, and you may always render further mischief on the part of the same man impossible.   The practical lesson to be derived from the objection is, not that perpetual imprisonment is impracticable, but that you must not put the management of prisons in the hands of weak or incompetent gaolers. Colonel Stace (Governor of Oxford Gaol from 1859 to 1863), in his evidence before the Commission, observes that it would be extremely difficult to manage a prison consisting exclusively of life men ; and he adds that it would require a very large staff and very strict discipline.   The suggestion of so easy and obvious a remedy is equivalent to saying that there is no serious difficulty in the matter.[4]

---

[4] The object is an important one, and the only inconvenience of a large staff is that it would cost more money than a

I think I am justified in saying that the
objection is fanciful, because it is evident upon
the face of the matter that the prisoner has the
strongest possible interest in being upon peace-
able terms with his warders, except upon the
supposition of a gaol so ill-managed as to afford
a reasonable hope of escape through the murder
of a warder.   The internal organisation of all
prisons affords means of punishing breaches of
discipline.   The gaoler could not say to a
prisoner for life, Your term of imprisonment
shall be increased, but he could and would say

smaller staff. In the Appendix to Lord Russell's ' Essay on
the English Government and Constitution,' I find it stated that
during the forty years from 1823 to 1863, 441 persons were
executed in England for murder. This is at the rate of eleven
a year, and if five be added for Ireland and Scotland, this
would give sixteen as the annual average for the kingdom ; and
if twenty years were assumed as the average duration of the
prison life under a system of life-imprisonment as the punishment of murder, there would be 320 murderers on an average
living within the prisons of the United Kingdom. If 200*l.* a
head should be taken as the average annual cost of maintaining
these murderers in prison under that exceptionally expensive
system of prison management, there would have been expended
at the end of forty years rather more than two millions and a
half of the public money, equal, perhaps, to a couple of months'
cost of a war with a barbarian prince in a remote corner of the
world.

to him that which in ninety-nine cases out of
a hundred would be perfectly effectual : ' Your
mode of life within the gaol shall be made still
more painful to you than it is already, if you do
not conduct yourself peaceably.'

Some of the witnesses before the Commission
insist chiefly on the point that the treatment
which it would be necessary to apply to prisoners
for life might drive them mad ; that separate
confinement, for example, on a man without hope,
might deprive him of his reason. But why, let
me ask, should life-prisoners be all treated exactly alike ? Some men might possibly be driven
mad by separate confinement if long persisted
in ; if so, why persist in it ? Why not allow of
intervals of exemption from the separate treatment ? There are many men who would certainly not be driven mad by separate confinement.
In no system of treatment applied to human
beings can you possibly lay down inflexible
rules on points of great magnitude. Why not
give the governorship of this class of prisons to
men of more than average skill, judgment, and
experience ?—these qualities are to be had, if

we choose to pay the market price for them—
and leave something to their discretion in the
treatment of the prisoners ?   The system of
what are called secondary punishments for great
crimes is of course not free from difficulties, but
the difficulties are very far indeed from being
insurmountable.   I am afraid that the principal
reason why there is such a weight of opinion in
favour of Capital Punishment is that it is a mode
of dealing with crime which is so exceedingly
easy.[5]   The death of the man cuts short all

[5] The disposition of governments to take short cuts to their
objects in preference to the longer and more intricate path is a
great and permanent source of evil, tending perhaps more than
any other cause to retard the progress of human improvement.
In the first place it produces and fosters the mental habit
amongst men of satisfying themselves with superficial views of
questions, to the discouragement of all systematic study of
moral and political science, especially among the very persons
who, as rulers of their fellow-men, depend for the efficient discharge of their duties upon their knowledge of those sciences.
Again, it produces amongst the men who constitute governing
bodies the habit of persuading themselves of the truth of propositions, however doubtful, the assumption of which is necessary as a justification of the course they are taking.   It leads,
again, to the frequent violation of great principles on the part
of the very body, one of whose most important duties it is, by pre-
cept, legal sanction, and example, to maintain great principles
unimpaired.   In political, as in private life, the short cut to
an object is generally the violent course, and, accordingly, vio-

difficulties.   The culprit once fairly dead and
buried, all puzzling questions in regard to his

lence is the usual expedient of the weak and the ignorant.
The flogging schoolmaster of forty years ago flogged because he
was incompetent to control by moral means, for which it was
necessary to study a great variety of dispositions, capacities,
and temperaments. His mind was not equal to this study,
whereas his arm was quite equal to the caning of half-a-dozen
boys in a quarter of an hour.   It would have been quite as reasonable to endeavour to flog the master into a knowledge of
boys, as it was to flog the boys into a knowledge of Greek
verbs.   It is the special business of a schoolmaster to know
boys, and Arnold and Temple, and some others, have known
them tolerably well.   It is the special business of rulers and
legislators to know men, and one ruler or legislator out of a
hundred knows something about them.   The rest neither know
them nor care to know them.   The moment a serious difficulty
arrives, they remove it by the immediate application of superior
physical force.   In nine cases out of ten the removal is only
temporary.   The evil is postponed, and comes back again in
the same form, or in some other form, and in increased dimensions in the course of a few years, or months, or days, as the
case may be.   By the method of extermination the earth might
at any moment be cleared of existing malefactors on the Car-
lylean clean-sweep principle ; but, unfortunately, the old set
so swept away would be perpetually replaced by a new set.
Political or social disaffection may at any time be put down by
the easy process of killing the disaffected ; but that process,
unfortunately, operates as a stimulant to the seeds which, at
some future time, will yield a still more abundant crop of
disaffection.   The French patriots who had the power in their
hands in 1792-3 thought to strengthen the cause of responsible
government against aristocratical opposition by murdering the
aristocrats.   That system was very successful for a year or two ;
as was, for a few months or weeks, the system set on foot by

treatment disappear for ever. They trouble us only so long as the man is still upon our hands, and we are responsible to him and to his family and to society at large for his treatment. So do puzzling questions in regard to the truth or falsehood of that verdict of guilty disappear, when the only man who has any strong interest in reopening that question has been removed from this world. If we are called upon to prove that our system of putting murderers to death is the best possible, all we have to do is to assume the truth of the following propositions— and who can conclusively disprove them ? 1st, The fear of death is the only fear which is sufficiently intense to deter from the commission of murder. 2nd, Juries are never led by their dislike of Capital Punishment to give false verdicts. 3rd, Innocent men are never hanged. 4th, A week or two of professed penitence for a great crime will secure the offenders pardon in another world. If we can only succeed in per-

those same French rulers, of preventing dear bread by sending to the guillotine the bakers who infringed the order which commanded them to sell bread cheap.

suading ourselves of the truth of these four propositions, we may go on hanging with a safe conscience and save ourselves a world of trouble and perplexity.[6]

It is taken for granted that depriving a man of hope (by which word, be it observed, is meant, in the case we are considering, only hope of release from confinement) will make him desperate in the sense of dangerously violent. There is a great deal both of ignorance of human nature and of confusion of thought in this view of the matter. If a man through extinction of the hope of release becomes desperate up to the point of suicide, so as to be perfectly indifferent to life, irritation or the desire of revenge may no doubt incline him to kill or hurt the persons who are the immediate instruments of his misery. But if its effect upon him falls short of the suicidal point, the extinction of hope is little likely to lead to any such result. Extinction of hope on one point, however important, does not

---

[6] It is a curious fact that, with few exceptions, judges have always contrived to persuade themselves of the truth of at least the three first of these propositions.

necessarily exclude hope on all points, and feelings, which are very weak at first, will, through
the gradual change of habits arising from a new
mode of life, go on progressively increasing in
strength.   There is a well-known disposition in
human nature to accommodate itself to a plain,
undoubted necessity, and to cling to all such
alleviations of pain as are not incompatible with
that necessity.   It is where the necessity is not
absolute ; it is in cases where there is some
hope left of escape from the main grievance, that
men become restless and irritable.   If the necessity is as certain, or nearly so, as that of ultimate
death, ninety-nine men out of a hundred, so
far from becoming desperate, eagerly grasp at
such sources of comfort or alleviation of pain
as still remain to them.   So long as the desire
for life remains, the desire remains to make life
as little painful as possible.   There is a certain
analogy between the case of a man who is
suddenly shut up in a prison, to remain there
for the rest of his life, and the case of a man
suddenly deprived of an inherited fortune, without the smallest prospect, either from exertions

of his own or from any other source, of obtaining another.   Such a man in the first agony of
his grief requires to be watched.   The force and
suddenness of the blow may lead to suicide or to
some other desperate act ; but at the end of a
certain time, most men accommodate themselves
in a great degree to the new circumstances.   The
prisoner finds that even in a prison there are
pleasures, or if not pleasures, degrees of pain ;
and the ruined man finds that even the coarse
daily labour required to earn his bread is not
altogether without enjoyment, and that it is at
least within his own power to make his new
condition more or less miserable.   If either the
one or the other, either the ruined man or the
prisoner for life, finds the new life so painful
that death is preferable, he may commit suicide ;
but, if his feeling of despair falls short of this,
he will strive to make the new life as little
painful as he can.   Now, at the end of a certain time, it is as sure as anything in human
nature can be, that from the mere force of habit
he will find the pain subside, and will discover
sources of pleasure which at first he never

dreamed of. If any one doubts this, let him read the autobiographies—of which there are several —of political offenders shut up in prisons. Some of these men have come to take a strong and lasting interest in things which, prior to the commencement of the prison life, would not have had power to attract their attention even for a few seconds, such, for example, as the daily course of life of a spider.

I quite admit that at first there would be more risk of insanity, suicide, or dangerous violence in a life-convict than in one under a shorter sentence, because the first shock to the mind of a prisoner of a life-sentence would be greater than that of a sentence which should not cut him off absolutely from all hope of ever being restored to the only interests and pleasures of which up to that time he has had any knowledge, but against that temporary risk it is easy to take the proper precautions. At the end of a comparatively short time, life-prisoners would become more tractable than prisoners for shorter sentences. Absolute irremediable necessity has in the long run a tranquillising rather than an irritating effect.   What chiefly unsettles a man's mind in a prison, as elsewhere, is the hope of getting back to pleasures or interests from which he has been suddenly cut off, combined with uncertainty as to the time of his getting back. All experience proves that men are not for any considerable length of time made miserable by dwelling on objects of desire which they know to be hopelessly beyond their reach.   A labouring man is much more likely to be irritated by the spectacle of the comparative comfort of his fellow-workman who earns five shillings a week more than he does than by the spectacle of the grandeur and luxurious living of his rich employer.   There is no lack of experience to guide us in this matter, for confinement in a prison is not the only incident in a man's life by which he may be deprived of personal freedom, nor is personal freedom the only thing which men intensely desire, the sudden deprivation of which, therefore, causes them intense pain.   A man is suddenly separated by death from a wife, a brother, or a friend to whom he is devotedly attached, and with whom all the habits and

pleasures of his life are bound up. He would
rather live in a prison with that companion than
in freedom without him. A man is suddenly
deprived of fortune and reduced to poverty.
Another man is, in the prime of life, deprived of
his eyesight, or of the use of his limbs and left
without a hope of ever again leaving his couch.
The separation from the occupations, interests,
and pleasures of his former life may be almost
as complete and sudden as that of the life-convict ; but experience does not show that, after
the first shock, such men become desperate in
the sense of dangerous to themselves or others.
The suddenness and completeness of the change
is for a certain time exquisitely painful, but each
successive day weakens the old associations and
strengthens the new ones. In ninety-nine cases
out of a hundred, if the man commits no desperate
act in the course of the first few months, he will
not do so at a later period. The only thing
which is likely to prevent or retard the steady
progress of that change in habits and interests
is uncertainty on the question whether the main
evil is absolutely irremediable or not, and whether

the return to the old life at some time or other,
near or distant, is or is not utterly hopeless.   It
is self-evident that doubt on that point must
tend more or less to keep up the old associations
and to keep down the new ones.   The mind of
the man who has not lost all hope will be
frequently turned to the question of the greater
or less efficacy of the various causes on which an
ultimate cure must depend, to the exclusion of
that other question : What enjoyments or alleviations, how many of them and of what kind,
are compatible with the new life ?   The pain of
the man who hopes for a cure is no doubt alle-
viated by that constant subject of interest, but
it is an irritating kind of alleviation ; alternate
fits perhaps of exaggerated confidence and exaggerated despondency.   It is a much more
mixed alleviation than the other, has more of
pleasure in it and more of pain.   Of that particular kind of alleviation the man without hope
has, of course, not a particle.   His alleviation is,
however, not the less certain because it is one
of a different kind, because it does not consist

H

of the excitement inseparable from an alternation
of hopes and fears.   His relief is that of a constant, very slowly increasing interest in the little
objects which make up his new life, objects
which are insignificant perhaps if taken separately, but which in the aggregate are important
in their influence on his mind and spirits from
the circumstance that his attention to them is
not distracted by other thoughts, and especially
not by any thought of the possibility of a cure
of the main evil.[7]

[7] Would he ever admit that impossibility into his mind ?
That question may of course be asked ; indeed, at page 31 of
the Evidence taken before the Capital Punishment Commission,
the Chairman suggests a doubt whether a life-convict could
ever be got to abandon active hopes of obtaining his liberty
sooner or later. 'Would he not,' says the Chairman, 'always
imagine that some circumstances might occur which would
shorten that imprisonment ?' and Sir George Bramwell, to
whom this doubt is suggested, observes that 'Prisoners are
like all the rest of us ; as long as we have any life in us we
have a hope of some change in some way or other happening.'
This is true : hope cannot be utterly extinguished so long as there
is life ; but it may be brought indefinitely near to the point of
extinction.   That depends upon the system which is adopted
and acted upon.   Men judge by experience, and also by what
they know of the state of the law ; and it is the duty of a
government (one which in England is very much neglected) to
take active measures to make the law, and the practice of its
administrators, where discretion is left to them, generally

From the above considerations I conclude
that there could be no serious difficulty in
managing a prison for life-convicts from any
cause but one, namely, the existence of a doubt
in the minds of the prisoners whether the sentence would really be carried out to the end.
In proportion as that doubt had real ground to
build on, would there be restlessness, irritation,
and disturbance in the minds of the prisoners
who would become in that same proportion
dangerous to themselves or others, at one time
from excitement, at another from despondency.
It follows that if life-imprisonment became the
legal punishment of great crimes, it would
become the duty of a government by every
means in its power to strengthen the belief

known.   Suppose, for the sake of argument, that by English
law the punishment of life-imprisonment for convicted murderers could be shortened only by a special Act of Parliament
in each particular case ; and suppose the fact, by systematic
measures of publication, to have become notorious that for the
fifty years preceding no such Act had ever been passed, except
in cases in which the innocence of the prisoner had been discovered and established, would not the impression on the
mind of the criminal public in regard to the possible release of
a convicted murderer be one scarcely distinguishable from an
utter absence of hope ?

in the public mind that there were to be no exceptions to the rule. A very small number of exceptions would suffice so greatly to weaken this belief as to produce incalculable mischief.

LETTER IX.

IN my last letter I endeavoured to show that there are no substantial difficulties in the way of carrying out the punishment of imprisonment for life. But it has been alleged that, let that question be decided as it may, Government would not have firmness to carry it out; that they would never, in fact, withstand the solicitations of the relatives and friends of the prisoner, backed up by the public feeling in favour of the liberation of sincere penitents. I will put the strongest case I can against my own view of this matter. I will suppose that a young man has committed a deliberate and unprovoked murder. There are no circumstances tending to lessen the enormity of his guilt. He is accordingly sentenced to imprisonment for life. At the end of a few weeks' confinement he becomes overwhelmed with remorse. This feeling continues, and finally leads to one absorbing desire which is to expiate his offence by exemplary conduct in his prison life. At the end of twenty years of undeviating devotion to this object, it becomes a matter of moral certainty with those who have charge of him that he might be restored to the world without the smallest risk of injury, so far as his individual conduct is concerned. Ought he not, thereupon, to be liberated ?[1] If society runs no risk from his liberation, how can you refuse to set him free ! The question lies between what is right in the individual case and the necessity of maintaining an important general rule. The lesser consideration must give way to the greater, and, in this case, it is of paramount importance to do nothing to weaken the deterrent effect of the punishment. A case is, of course, possible in

[1] In this argument I assume that the effect of the liberation of the twenty-years penitent would be to relieve him from pain ; but in many cases it would certainly not be so. A continuance of the prison life, with which all his thoughts and habits had for so long a period been bound up, would, in a majority of cases, probably be preferable (as a mere question of pain and pleasure) to the entering upon a new life in the world in the peculiar situation in which the fact of his great crime of twenty years before would place him.

which it would be useless, so far as danger to
society from the individual man is concerned, to
detain him longer, and if so, it might seem to
be cruelty to do so.   But it is better to be cruel
to an individual man, or even to an individual
family, than to be cruel to society by weakening the securities on which their safety from
personal violence depends.   Everything turns
upon the greater or less degree of importance of the rule.   The evil of exceptions is
in this case too plain to need much argument.
Men under temptation to commit great crimes
would put the matter to themselves in this way:
'What has happened in the case of A. may
happen in my case.   I can be quiet and orderly
in prison as well as he.   I should gain nothing
by being otherwise.   I can as easily as he gain
the confidence of the governor and the chaplain.
If he has been released at the age of forty, after
twenty years' confinement, I may be released
after the same period, or sooner, if I play my
part well.'   The first exception would be a
precedent for other exceptions, and, considering how difficult it is to distinguish between

genuine repentance and sham repentance, it would not be long before some exception to the rule led to disastrous consequences. It would then be too late to say, ' There shall be no more exceptions.' It would take a very long continuance of undeviating adherence to the rule to re-establish the confidence of the public and to destroy the other mischievous effects of those first few exceptions. Supposing even that, by rare good fortune, none but genuine penitents should have been released, still the mischief would not be much diminished. The public would never know with certainty that the repentance had been genuine, and, indeed, men meditating murder would seldom or never trouble themselves with that question ; would seldom or never look beyond the broad fact that out of twenty murderers sentenced to life-imprisonment, one, two, three, or more had been released at the end of a certain number of years. If, in the case of very atrocious crimes, such as deliberate murder, the hope of returning into society should be admitted, more would on the whole be lost by weakening the deterring power of the punishment than would be gained by receiving back a reformed citizen into society. The more this reason against the occasional liberation of repentant murderers under a system of perpetual imprisonment is considered, the more conclusive, I believe, it will appear. If relations and friends, however powerful, should intercede in favour of a reformed murderer, it would, of course, be necessary to turn a deaf ear to their solicitations. If the general public should back up these solicitations, it would be necessary to do what was right in the teeth of the public feeling. The unpopularity of a law, of a rule, or of a course of conduct in some particular case, is not a conclusive reason against it. If a law should be unpopular to the extent of making it impossible, or in a very high degree difficult, to execute it, it may be an unfortunate necessity to wait until the public shall have become more enlightened ; but mistaken public feeling falling short of that extreme point ought, of course, to be resisted.[2]   If the law or rule is

---

[2] An author quoted by the Secretary of State for Justice in Portugal (see page 531 of the ' Report of the Capital Punish-

intrinsically good, sooner or later there must be plain evidence of its goodness, and that is the best of all remedies for popular clamour. Adverse public feeling is not conclusive against any punishment, unless, by extending itself to juries, prosecutors, or witnesses, it leads to impunity for crime. If it were as undoubtedly expedient as I believe it to be the contrary, that murderers should be put to death, the public, however adverse to that punishment they might be, would ultimately be made to see that it was expedient. It would be the same under a system of imprisonment for life. There is no permanent impossibility of making plain to the public mind the importance of maintaining inviolate rules which, in matters of great magnitude, have been

ment Commission,' 1864-5) says : ' Legislation ought not to go before society, it ought to confine itself to follow it.' This is not an unfashionable doctrine with certain politicians in England ; but if legislators are chosen for their superior wisdom, it is almost equivalent to saying that the wiser portion of society shall not go before the less wise. In one sense, and in one only, is the saying true. If the moral consent and approbation of society is indispensable to the successful working of a new law, then that new law, however wise and desirable in itself, must be postponed until society has been educated up to the point of perceiving its wisdom.

made for the protection of the public. But, in truth, no fear can be more fanciful than the fear of a public clamour for the release of a repentant murderer. The public would know nothing of his repentance, and no good could be done by acquainting them with it. It could only increase the difficulty of administering prisons, and might in other important respects be mischievous, if gaolers were to take the public into their confidence. It may be right that the general condition and system of management of the prison should from time to time be made the subject of a public report, and that, when a prisoner dies, the fact should be published ; but minute details in regard to the particular condition, mental and bodily, of each individual prisoner, especially if such details were extended to his religious feelings, would be worse than useless. In the absence of such particular information the public would be as little competent, as they would be little disposed, to thrust their views and wishes on the administrators of the law.

It may be said that adverse public feeling might be as serious an obstacle to the administration of the law in the case of perpetual imprisonment as in that of death ; that if one jury will bring in a wrong verdict to save themselves the pain of being instrumental in the hanging of a man, another jury may bring in a wrong verdict to save themselves the pain of shutting him up for the remainder of his life. That condition of public feeling is, of course, conceivable, but it has certainly not hitherto, so far as we can judge, had any existence. No one supposes that there is any feeling against perpetual imprisonment in the case of a murderer on his trial. The supposition is that the feeling would arise at a much later period in the case of a repentant prisoner. No failure of justice could in that case arise from that mistaken popular feeling, and there could, therefore, be no necessity for yielding to it.

It may be said that a minister of state, acting for the Sovereign in the exercise of the prerogative of mercy, could not always be trusted to resist the popular feeling in the case of a repentant murderer ; that if one minister had sufficient strength of judgment and of character to stand firm, his successor might be a weak man, morally unable to withstand solicitation, or intellectually unable to understand the kind and degree of benefit which a community derives from maintaining great principles unimpaired. There is, however, no more reason to apprehend such dangerous weakness on the part of a minister of state in the case of the punishment of great crimes than there is in hundreds of other cases against which it is found in practice unnecessary to take precautions. If precaution is necessary, it may, of course, be taken in this case as in any other. The prerogative of mercy in murder cases might be placed in the hands of the supreme power of the State, in which case a convicted murderer could be liberated only by a special Act of Parliament.

There is, of course, one case which must be an exception to the carrying out of all sentences of imprisonment, whether for long periods or for short, that case namely in which proof should arise that the conviction had been erroneous, that the man is innocent of the crime for which he has been suffering. That would be the one

single admissible exception to the carrying out
of the sentence of life-imprisonment on convicted
murderers. Indeed, if that could be proved
which never can be proved, namely, that society
had a very strong permanent interest in retaining in confinement to the end of his life a man
ascertained to be innocent of the offence which
first consigned him to prison, it might be right
to sacrifice that one innocent man for the certain
good of thousands of other men. The reason
why it never was and never will be right so
to do is that society can have no such interest,
can by no possibility have any interest plainer,
stronger, and more fundamental than that which
she has in the protection of innocence from un-
merited suffering. To release an innocent man
from an unjust imprisonment, if the cause of the
release is made public, can by no possibility
operate in any way, direct or indirect, as an
encouragement of the crime for which he was
mistakenly convicted. But the case of the penitent criminal is entirely different. This release
must necessarily more or less operate as an
encouragement of the crime of which he was

undoubtedly guilty, and is mischievous in other ways ; for, in the first place, the genuineness of the penitence and the absence of all direct danger to society from his release, are not capable of any conclusive proof ; and, even though the penitence should be real, the idea would always arise in the mind of the man meditating the commission of a similar crime that he also might become a true penitent, or might be clever enough to pass off false penitence for true.

LETTER X.

In your reply to my last letter, you remind me
that at the beginning of my letter No. 8 I
referred to the three principal objections to imprisonment for life urged by witnesses before
the Capital Punishment Commission, and that
the first of those objections was that as a punishment it was not severe enough to be efficacious ;
and you then proceed to observe that the whole
course of the argument contained in my two last
letters, in disproof of the alleged difficulty of
carrying out perpetual imprisonment in practice,
affords a strong, however unintentional, confirmation of the soundness of that objection ;
for that my argument in reality rests upon the
assumption that imprisonment without hope of
release is, on the whole, less painful than imprisonment (whether nominally for life or for a
shorter period) with hope of release, in which

case, *à fortiori*, it must be less painful than death, and, if less painful, then less deterrent ; and that, inasmuch as the main consideration is which is the most deterrent punishment for murder, if death be admitted as the most deterrent, it then seems scarcely worth while to go on with the other arguments against it. And you then refer me to an observation of Mr. Justice Byles, in his evidence before the Capital Punishment Commission, in confirmation of this view of the matter. To Mr. Justice Byles's observation I will come presently. In the meantime I must observe that what I allege with regard to imprisonment without hope of release is, not that on the whole it is less painful, but that the pain, be it greater or smaller, is of a different kind, is less productive, *on the whole*, of excitement, irritation, violent mental disturbance, less likely, therefore, to lead to madness, suicide, or outrage. I have not denied that during the first months of life-imprisonment there might be a dangerous feeling of despair arising from the sudden change to a life of restraint and privation, combined with the absence of all hope of relief, but I have

I

endeavoured to show that it is the tendency of hopelessness on one point to stimulate hope on other points, and thereby to diminish rather than increase that violent mental disturbance which is the forerunner of suicide, madness, or outrage ; that the dangerous mental condition of a life-prisoner would only be temporary ; that his mind would from the necessity of the case, as time went on, dwell less and less on the idea of escape from the prison life as a possible event, and would come to dwell more and more on the means of making a prison life endurable. His ultimate mental condition might be no less painful, but it would not be one of dangerous irritation. What I contend for is that it is the element of uncertainty in punishment that tends to produce violent disturbance in the minds of prisoners, which the element of certainty tends to allay, and that from this cause it will always be more difficult to execute sentences of life-imprisonment when there is uncertainty as to their being carried out to the end than when there is no such uncertainty.

But the chief delusion under which, in common with so many other persons who have written and spoken on this subject, you seem to me to labour, is that which lurks under your words ' *if less painful, then less deterrent.*' All punishments are painful, and deterrent because painful ; but the deterring force is very seldom in direct and exact proportion to the pain. A punishment may inflict a great deal of pain, and not be very highly deterrent ; whilst another may be in a much greater degree deterrent, and yet inflict much less pain. Punishments are deterrent in proportion as they are terrifying ; but terror is the anticipation of pain, not the pain itself. A man's expectation of pain from a certain treatment is not always exactly borne out by his subsequent experience of it. It may turn out to be less severe than he had expected, or more severe ; and we are sometimes able in the case of a given punishment to foresee in which direction a man is likely to miscalculate. This is the most important point in the whole controversy, and it is now, therefore, necessary to go into the question of the circumstances on which the deterrent effect of punishment depends.

One thing—the most important thing of all—is
self-evident, viz. that the pain of a punishment
is deterrent only in so far as it is known ; in so
far as it can be readily and easily estimated ; in
so far only as it is likely to be brought home to
the mind or, so to speak, to be felt by anticipation by the man who is under temptation to
commit a crime. You might shut a man up
in a prison and exercise all the ingenuity you
possess to make his life wretched ; you might
heap upon him everything that could give him
uneasiness, and withhold from him everything
that could give him relief ; but if you either
could not or did not take effectual steps to bring
this system of prolonged torture under the notice
of the public, in such a way as to enable a man
to understand and appreciate the real sufferings
of your victim, you would not by all your
ingenuity be increasing the deterrent effect of
his punishment by one iota. So you might
shut up a man in a prison and make his life as
comfortable and pleasant as is compatible with the
safe custody of his person, without diminishing
by one iota the deterrent effect of his punish-

ment, if you kept the public ignorant of this
your particular mode of treating your prisoners.
Practically, in a civilised country in the nineteenth century, imprisoned criminals are neither
pampered nor tortured.   The knowledge how
little or how much they really suffer is derived
in some degree from the report of released
convicts ; but nothing either that the released
convict or the gaoler can tell in regard to what
goes on in the inside of the prison adds much
to the sort of general idea which exists in the
public mind in regard to the kind and degree of
that suffering.   The deterrent effect of a punishment is identical with that sort of general picture
of suffering which the men who meditate the
commission of crimes form in their own minds.
When the punishment consists of imprisonment,
the governor of a prison can say little that shall
add to the effect of that picture.   Every man
knows what it is in its leading characteristics.
He knows that imprisonment is loss of liberty,
forced labour, coarse food, subjection to the will
of other men, and absolute deprivation of the
pleasures of his present life.   Each man, accord-

ing to his character, habits, and temperament, will form a different estimate of the degree in which such a punishment will be painful to him. If we wish to estimate correctly the deterrent effect of imprisonment as the punishment of murder, we must look first to the kind of men who are likely to commit murders, and we must consider how far the general idea, which I have stated, of that punishment, with that important element of life-duration added to it, is likely to affect their imaginations; we must begin by remembering that that element of life-duration will go far to render of no effect any reports throwing doubt on the supposed severity of the punishment, which they may receive directly or indirectly from released convicts, whose testimony in regard to the pain of the prison life will, as I have shown, be modified in a great degree by that particular kind of alleviation which is derived from the prospect and the fact of ultimate release, and in a much less degree by that other kind of alleviation which is derived from the effect of habit in reconciling a man to a life which was at first intensely painful.[1]

[1] 'What chance is there of this prison life ever becoming

Now, murderers in England may be divided into three classes according to the nature of the motive which has impelled them to the crime. There are, first, the murderers for gain. They are the most deeply depraved, the most habitually wicked, and if not professional criminals whose business in life it is to prey upon society, yet partaking a good deal of the character of that class. There are, secondly, those who have been impelled to murder by the passion of anger in some form or other, including most of the men who murder their wives ; and there are, lastly, those whose crime is closely connected with the sexual passion. In one or more of these classes a murderer in England may, with few exceptions, be placed. Now, there are some important characteristics which are more or less common to them all. They are for the most part eager in the pursuit of their objects, most of them hate hard, regular labour, many of them indulge

endurable ? ' is the question which the man who is on the verge of a great crime might be disposed to ask of the released convict. The answer he would get would be this, ' I don't know. It became endurable to me because I knew I was to be let out sooner or later, and I am very glad to be where I am, and have no wish to go in again.'

habitually in exciting pleasures, all of them
intensely hate restraint or subjection to the will
of other persons, and they are all deficient in
that particular kind of patient courage which
bears up against physical privation. Now, the
life of a prison is, as I have said, a life of
restraint, of forced labour, of the privation of
exciting pleasures, of subjection to the will of
others, and the men whom I have just described
know that it is and must be so. It cannot,
therefore, be otherwise than in a very high
degree terrifying to them. On entering the
prison, they know that they will find themselves
deprived of all hope of getting their own will in
opposition to the will of another man; of enjoy-
ing pleasures or comforts which another man
has determined that they shall not enjoy; of
being relieved from tasks which another man
has set them; of ever, soon or late, being delivered from this state of insufferable thraldom.
This is the idea which they will form of imprisonment for life: and the last idea which is
likely to suggest itself to them is that constant
subjection to the will of other men will, by lapse

of time, lose a good deal of its bitterness, that
pleasures which are now all in all to them will,
by lapse of time, cease to have any power over
their imagination ; that the allotted task which
now they loathe will end by becoming a relief
to them ; that—by mere force of habit, and by
the mere effect upon their minds of a palpable
necessity from which there is no escape except
in death—a course of `life which at first pre-
sented itself to their imaginations, and which
for a certain time was in fact almost unbearable,
will ultimately become not only bearable, but
not devoid of a certain class of real, although
unexciting, enjoyments.

This progressive change of feeling, the
consequence of a corresponding change of habits,
is one which, to a person who has reflected
much on the constitution of the human mind,
presents itself as in a considerable degree a
matter of certainty ; whilst to the mind of the
man who is capable of meditating the commission of a great crime (one who by that very
supposition is of a low order of intellect, habitually under the influence of the feeling and pas-

sion of the moment, and very little capable of
drawing remote inferences from circumstances of
which he has no experience), it will be utterly
unintelligible.

If this view of the matter is correct, we have
in imprisonment for life the two qualities which
are most to be desired in punishment, viz. a
great power of terrifying in the prospect, and a
gradually diminishing infliction of pain in the
reality.   The man who is meditating a murder
will look upon it as a condition of life which no
lapse of time can make otherwise than a torment, whilst the man who has had a long experience of it will know that the alleviations of
the torment have been becoming year by year
greater and more numerous.   The supposition
that the pain actually endured may be taken as
the correct measure of the deterrent force of a
punishment must disappear from the minds of
judges and legislators before there can be sound
legislation on this subject.   Mr. Justice Byles
(page 626 of the ' Report of the Capital Punishment Commission ') puts the argument against
imprisonment for life in the shape of a dilemma.

You must either preserve the prisoner's health in mind and body, he says, or you must destroy it.[2] If you destroy it the punishment is

[2] Mr. Mill (in his speech of April 21, 1868, on Capital Punishment) observes that 'few would venture to propose as a punishment for aggravated murder less than imprisonment with hard labour for life.' This would, of course, be the sentence passed upon the convicted murderer ; but there might be cases in which, when the prison treatment came to be applied to a particular man, it would be found necessary to modify that treatment on certain points, especially on the point of hard labour.   To require from a particular prisoner the same amount of daily labour as from his fellow-prisoners—indeed, to require from him any amount, however small, of hard labour—might in its effect be to kill him by slow torture, and that, as Mr. Justice Byles truly observes, is not to be tolerated in a civilised country.   It is imperative to leave some discretion on points of this kind, as on many others, to the governors of prisons ; imperative also to subject the exercise of that discretion to official supervision and control.   The difficulty is not one peculiar to the case of imprisonment for life.   A man sentenced to a twelve months' imprisonment might, at the time of entering the prison, be of a bodily constitution such as to be killed by slow torture before the expiration of his term if he were subjected, in all its rigour, to the ordinary prison routine.   These are cases of rare occurrence, which present no difficulty other than that which attaches to the exercise of discretion on all important subjects by beings of fallible judgment and imperfect goodness. Governments must take the trouble (and I admit that the trouble is not small) to obtain adequate securities for a skilful exercise of discretion in such matters, a discretion which shall hold an even hand between cruelty on the one side and weakness on the other, cruelty in inflicting a worse pain and a different pain from that which the law intended, weakness in losing

death by slow torture, and therefore not to be tolerated in a civilised country ; if you preserve it, then ' such is the power of the human constitution to adapt itself to circumstances, that the longer the imprisonment the easier the prisoner bears his hardships and privations, till at length imprisonment, with all its miseries, becomes tolerable if not agreeable.'

In the very next sentence Mr. Justice Byles makes another observation, a very true one, which I think altogether destroys the force of this argument, for he observes that the slow torture system would fail to deter, ' because the uninformed and unthinking masses

sight altogether of the fact that the prisoner is there as a recipient of punishment, and not as a subject for the application of science to the maintenance of the most perfect and durable state of physical health. There must be no miserable sacrificing of objects affecting so deeply the welfare and improvement of mankind, to questions of a few thousands of pounds sterling more or less of national expenditure. If governments are wanting in the requisite degree of skill and industry, and peoples in the art of obtaining better governments, there is, of course, nothing to be done, and mankind must go rubbing on as they are for a few centuries longer.

I need not add that the deterrent power of life-imprisonment would not be impaired by such exceptional relaxations of rigorous treatment, for the public would know, and ought to know, nothing of them.

do not witness, and therefore do not imagine or dread, the sufferings endured by a prisoner.' But surely the same want of thought and information on the part of the masses which would operate to prevent any enhancement of the deterring force of the punishment if pains were taken to increase its severity, would operate to prevent the deterring force of the punishment from being impaired if—from a cause so obviously beyond the appreciation of uninformed and unthinking men as the effect of changed habits upon the feelings—the severity of the punishment should, in fact, be diminished.

Nothing can be more just and more in conformity with experience than both the observations of Mr. Justice Byles which I have quoted ; the first, as to the force of habit in reconciling men to a mode of life which in the first instance was intensely painful to them ; the second, as to men not being influenced by sufferings which they do not witness or which are not in some shape or another made apparent to them ; but the second observation is as true of mitigations as of aggravations of suffering. It is equally true whether the pain is found on trial to be greater or to be less than the man whom it is sought to influence believed it to be. Nothing can be more certain than these two things. First, that in the nineteenth century, in a civilised country, tolerably well governed, prisoners for life will neither be tortured nor pampered ; and secondly, that under a reasonable system of prison discipline, falling neither into cruelty on the one hand nor weakness on the other, the sufferings of life-prisoners—whatever the governor of the prison may wish or intend—will, in fact— especially if there should be no hope of release— be mitigated to a very considerable extent by the mere lapse of time, giving constantly increasing effect to a new set of habits. Such mitigation is not merely a probable, it is a certain concomitant of imprisonment for life, and so far from being an objection to that punishment it is a recommendation of it. It is a saving of pain without any weakening of the force of the example.

LETTER XI.

AMONGST the objections to the punishment of death urged by Jeremy Bentham in his address to the French people in 1830, there is one which he designates '*Tendency to produce Crime,*' but these words do not sufficiently explain the nature of this objection, and it can scarcely, without an illustration, be made intelligible. One or more persons (let me say A. and B.), having perpetrated some great crime, are exposed to the risk of detection through the evidence of C., who is cognisant of the circumstances of that criminal act of theirs. They are of course under strong temptation to extinguish for ever this risk by the death of C. To compass his death by a false accusation is immeasurably less dangerous to them than to murder him, and if they play their game well any denunciation by him of their wicked conspiracy against his life may be made to appear as revenge, or, as the last resource of a desperate man who has no substantial answer to the accusation preferred against him. The man once convicted and executed, they are safe from the danger which pressed upon them. It is a fearful thing to reflect upon the opportunity which capital punishment may give to malefactors to destroy with impunity the life of an innocent man who happens to stand towards them in some relation which threatens their safety, or who, without standing towards them in any such relation, may yet by a skilful arrangement of circumstances, some or all of them established by perjured testimony on their part, be involved in an inextricable web of circumstantial evidence which shall fix upon him guilt which is in truth theirs. Englishmen are very apt to overrate the conclusiveness of circumstantial evidence ; they are apt to forget that the reality or significance of the circumstances rests upon testimony, and that testimony may be false ; false in two ways : 1st, by the invention of facts which had no real existence ;

2ndly, by the suppression of facts which, if known, would materially alter the conclusions derivable from other facts. A knife, a comb, a handkerchief, or some other article which C. was in the habit of carrying about with him, is found close to the spot where lies the body of a murdered man, and C. is sworn to as having been seen in the near proximity of that spot about the time when the murder was committed. In C.'s house, too, is found some article of value which is known to have belonged to the murdered man. But the story as to proximity may have been invented, and the articles stolen for the express purpose of being so disposed of, by the real authors of the murder, in order to throw suspicion upon an innocent man and thereby divert it from themselves. What it is important to point out in regard to such a supposed conspiracy is this, that if it succeeds on the trial the real authors of the crime are made safe in the course of a few weeks by the death of their victim. It may easily have a temporary success, and the only chance for its ultimate exposure is the continuance in life of the man who alone has

K

any very strong interest in its detection, and
who is best able, if time is given him, to throw
new light on some or all of the circumstances on
which the false conclusion rests.   In the short
interval which elapses between conviction and
execution, what chance has an innocent man of
convincing any one of his innocence by simple
asseveration ?   What chance of proving it when
the very first step in the process of proof must
be to set on foot a systematic and elaborate
search for evidence ?   Give a man who has an
overpowering interest in the success of his search
sufficient time, and he may succeed ; but hang
him in three weeks from the day of the sentence,
treat his protestations of innocence as the last
vain struggles of a desperate man to escape from
punishment, make no response to them but by a
proffer of religious aid ; do this, and the final,
complete, and permanent success of the conspiracy is established ; its authors are at ease, with
nothing to disturb their peace, except the consciousness that an innocent man has by their
villany suffered death for their crime.   The
execution over, if their remorse does not lead to

the detection of the conspiracy, nothing else is likely to do so.

It will be said that a conspiracy against the life of an innocent man is an event so rare as to lose all significance as an argument in the discussion of the question of Capital Punishment, but it must be remembered that, although absolutely very rare, it may not be so relatively to the sum total of trials for murder in a civilised country, and that the relative, not the absolute number of cases is what it is material in this discussion to consider. That the number of such cases should be underrated is almost certain. Assuming the existence of such a conspiracy, its temporary success is by no means a very improbable event, and, if successful at first, it is almost sure, through the death of the one only person who has a very strong interest in its detection, to be successful to the end, and thus to remain, *as a matter of fact, for ever* unknown, The maxim ' de non apparentibus et non existentibus eadem est ratio ' is a very deceptive one in cases of this kind, and the number of persons who have suffered death on the scaffold, whether victims of a conspiracy having for its object to divert suspicion from the real criminals or victims of the innumerable aberrations of human judgment, is probably much larger than it is supposed to be. When a trial for a capital offence has been concluded by a verdict of guilty acquiesced in by the judge, it is quite certain that all parties directly or indirectly connected with the matter, from the judge down to the general public—the supposed criminal alone excepted—would be strongly averse to a reopening of the question of fact in any shape or in any degree. This, so far from implying blame to any one, is inevitable, and on the whole desirable ; at least, it is better that no cases should be reopened than that all cases should be reopened. Nevertheless, inevitable and right on the whole though it may be, it is a state of things which, when taken in connection with the subsequent death of the supposed criminal in the course of a few weeks, is almost fatal to the chance of his innocence—if innocent he was—ever becoming known to the world. It is not in human nature that when a jury have satisfied themselves that

the evidence is sufficient to warrant a conviction,
and when the judge has concurred in that view,
they should not—both judge and jury—feel the
strongest reluctance to admit into their minds
any, the very smallest particle, of doubt of the
prisoner's guilt ; and indeed any public expression of a doubt, however small, would be fatal
to the possibility of putting the convicted man
to death.   Accordingly, in passing sentence,
judges almost invariably—and I cannot say im-
properly—refer to the prisoner's guilt in terms
which imply a certainty not inferior in degree to
that which a man has of an event of the reality
of which he has had within the last half-hour the
evidence of his own senses.   The feeling of the
general public is one of strong alarm and horror
at the bare idea of a murder appearing to remain
unpunished ; the public therefore is also in a
strong degree reluctant to admit doubt into their
minds when a verdict of guilty has been pronounced, and (the man once executed and all
possibility of reparation, if a mistake has been
committed, at an end) that reluctance is of
course increased tenfold.   After the final cata-

strophe, any defect in the evidence must be flagrant indeed which is likely to be followed by a wish to subject that evidence to further and more searching tests.   No blame attaches to any one in all this : it is inevitable and right.   The fault lies with the law of Capital Punishment, not with the administrators of the law.   Upon a probability of guilt in a greater or less degree removed from certainty, men are and must be punished.   If absolute certainty were required, Criminal justice must come to an end and society fall to pieces.   But, although the public conscience is and must be satisfied to punish upon a probability, it need not, and I think it ought not to, be satisfied to *kill* upon a probability.   One serious objection (and I wish it were the only or the most serious objection) to the killing is that it for ever shuts the mouth of the man who, in reply to your verdict of guilty founded on evidence under which, in many cases, you cannot deny that there may lurk misconception, inconclusiveness, or perjury, still protests that he is innocent, and that, if time were given to him, it might be possible for him

to prove it. But, it will be said, if cases once
disposed of in criminal courts are not to be reopened, what greater chance would an innocent
man have of bringing out the truth from his
prison cell than from his grave ? The reply
is that the reasons against reopening the case
are far stronger in the latter case than in the
former. The prisoner dead and reparation impossible, the principal object of reopening the
case is at an end. All proper precautions may
be taken in deciding for or against reopening a
case. It is precisely where the innocence of the
convict is a fact that his personal representations
laid before a proper officer are likely to bear upon
them such marks of truth as to warrant a further
investigation. Any public proceeding founded
on the result of such investigation would of
course be contingent upon a competent person
on whom that duty would officially devolve
being satisfied of its propriety.

Mr. Mill, in his speech of April 21, 1868,
in the House of Commons, admits that the objection to the punishment of death arising from
the impossibility of making reparation to a con-

demned person who should afterwards be proved
to be innocent, cannot entirely be got rid of ;
but he thinks that in England our rules of
evidence and the feeling in the minds of all
persons connected with a criminal trial are so
favourable to the admission and thorough investigation of all doubts, however trifling, which
may arise in regard to the prisoner's guilt ; he
thinks too that this feeling is so exceptionally
strong in the minds of judges and juries when
the case is one which involves an irreparable
punishment so shocking to the imagination as
that of death, as to take away much of the weight
which would otherwise attach to the objection.
This is substantially true, but I think Mr. Mill
in some degree overrates the excellence of our
system of Criminal procedure, and thereby in
some degree underrates the risk which an innocent man runs upon a trial for his life.   I grant
that the innocent man has nothing to fear from
our procedure except in so far as it is an imperfect process for the discovery of the truth ; but
in this point of view he has a good deal to fear,
for errors in criminal trials arising out of the

mere imperfection of human judgment and
human systems will probably be as often adverse
to innocence as favourable to guilt.   A criminal
trial in England is often spoken of as the nearest
approach to perfection which the infirmity of man
admits of, but I cannot look upon it in that
light ; for it seems to me to labour under a grave
and obvious defect at its very foundation.   Its
imperfection as a process for the discovery of
the truth does not arise from its not providing
sufficiently searching tests of the trustworthiness
of the evidence which is brought before the
court, nor from partiality or defective judgment
on the part of judge or jury, but from the want
of any sufficient machinery for bringing before
the court *the whole* of the evidence which is
really accessible, and which would be forthcoming, if there were any one whose special business ·
and duty it was to call for it.   That there is
no sufficient machinery for this purpose must
be evident to any one who considers the theory
of a criminal trial in England.   The parties
concerned in it are four in number : 1st, the
conductors of the prosecution ; 2nd, the con-

ductors of the defence; 3rd, the judge and jury;
and 4th, the prisoner.

The business of the first is to prove the
guilt of the prisoner, and of the second to prove
his innocence ; the business of the third—that is,
of the judge and jury, and in practice it seems
to be limited to this—is to see fair play between
these two and to decide impartially and intel-
ligently between the two opposing cases presented
to them.   Now, upon the face of it this is not
as perfect a machinery for the discovery of the
truth as it might be, for in all enquiries the
best chance of truth is to be found in an examination of the *whole* of the material evidence,
and this system neither does all it might do in
the search for evidence, nor all it might do to
bring it into court when it has been found.   In
· reply to this it may be said that all material
evidence must either be adverse to the prisoner,
in which case it is morally certain to be brought
before the court by the conductors of the
prosecution, or favourable to the prisoner, in
which case it is equally certain to be brought
before the court by the conductors of the

defence.   But in practice this is not so.   Facts
favourable to the prisoner, known to the conductors of the prosecution, are not always known
to the conductors of the defence, and *vice versâ*.
Evidence which bears upon the case is sometimes withheld.   The question what evidence
shall and what evidence shall not be brought
forward rests entirely with the official or professional persons conducting the case for or
against the prisoner.   Their discretion in that
respect is seldom interfered with by judge
or jury.   But inasmuch as the object of these
persons is to make good either the affirmative
or the negative of a particular proposition, and
not merely to ascertain the truth, and inasmuch
as they do not always know beforehand what
will be the practical effect of the testimony to
be given by a particular witness, the exercise of
that discretion does and must often lead them
to the conclusion that as a matter of prudence
or convenience it will be wiser to keep a particular witness out of court altogether.   Quite
right perhaps in the interest of their case, but
not at all right in the interest of truth and

justice.   This is more particularly the case with the conductors of the defence.   It might have been supposed that evidence favourable to the prisoner would never be withheld ; but this is not so ; for it is not only certain that counsel for the defence do occasionally injure their clients by a mistaken fear that certain evidence is dangerous and had better be kept back, but it is scarcely possible that it should be otherwise, and that mistakes should not from time to time be made.   For it must not be forgotten that the prisoner's counsel may be quite as ignorant of the truth on the question of his client's guilt or innocence as the rest of the world, in which case he almost necessarily forms some theory of his own on the subject, which, if unfounded, may entirely mislead him in regard to the probable effect of certain testimony on the case which he is conducting.

Three important things have to be done before a jury can be called upon to say whether A. is guilty or innocent of the crime laid to his charge : 1st, the evidence has to be sought for ; 2ndly, it has to be arranged and brought

into court ; and 3rdly, it has to be dealt with
when in court.   I believe the last of these things
to be nearly as well done under our Criminal
system as it is possible to do it, but of the two
first the same thing can certainly not be said.
The search for evidence in a murder case is
conducted by persons who cannot be trusted to
take a very high view of the great principle or
purpose of the duty entrusted to them.   They
are persons not unapt to jump to conclusions
on insufficient grounds, more anxious that no
murder shall be committed without some one
being found by the verdict of a jury to have
committed it, than that guilt should always be
laid bare and innocence always protected ; very
much indisposed, after having taken a great deal
of trouble in following up one clue, to admit
into their minds any proof that it is leading
them in a wrong direction and that they must
abandon it and take to another ; and again,
when they believe that they have collected
enough of evidence to prove their case against
a particular person, very little disposed to pursue

their enquiries any further.[1]   But if the securities against innocent men suffering, guilty men
escaping, and the truth remaining undiscovered,
are to be made as perfect as possible, it is plain
that this is not exactly the spirit in which
evidence must be sought for.   More effectual
means must be taken than any which now exist,
that no evidence bearing on the case shall remain
undiscovered, and that all such evidence when
discovered shall be brought before the court.
An ordinary police force cannot be safely trusted
with the performance of so important a duty,
except under the immediate and constant direction of an officer of a very high order of
intelligence and character, specially appointed

---

[1] Those who call to mind the case of Pelizzioni, who, but
for the interposition of a highly intelligent and public-spirited
fellow-countryman, would have been hanged for an act which
he did not commit, the mass of material evidence which was afterwards forthcoming, and which ought to have been obtained before
the man was put upon his trial—at all events, before a jury was
called upon for a verdict ; those also who remember the case of
a woman murdered, some years ago, in a house of ill-fame in
George Street, St. Giles's, and the more recent case of the
murder of a housekeeper in Farringdon Street, will scarcely, I
should think, resist the conclusion that our Criminal system, in
so far as regards its two first important elements, the search for
evidence and its production in court, is lamentably defective.

for that purpose, and so appointed as to make it a matter of certainty that his object shall be strictly identical with that of the judge, bringing the case before the court in its entirety. So long as this is left in any material degree dependent upon the discretion of police officers, solicitors, and advocates, a criminal trial in England, when all has been said for it that can be said, will still be very far removed from what it ought to be, a much less effective process for the discovery of the truth than it might be made.

LETTER XII.

IN some cases there is, over and above the objections to capital punishment which apply to all cases, a special objection arising from this, that the fear of death is not the kind of motive which operates with any force on the class of persons whom you wish to deter. One of the greatest impediments to a sound system of Criminal jurisprudence is the prevalent notion that offences, in the very highest degree injurious to society, should, as a matter of course, receive the severest punishment known to the law. But suppose that severest punishment should be of a kind which we have found by experience not to be very much dreaded by the kind of men who are likely to commit the offence. We ought, then, clearly to seek for some other. Mr. Lawson, in his examination before the Capital Punishment Commission of 1865, having

stated it as his opinion that the punishment
of death should be totally abolished, is asked
(Question No. 3104), whether it would be
possible to abolish the punishment of death for
high treason ; for the murder of the Sovereign,
for instance ?   He replies, ' I certainly would
abolish it in cases of treason also ; ' but afterwards (in reply to Question No. 3105) he says,
' you might except that if you thought proper,'
and (at No. 3106) ' I should not object to ex-
cepting it ; but it would rarely, if ever, occur.'
But why not object to it, if it is the wrong kind
of punishment?   The one conclusive reason
against punishing the murder of a Sovereign
with death, is that the murderers of Sovereigns
are almost invariably persons who are little, if
at all, affected by the fear of death.   They are
either insane, or belong to the class of men who
are prepared to devote their lives to what they
—truly or falsely—believe to be a great cause.
In either case they have in them much of the
spirit of martyrs.   Contempt is the thing they
fear.   If you wish to prevent the assassination
of Sovereigns, treat the assassin as a madman—

which in many cases he really is,—consign him
to a lunatic asylum, or sentence him to imprisonment for life as a criminal having dangerous
morbid proclivities, requiring a treatment similar
to that of a lunatic, and you will do much
more to prevent political murders than by
hanging him, or even by torturing him first and
hanging him afterwards. The men who are
led by some intense paroxysm of the sexual
passion, to commit a murder—such men as
Townley, for example—would have more dread
of life-imprisonment than of death. Such men,
when their desire cannot be gratified, are constantly seen to court death. Their crime is in
the very highest degree atrocious, but death is
not the appropriate punishment for it.

A special study should be made by legislators
and rulers of the cases in which men commit
murders and immediately give themselves up.
Such men are not always proof against the
terror of death, when the last scene on the scaffold draws near, but the act of giving themselves
up proves conclusively that the fear of death is
inadequate to deter them from the commission of

the crime.   What kind of punishment would
deter them ?   That is what we should endeavour
to discover.   Enthusiasts, religious or political,
and the slaves to violent passion, whether of
anger or of love, are generally but little acted on
by the fear of death.   To the latter, life is often
felt as a burden so long as they are deprived of the
object of their desire, or are unable to liberate
themselves from some overpowering cause of constant, intense personal annoyance or irritation.
In the character of enthusiasts there is often
a mixture of strong conviction with personal
.vanity, and they are apt to look upon that death
upon the scaffold as the last and greatest proof
which they can give to their own conscience and
to the world, of their devotion to a great cause.

In November 1867, three men, by name
Allen, Larkin, and Gould, were executed at
Manchester for murder.   They were Fenians,
and had been engaged in a forcible rescue of two
men, also Fenians, who were being removed in
the prison van to the Manchester gaol.   Armed
with pistols, they had taken an active part in
the rescue, and one of them was sworn to as

having fired the shot which resulted in the death of one of the police officers.   This is murder by English law, which, when the prisoner is engaged in some illegal act, does not require any proof of malice towards the particular man who has been killed, or indeed any deliberate intention of taking away life at all.   Some efforts were made to save the lives of the prisoners, but they were unsuccessful.   But the effect of putting these men to death, instead of sending them to prison, was very lamentable, and very much what might have been expected.   In Ireland they were looked upon as political martyrs, dying for their country ; as victims of political vengeance, not as victims of what the 'Daily News' very properly called the 'cause of organised society.'   The feeling, even in England, which, when the offence was committed, was one of unmixed indignation at so gross and open an outrage upon the very principle of civil government, was, of course in some degree, diverted by that feeling of compassion mixed with horror which is inseparable from the taking of human life, where the offence is not one which is indicative of any very profound depth of moral depravity. The disaffection in Ireland was, of course, increased, and the disposition in England, such as it was, to sympathise with Fenianism, certainly not diminished. A lady of high rank, of the Catholic persuasion, sent 100*l*. for the use of the surviving relatives of the three men, accompanied by a letter full of tender and almost respectful expressions of sympathy. The entire want of sympathy with the cause of Fenianism on the part of the Catholic clergy was, of course, diminished. Here again death does not seem to be the right punishment. It is not a punishment appropriate to the case of persons whose offence is mixed up with objects with which any considerable fraction of a community sympathise, especially where the sympathisers are separated in territory, religion, race, and traditional political feeling from the rest of the nation. The feeling of that disaffected portion of the community is already not so much the salutary fear of subjects, as the bitter hatred of enemies, a feeling which a government should make every effort to extirpate.

Death by violence, not deliberate executions after trial by the ordinary law, is the appropriate and ordinary incident of a state of open warfare ; such executions will, therefore, by the mere force of association, be looked upon by the disaffected rather as acts of vengeance to be met, when opportunity offers, by retaliation, than as acts intended for example arising out of the ordinary administration of justice. I admit that the administration of justice is not to be left at the mercy of the angry feeling of unreasoning disaffection, but I contend that the policy of a wise government in such a case would be—especially when the offence to be punished was itself one of violence—to dissociate their administration of the law as much as possible with violence and bloodshed. If, too, example be the main object of punishment, a government should bear in mind that they are dealing with men who, by joining in an enterprise full of personal danger, have given proof how little they are acted on by the fear of death.

LETTER XIII.

I WISH to say a few words to you on the subject
of insanity in connection with Criminal law.
It is unfortunate that the various modifications
of sense in which the word 'unsound' may be
applied to a man's mind have thrown a good
deal of confusion into this matter.   In a purely
moral sense all men who commit murders or
other atrocious crimes may be said to be' of
unsound mind, but the perpetrators of such
crimes who are of unsound mind in such a sense
as to make it unjust or impolitic to punish
them are very few in number.   The question of
insanity is, in courts of Criminal justice, usually
submitted to this test : ' When the prisoner perpetrated his crime was he morally responsible
for his actions ? did he understand the difference
between right and wrong ? If not, then he is

a madman.   If he did, then he is of sound mind
and must be punished.'   But the question of
knowledge of right and wrong in Criminal
courts is as full of difficulty as that of sane or
insane.   Suppose the case of a man who is an
absolute slave to his passions, perfectly indifferent to the good of others, utterly insensible
to all feelings of horror or compassion at the
sight of human suffering.   Such a man is in a
moral sense a monster, and might be capable of
committing a barbarous murder on a very trifling
provocation, or to obtain some very trifling
enjoyment ; and unfortunately such cases are
not entirely without precedent.   It might be
perfectly true, in a certain sense, to say of ·such
a man that he is a madman, for he certainly does
not know the difference between right and wrong
in any practical sense ; but he knew as well as
you or I could have done, when he committed
that barbarous murder, that it was an act
punishable by the laws of his country.   In that
sense he knew it to be wrong and would have
abstained from committing it had he not hoped
to escape detection.   Such a man is not at all

insensible to the dread of punishment: on the
contrary, there is no man whom you might so
certainly act upon by the fear of pain, and therefore—sane or insane as you may choose to call
him—there is no kind of man whom it would be
so necessary for the good of society to punish ;
for, make what supposition you please with regard
to the force with which violent and habitually
uncontrolled passion may pull him in the direction of the crime, it is clear—since pain is his one
great evil and pleasure his one great good—that
the fear of punishment will in a greater or less
degree pull him in the opposite direction, that is,
away from the crime. This is all that is needed
to prove the necessity of punishing him ; for,
although the force of the example would fail of
its effect in some cases, it is absolutely certain
that it would succeed in others.

Another man murders his children and
maintains that it was not wrong to do so. He
does not deny that as a general rule it is wrong
to kill one's fellow-creatures, but he affirms that
there are exceptions to the rule, and that this is
one of them ; that it is better to destroy the life

of your children than to leave them in a world where there seems to be no means of maintaining them in reasonable comfort. You know that the man's reasoning is utterly fallacious, and that his practical conclusion would lead to consequences fatal to the very existence of civil society; but you also know him to be perfectly sincere. You might therefore be justified in pronouncing that he did not know the difference between right and wrong, and was of unsound mind; but this man, like the last, is not insensible to the fear of punishment, and you would not be justified in leaving him unpunished.

A third man plainly labours under monomania. He is persuaded, for example, that he is commissioned by God to destroy all persons who hold some particular religious opinion; who deny, for instance, the doctrine of the Atonement. In pursuance of his supposed commission he kills A. B. There is no evidence indicating unsoundness of mind on any other point, and nothing to show that he labours under any delusion in regard to the fact that murder is an act punishable by the laws of the country.

You would of course punish him as a murderer.

A fourth man maintains that he lies under
the strongest moral obligation to kill all people
who by leading an immoral life are giving a bad
example to their neighbours.   This is another
form of monomania, not indicating that the man
deceives himself in regard to the legal prohibition
of murder.   He would of course be punished
like the rest.

Now this question arises : Is there any case
whatever in which a man, having committed a
murder and being, at the time he did so, perfectly
capable of understanding (and with respect to
whom, therefore, it may fairly be assumed that
he did in fact understand) that he was violating
the law, ought to be relieved from punishment,
either on the ground that his apparent motives
are unintelligible, indicative therefore of an unsound mind, or on the ground that one or more
medical men have pronounced him to be mad ?
It seems to me that there is no such case, and
that the only safe test of insanity in courts of
Criminal justice is the capability or otherwise in

the mind of the offender to understand that the
offence is illegal and punishable.[1]   There are
men who are wholly incapable of understanding
this or of making any reasonable calculation of
the probable consequences of their actions in the
way of pleasure or pain to themselves.[2]   Such

[1] In 1858 James Atkinson was tried at the York Assizes for
the murder of a young girl to whom he was attached. He
stated on his trial that ' he murdered her because she would
not have him.' He was acquitted as insane on the evidence of
three medical gentlemen who had had an interview of two hours
with him. Seven years later, in 1865, Dr. Hood, Resident
Physician to Bethlehem Hospital, under whose care Atkinson remained for upwards of five years after his acquittal, stated
(Capital Punishment Commission, 2817) that he showed no one
symptom of insanity during the whole of that time. If, on the
face of the matter, a prisoner has acted, as in this instance, on
one of the commonest of the motives which impel to murderous
outrage (disappointment of the sexual passion, for example), it
seems difficult to resist the conclusion that he was capable of
being influenced by the fear of punishment. Accordingly nothing can be more dangerous than acquittals on the ground of
insanity in such cases as that of Atkinson.

[2] Incapability of that kind may, of course, be permanent,
or it may be only temporary. In a fit of delirium tremens, or
of drunkenness, a man may for a short time be utterly incapable
of any reasonable perception of the nature and consequences of
his actions. Nevertheless there are some such cases (that of
the drunkard, for example) in which it may be a question
whether punishment ought not to be inflicted, for the outrage
may have been the direct and speedy consequence of indulgence
in stimulating pleasures by one who was perfectly sensible of

men are of unsound mind in the extreme sense
of the word, and being wholly impervious to
fear of punishment or hope of reward, are not
to be influenced by example.   To punish one
such man who has committed a murder will
not deter another such man from committing a
similar act; but amongst the men who, being
insane up to a certain point, are not insane up
to the point of incapacity to apprehend the fact
that certain acts are punishable by law, the
actual punishment of one will act as a deterrent
on the others.   Let the test of insanity in
Criminal courts be what it may, however, there
will of course in practice be doubtful cases, and
the substitution of life-imprisonment for death
as the punishment of murder would have this
advantage, that it would put an end at once and
for ever to all the difficulty which is now felt in
those numerous cases in which doubt arises of
the prisoner's sanity.   A medical witness thinks
he sees something in the man's conduct when he

the probable consequences of such indulgence.   In this case, as
in others, the punishment of one deters others at the right
moment.

perpetrated the crime, or afterwards, to indicate
unsoundness of mind ; or it may be that the
extreme barbarity of the murder seems to be
out of all proportion to any conceivable motive
for its perpetration, and insanity is inferred from
that. It may be very difficult during the short
interval which intervenes between the man's
apprehension and his execution to set that
question of insanity entirely at rest. Accordingly, it is not surprising that a humane
physician, or a humane jury, where they think
the sanity of the man is in any degree doubtful,
should shrink from sending him to the scaffold
within a fortnight or three weeks from the day
of his sentence. They could by no possibility
shrink from sending him to a prison ; for, if
sufficient time were allowed, all doubt in regard
to his mental condition would be removed.
Once within the prison walls, at the end of a
certain time, one of three things would happen.
Either all doubt of his insanity would disappear,
in which case he would be removed to a lunatic
asylum ; or his sanity would be made apparent,

in which case he would undergo his sentence to the end ; or the question would still remain doubtful, in which case he would still be retained in the prison, his treatment there being so far modified as to meet that case of doubt.

LETTER XIV.

You tell me that as a matter of strict argument
my last letter [1] is not perfectly clear to you.   I
will therefore put the question before you again
in a more condensed and, therefore, perhaps in a
clearer form.   In a community of Christians,
who believe in a future state of reward and
punishment, to be determined by conduct in this
world, it is morally impossible that the administrators of the law, when they are about deliberately to put a man to death, should be indifferent
to his fate in the next world, should look upon
that question otherwise than with deep anxiety.
For, on the face of the matter, it would appear
that a murder, if it is so bad a crime as to make
the man who has committed it unfit to remain
longer in this world, will be punished in a world
to come.   Hence necessarily arises an intense

[1] See Letter VII.

desire on the part of judges, gaolers, ministers
of religion, &c., to obtain from a murderer under
sentence of death, expressions of sorrow for his
crime, of penitence, of supplication for pardon
addressed to God, such as to afford some particular ground of hope to be set against the
opposite presumption tending to exclude hope.
This feeling, when superadded to that instinctive
feeling of compassion produced by mere intercourse with a man who is to be deliberately
removed from this world in the course of a few
weeks or days, must of necessity lead to such
tenderness of treatment of a convicted murderer,
and to so strong an indisposition to discourage
in his mind the hope of Divine pardon, as to lead
frequently, if not generally, to absolute expressions of confident belief on the part of the
convict of his being admitted to happiness in
another world. It is plain that all this runs
entirely counter to the main object of all Criminal
law, that of deterring from crime ; in so far at
least as it is known to the public. But in the
present age of publicity in regard to all matters
of social interest, it must be known to the public,

unless the administrators of the law set up a
system of profound secrecy in their treatment of
murderers under sentence of death, which would
be attended by evils of another kind, and would
not after all prevent individual expressions of
confident belief of the man's pardon in another
world.   Indeed there is, under all circumstances,
a predisposition to that belief; because the idea
of depriving a man at one blow both of life in
this world and of all hope of anything but
misery in a world to come, the idea of killing
both body and soul together, is too painful to be
endurable.   I blame no one for all this gentleness
and care and tenderness, for all this anxiety to
prevent the perpetrator of some diabolical crime
which makes the blood run cold with horror,
from despairing of his prospects in another
world ; on the contrary, I should think judges,
chaplains, and gaolers deserving of great blame
if they acted otherwise.   They act according to
the true instinct of a good man who cannot,
if he would, be indifferent to the eternal fate of
his fellow-man.   I blame only the law inflicting
death, which places its administrators in the

unavoidable position of so acting as seriously to
impair that great social purpose for which they
have been placed in situations of grave trust ;
that purpose being the prevention of crime.[2]

[2] In August 1869 a man named Jonah Dethridge was executed at Dorchester, for the brutal and deliberate murder of a
warder at the Portland convict establishment, where he was
undergoing a sentence of seven years' penal servitude for felony.
In the account of the execution given by the *Daily News*, it is
stated that the convict on his trial and sentence treated the
whole affair with the utmost indifference, preserved a dogged
silence in gaol up to the last moment, persistently refused to
accept the consolation and advice offered to him by the ministers
of religion, slept well on the night, and ate a hearty breakfast
on the morning immediately prior to the execution, and maintained a sullen, undaunted self-possession up to the very last
moment of life.   On the scaffold the following scene took place :

The Rev. J. Mann ascended the scaffold quickly, took Dethridge by the hand, and in an earnest tone said, ' Try to pray ;
pray to the Lord to have mercy on you.'

The cap was not low enough to obstruct Dethridge's utterance, and he exclaimed, in a rather fierce tone, ' Who must I
pray to ? Who has brought me here ? That is what I want to
know.   Has God brought me here ? '

Mr. Mann, imploringly—' I want you to try to be saved.
The Lord have mercy upon you.'

Calcraft then pulled the cap entirely over his face, and
Dethridge exclaimed, ' What are these men here now, and what
are they come for ? '

Mr. Mann—' Try to pray ! try to pray ! '

The rev. gentleman then shook hands with him, and said,
' Good bye, God bless you,' and left the scaffold.

To Calcraft the convict muttered, ' What does he say ? '

Calcraft—' Pray to the Lord to save you.'

M 2

The injury produced is twofold. First,
injury to society in the shape of encouragement

Dethridge, in a scornful tone—'Pray to the Lord to save
me!'

Calcraft shook Dethridge's hand, while doing which he gave
a professional glance to see that the rope was properly adjusted,
&c., &c.

The chaplain performed his duty, and could not have spoken
differently to this horrible ruffian; but why should a minister
of the Gospel be placed by the law in such a position as to be
compelled publicly to use language which implies the possibility
of a life of immorality, irreligion, and crime of the very worst
kind, being atoned for, in the eyes of a perfectly wise and just
Judge, by half a dozen words of supplication forced from him
by the urgent entreaties of a clergyman during the one or two
minutes immediately preceding his being suddenly deprived of
life? Those words, if they had been uttered, could not, in the case
of Dethridge, represent any real repentance existing within his
breast. If to be the victim of the most deadly injury which one
human being can suffer at the hands of others, could entitle
Dethridge to Divine forgiveness for his own crimes, he might
have urged that plea, but it would then have taken the form,
not of a prayer, but of a protest, a protest against the cruelty
of cutting him off from all possibility of atoning for his crimes,
except by a short, unmeaning form of words (unmeaning under
such circumstances), having none of the reality of penitence.
But you may ask this question, 'When, in the course of nature,
men who in their lives have not scrupled to set at defiance all
laws, human and Divine, which interfered with their pleasures,
lie upon their death-beds, do not clergymen address to them
words similar to those which the Wesleyan minister at Dorchester addressed to Dethridge?' I cannot say. We know but
little of what takes place on such occasions; but we do know,
in its most minute details (even under the present system of diminished publicity at executions), all that is said and done by the

to great crimes by suggesting to the public mind that the perpetration of a great crime is by no means an insurmountable bar to happiness in a future life. Secondly, gratuitous injury to the criminal by suggesting to him hopes of pardon in another world, on grounds which, judged by the fundamental doctrines of our religion, we can scarcely deny to be delusive, at the same time that we deprive him of the opportunity of establishing that hope on grounds which, judged by the same doctrines, we believe to be effectual.

Mr. Visscher, a member of the council of state in Belgium, in the course of his examina-

sufferer and by each of the actors at the putting to death of a criminal, and this at least is certain, that the effect on the public mind, of words which, whether spoken by the bed-side or on the scaffold, seem to give some warrant to the doctrine that crimes which are too bad to be forgiven by men may not be too bad to be forgiven by God, can only, in their effect on the public mind, weaken the force of the motives which deter men from sin. There is, too, a plain inconsistency between the words of grave doubt which we so often hear from the pulpit in regard to the prospects in another world of moderately good men, and the strong assurance of the impossibility of assigning limits to the Divine mercy, which are made to the very worst men upon the scaffold, an inconsistency which, in its effect on those who reflect upon it in connection with human conduct, can scarcely be otherwise than dangerously perplexing.

tion before the Capital Punishment Commission
of 1865, observes, 'it is worthy of a civilised
nation to require a system which, while it pro-
tects society, looks to the improvement of the
criminal.' True; and capital punishment not
only refuses to do anything to assist in the
improvement of the criminal, but it says to the
criminal, 'we will prevent you from doing anything for your own improvement. You might
perhaps repent and prove by a life of virtue
(for a good life is possible everywhere, within
or without the walls of a prison) the sincerity
of your repentance ; but we will prevent that.
You may make a death-bed repentance, if you
like, but nothing more. Whether a death-bed
repentance will avail you anything in another
world we do not know ; but this we do know, that
if our religion is true, it is immeasurably less
likely to avail you than a repentance proved by
years of amended life and sorrow for past sin.
The real, genuine, tried repentance would be
possible if life were left you, but it is not possible, because we are going to deprive you of
life.'

If it is a necessity of society that a Christian legislature should virtually hold such language as this to convicted murderers, we must submit to it; but the necessity ought at least to be proved beyond all possibility of doubt.

LETTER XV.

In your last letter you ask me whether I have read Mr. Mill's speech in the House of Commons in opposition to the Abolition of the Death-punishment, and whether I do not think there is great force in his arguments? The most useful answer I can make to your question is to quote those passages of the speech which seem to me to have most argumentative weight, and to make such observations upon them as occur to me ; but in so doing I fear it will be impossible for me to avoid to some extent repeating in substance what I have already said in former letters.[1]

The first passage I will quote is—

I defend this penalty when confined to atrocious cases, on the very ground on which it is commonly attacked—on that of humanity to the criminal ; as beyond comparison, the least cruel mode in which it is

---

[1] See Letter III.

possible adequately to deter from the crime. If, in our
horror of inflicting death, we endeavour to devise some
punishment for the living criminal, which shall act upon
the human mind with a deterrent force at all compar- ·
able to that of death, we are driven to inflictions less
severe indeed in appearance, and therefore less efficacious, but far more cruel in reality. Few, I think,
would venture to propose, as a punishment for aggravated murder, less than imprisonment with hard labour
for life. That is the fate to which a murderer would
be consigned by the mercy which shrinks from putting
him to death. But has it been sufficiently considered
what sort of a mercy this is, and what kind of life it
leaves to him ? If, indeed, the punishment is not
really inflicted, if it becomes the sham which a few
years ago such punishments were rapidly becoming,
then, indeed, its adoption would be almost tantamount
to giving up the attempt to repress murder altogether.
But if it really is what it professes to be, and if it is
realised in all its rigour by the popular imagination—as
it very probably would not be, but as it must be if it
is to be efficacious—it will be so shocking, that, when
the memory of the crime is no longer fresh, there will
be almost insuperable difficulty in executing it. What
comparison can there really be, in point of severity, between consigning a man to the short pang of a rapid death
and immuring him in a living tomb, there to linger out
what may be a long life in the hardest and most monotonous toil, without any of its alleviations or rewards,
debarred from all pleasant sights and sounds, and cut
off from all earthly hope, except a slight mitigation of
bodily restraint, or a small improvement of diet ? Yet

even such a lot as this, because there is no one moment at
which the suffering is of terrifying intensity, and, above
all, because it does not contain the element, so imposing
to the imagination, of the unknown, is universally reputed a milder punishment than death, stands in all
codes as a mitigation of the capital penalty, and is
thankfully accepted as such. For it is characteristic
of all punishments which depend on duration for their
efficacy—all, therefore, which are not corporal or pecuniary—that they are more rigorous than they seem ;
while it is, on the contrary, one of the strongest recommendations a punishment can have that it should seem
more rigorous than it is ; for its practical power depends
far less on what it is than on what it seems. There is
not, I should think, any human infliction which makes
an impression on the imagination so entirely out of proportion to its real severity as the punishment of death.
The punishment must be mild indeed which does not
add more to the sum of human misery than is necessarily or directly added by the execution of a criminal.
As my honourable friend has himself remarked, the
most that human laws can do to any one in the matter
of death is to hasten it ; the man would have died at
any rate not so very much later, and on the average, I
fear, with a considerably greater amount of bodily
suffering. Society is asked, then, to denude itself of
an instrument of punishment which, in the grave cases
to which alone it is suitable, effects its purpose at a less
cost of human suffering than any other, which, while it
inspires more terror, is less cruel in actual fact than
any punishment that we should think of substituting
for it.

Mr. Mill's argument in this passage seems to me to require more explanation than he has given to it; for he assumes that men are intensely terrified by a punishment which he declares to be comparatively mild, and much less strongly affected by a punishment which he declares to be comparatively cruel. The statement is not necessarily untrue because it is a paradox, but it must be followed out into all its particulars before it can be ascertained how far it is true in any sense which materially affects this question, the question I mean of the deterrent efficacy of death on the scaffold when compared with life-imprisonment as the punishment of great crimes, and no doubt a debate in the House of Commons is not a very convenient occasion for the discussion of a question of which the solution lies so little upon the surface. If death is at once the most terrifying and the mildest of punishments (the fear-producing impression on the imagination being out of all proportion great as compared with the real pain inflicted on the criminal), it follows that it is the best of punishments for great crimes, for it is the object of a wise legislator

to deter from crime as effectually as possible at
the least possible cost of pain. But Mr. Mill has
omitted from his argument two considerations,
which if included would, I think, materially alter,
if not reverse, both his conclusions ; for in estimating the real pain, he seems to me to have
overlooked the one thing which constitutes the
severity of the death-punishment, and in estimating the effect upon the imagination, to have
overlooked the fact that the fear of death varies
in intensity under different circumstances ; varies
so greatly as to be overpowering at one time and
almost non-existent at another. Mr. Mill speaks
of the death-punishment in terms which would
lead us to suppose that his conception of its
pain is confined to the mere deprivation of life
by a process which, at the end of a few seconds,
produces insensibility. He speaks of it as the
‘ short pang of a rapid death.’ ² But the real pain

---

² Nothing can be more expressive than this short description
of death on the scaffold, except, perhaps, that other description
of life-imprisonment as ‘ the immuring of a man in a living
tomb,’ but, as applied to the present question, both descriptions
are, I think, misleading. The first is true only of the final
minute or two minutes of the transaction on the scaffold ; the
other is more likely, I think, to be true as descriptive of the

of the death-punishment is not to be found upon the scaffold ; it is to be found within the prison walls, in anticipation of the scaffold ; in that mixture of anxiety and terror which goes far to absorb all the other faculties of the mind during that terrible interval between arrest and trial, and that still more terrible interval between sentence and execution. Of that prolonged agony, in which minutes pass like hours, no one can form a true estimate but the man who has endured it.   No doubt it is possible to imagine it ; but it does not belong to that class of pains which easily present themselves to the imagination of a man when the case is not his own. His mind fixes itself rather upon the event itself than upon that terrible three weeks of agitation and restlessness preceding the event.   He thinks a great deal of the approaching scene upon the scaffold, and very little of those long, weary hours within the prison cell.   The death of the scaffold

mental anticipation of a prison life as contrasted with a present life of excitement, liberty, and hope, than of a prison life presenting itself to the memory of a man who has known it long enough to have become in some degree reconciled to its hard, unexciting, monotonous routine.

is in truth, to most criminals, a long torture, not
the less real because some of those who endure it
have enough of pride and command over themselves to repress their feelings in the presence of
witnesses ; or, by a certain dignity of demeanour
at the last scene of all, are able to keep up for a
few minutes the appearance of courage or indifference.   You may tell me perhaps that this is an
exaggerated view of the intensity of the fear of
death, and you may remind me of the numerous
cases in which men lie upon their death-beds
without any apparent dread of the event which
they know to be close at hand ; but in those
cases there is generally either acute physical pain,
or strong religious faith, or prostration of the
powers, bodily or mental or both, the effect of
disease ; whereas in the case of the criminal there
is nothing either in body or mind to weaken
sensibility or to divert attention from the im-
pending fate.[3]

[3] I extract the following passage from the Rev. Lord Sydney
Godolphin Osborne's evidence before the Capital Punishment
Commission of 1865 (No. 3261) : ' When death is inevitable and
close at hand, it is usually met without the slightest exhibition
of fear.   I have, from circumstances, been present at the death-

If, by underrating the real pain, Mr. Mill had
underrated the terrifying power on the public
mind—the efficacy therefore in deterring from
crime—the force of his reasoning in favour of the
death-punishment might have remained undimi-

hour of a very large number of my fellow-creatures ; only in one
case did I ever see fear of death.'

This statement does not seem to have been intended—indeed
could not have been intended—to apply exclusively to criminals
dying on the scaffold, for the alleged fact, so limited, would
have been disproved by the history of executions, which furnish
us with many examples of both kinds, of criminals dying without any signs of fear, and of others dying with unmistakable
signs of intense fear.   The firmness on the scaffold is, no doubt,
in most cases that of a man who intensely dreads the contempt
of the class with whom he has been associated during his life, a
class of men who, as Lord S. G. Osborne observes, 'admire in
a fellow-creature what they prize in a bull-dog or fighting
cock, pluck.' ('They would despise the man who does not die
game, and the man about to die knows it.')   That kind of self-
love which dreads the contempt of those with whom we habitually live, or have lived, is perhaps the very strongest and most
durable passion in the human breast.   It sheds no ray of light
on the thoughts of the criminal in the solitude of his cell ; but
not unfrequently it carries him with éclat through the last imposing scene on the scaffold.   That it should do so, that a few
minutes only before a man leaves this world for ever, his conduct
should be capable of being influenced by the thought of the impression to be produced by that conduct on the survivors, is one
of those facts in human character which (on whatever principles
we may endeavour to account for it) is too well established by
direct experience to be controverted.

nished ; but this is not so. For those pains of
terror and anxiety which he has omitted from
his estimate, pains inseparable from the death-
punishment, and of overpowering effect upon the
man who is waiting in his cell for the day of his
execution, may almost be said to be non-existent
in the man who is meditating the commission of
the crime. This last man knows nothing from
his own experience, nothing from the report of
others, of those pains of terror and anxiety, for
they have no external signs indicating their real
intensity. They are such as in a great degree
to elude the observation even of the persons who
are in close attendance upon a prisoner, and to
the outside world, including all those whom it is
the special object of society to frighten by that
death-punishment, they remain a closed book.
The pain of the fear of death to a man meditating
the commission of a murder is the pain which
he himself endures at the moment when the idea
of that punishment as a possible consequence of
his crime rises up in his mind. It does not
occur to him at such a moment that the vague
feeling of uneasiness of which he is actually con-

scious might, through proximity and certainty[4] of the dreaded event, rise to the point of unendurable torture.   In short, to the man who is meditating the commission of the crime, the fear of death has scarcely a particle of that deep, pungent, gnawing, incessant pain which it has to the man who, having been convicted of the crime, is to be executed at a certain hour, on a certain morning, ten days or a fortnight hence.   In so far as the real pain of the death-punishment consists of anxiety and terror, those only will estimate it at its full value to whom it comes

[4] It would be more correct to say 'probability very nearly approaching to certainty.'   As long as there is life there is hope, more or less, and even the murderer who has been sentenced to death without any recommendation to mercy by the jury does probably not utterly abandon hope till the sad procession from the prison to the scaffold moves forward.   Anxiety implies some degree of uncertainty of the dreaded event.   When doubt ceases, anxiety ceases, and when anxiety ceases it is often replaced by a spasmodic effort of courage, which, when sustained by the spectacle of that dense mass of absorbed spectators, enables so many bad men, and even weak men, to die with all the imposing fortitude of martyrs in the best of causes.   The Duke of Monmouth, of whom Macaulay tells us that he crawled, and wept, and begged for life at the feet of his uncle, life at any price, at the price even of his religion, betrayed no dishonouring signs of fear at the last scene of all, when all hope was at an end.

too late to prevent the perpetration of the offence.

There is, I think, less of truth in the rule laid down by Mr. Mill that punishments which depend upon duration for their efficacy are more rigorous than they seem to be, than there is in a rule which should lay down the exact reverse of that proposition. The pains of life-imprisonment depend upon duration for their efficacy. I have stated in a former letter what those pains are. They may be summed up as follows : 1st, hard, regular labour ; 2nd, coarse food ; 3rd, depriva- tion of all exciting pleasures ; 4th, absolute subjection to the will of another man ; 5th, an entire want of variety in the events of their life. To every man the bare idea of such a life must be painful ; specially painful to the habitual criminal whose mode of life has been, by his own choice, as much as possible the opposite of all this. The idea of one day of such a life, however, would have no terror for a man ; of one month, not much ; of ten years, great terror ; of the whole remainder of life without hope of relief, terror of the greatest intensity. The terror

would be very much in proportion to the duration,
and would be immensely aggravated if it were
clearly understood that, whether long or short, it
was to be a life-duration.   Mr. Mill would not,
I suppose, disagree with this, but he would say,
let the duration be what it may—ten years, or
twenty, or the remainder of the natural life—the
real pain would be greater than the expected
pain.   I dare say that, at first, the reality would
come quite up to the anticipation, but I
very much doubt whether it would go beyond
it.   With ninety-nine men out of a hundred
I believe the anticipation would be substantially accurate ; for although the criminal should
have had no direct experience of a prison life,
what he does know, from direct experience, are
the comforts, pleasures, indulgences of the life
he has been leading, and he cannot but know
that the entire deprivation of these is what constitutes the wretchedness of a prison.   Stimulating food, stimulating drink, tobacco, sensual
pleasures of another kind, the pleasure of indo-
lence, the pleasure arising from the power of
gratifying desires as they arise, the pleasure of

unrestricted intercourse with persons of similar tastes and habits, the pleasure of variety in the incidents of life, the pleasure arising from freedom in the prosecution of his objects (which unfortunately is not always less of a pleasure because the object is low and unworthy) ;[5] all these will be cut off wholly and at one blow on entering the prison gates. There can be no misconception on the subject. Life-imprisonment ! Not one man in a hundred will have power to shut his eyes to the wretched prospect suggested by those words ; but it is equally true that not one man in a hundred will be capable of foreseeing that as years roll on the terrible reality will become progressively less and less painful and irritating, not because the lost pleasures will come back, but because the mere lapse of time will gradually bring forth such small alleviations and comforts as are not incompatible with hard, regular,

---

[5] I do not, of course, mean to say that all the persons whom it is specially desirable to deter from crime by the fear of punishment are indolent, smoke tobacco, drink spirits, and are sensualists in other ways, but I mean that, as a rule, the pleasures I have enumerated are in different degrees, and in different combinations, the special pleasures of that class of persons.

compulsory labour, and will also slowly weaken the power of lost pleasures over the imagination. I do not mean to say that a gaoler, who should have a prisoner handed over to him with instructions to make the remainder of his life as painful as possible, might not, by frequent changes of irritating treatment, succeed in keeping up the misery of his victim at, or even above, the point at which it stood in the first years of his confinement, but that supposition has no practical bearing upon the question we are discussing, for the treatment of the inmates of a prison is to a great extent one of prescribed routine. However painful that treatment may be at first, unless ingenuity is exercised to prevent the natural effect on mind and body of constant repetition, routine will necessarily bring with it mitigation of pain, very slow I admit in some cases, but in almost all cases sure. There can be no doubt that if you were to question a man in regard to his feelings and sensations, whose life from having been one of indolent freedom and habitual indulgence in exciting pleasures had, in consequence of a sentence of life-imprisonment, become one of restraint, coarse food, hard labour, and deprivation of exciting pleasures, you would, *ceteris paribus*, find him in a much less acute condition of depression, irritation, and physical suffering in the tenth than he had been in the first year of his confinement.

Life-imprisonment is, I admit, entirely wanting in that one moment at which the suffering is of ' terrifying intensity and in that element of the unknown so imposing to the imagination,' which Mr. Mill speaks of as being the chief characteristics of the punishment of death ; and if these could be transferred from the imagination of the convict in his cell to that of the free man meditating the commission of the crime, the punishment of death would in its deterrent efficacy be all, or nearly all, Mr. Mill believes it to be ; but to this, all experience and all knowledge of human nature is opposed. Mr. Mill seems to me to have overlooked in his argument that peculiarity of the idea of death arising from its familiarity to the mind as that of an event inevitable and yet uncertain as regards the time of its occurrence, which has been so well illustrated in the well-known fable of La Fontaine.

> Un malheureux appelloit tous les jours
>   La Mort à son secours.
> Ô Mort! lui disoit-il, que tu me sembles belle,
> Viens vite, viens finir ma fortune cruelle!
> La Mort crut, en venant, l'obliger en effet.
> Elle frappe à sa porte, elle entre, et se montre.
> Que vois-je! cria-t-il; ôtez-moi cet objet!
>   Qu'il est hideux! que sa rencontre
>   Me cause d'horreur et d'effroi!
> N'approche pas, ô Mort! ô Mort, retire-toi!

Nothing can be more true than this picture of the complacency with which death may be contemplated or even invoked when at a distance, and of the horror which it inspires when near at hand.

I will now quote another passage from Mr. Mill's speech.

> For what else than effeminacy is it to be so much more shocked by taking a man's life than by depriving him of all that makes life desirable or valuable? Is death, then, the greatest of all earthly ills? Is it indeed so dreadful a thing to die? Has it not been from of old one chief part of a manly education to make us despise death? teaching us to account it, if an evil at all, by no means high in the list of evils, at all events,

as an inevitable one; and to hold, as it were, our lives in our hands, ready to be given or risked at any moment for a sufficiently worthy object. . . . I cannot think that the cultivating of a peculiar sensitiveness of conscience on this one point, over and above what results from the general cultivation of the moral sentiments, is permanently consistent with assigning in our own minds to the fact of death no more than the degree of relative importance which belongs to it, among the other incidents of our humanity. The men of old cared too little about death, and gave their own lives and those of others with equal recklessness. Our danger is of the opposite kind, lest we should be so much shocked by death in general, and in the abstract, as to care too much about it in those individual cases, both other people's and our own, which call for its being risked.

In this passage Mr. Mill seems to me not to have made that very necessary distinction between sensitiveness in regard to our own lives and sensitiveness in regard to the lives of others. ' Has it not been,' he says, ' from of old one chief part of a manly education to make us despise death, teaching us to account it, if an evil at all, by no means high in the list of evils? Ought we not to be ready,' he says, ' to give or risk our lives at any moment for a sufficiently worthy object ?' ' Yes,' will be the universal answer,

'this *is* one of the first and greatest of the
lessons of a manly education ;' but men who
can be trusted not to overrate the sufficiency
of the occasion on which their own lives may
properly be given or risked, cannot be trusted,
when a judgment has to be formed in a case
which involves the lives of others. No one
who knows anything of the history of the
French revolution will say that Danton was
naturally a cruel man, or that he was otherwise than sincere in his devotion to the one
great object which he professed, the good of his
country. In September 1792 he and his fellow-
patriots connived at—if they did not perpetrate
—the murder of some thousands of innocent
persons, to save the cause of good government in
France, *as they believed* ; in 1572 the great Catholic
leaders made a grand slaughter of French Protestants, to save what *they believed* to be the cause
of true religion ; but who is there at this day who
believes that, if the price to be paid had been
their own lives instead of being the lives of
others, the judgment of these men, as to what
the salvation of their country or the cause of

true religion required, would not have been very different?

Indomitable courage in risking his own life is perfectly compatible in every man with the most sensitive tenderness in regard to the lives of others. Take up an English newspaper on the occasion of one of those terrible explosions in coal mines, which have become so frequent. It will tell you in what sense an English miner of the real heroic stamp understands the great lesson in regard to human life. That miner holds his own life so cheap, and is so tender of life in general, that he will descend into that mine at the most deadly risk to himself, rather than that the smallest chance should be lost of saving one single fellow-workman out of those fifty or one hundred who have been struck down by that explosion. No one will object to Mr. Mill's lesson, if it be taught in the spirit of that miner. But unless that important distinction between our own lives and the lives of others be constantly kept in view, that lesson becomes in the highest degree dangerous. If men are to be taught to ' assign in their own minds to the fact

of death no more than the degree of relative
importance which belongs to it amongst the
other incidents of our humanity,' and to be left
to make their own estimate of the comparative
value of their own lives and of those of other
men, is there not great risk of dangerously
weakening those feelings and principles which
form the counterpoise to the particular temptations which impel a murderer to his crime? We
may conceive a murderer, on the eve of the
commission of his crime, applying to himself,
with fatal effect, the arguments by which Mr.
Mill enforces his lesson, that death stands so low
in the list of evils to which humanity is subject.

'The most that the law can do against me
in the matter of death,' he may say, ' is to
hasten it. I should die at any rate not so very
much later, and probably with a greater amount
of bodily suffering ; and is it, after all, so
dreadful a thing to die ? And if life is risked
by other men for objects which they consider
worthy, why not by me for an object which,
whether worthy or not in the estimation of
others, is at all events one which, if unattained,

deprives me of all that makes life desirable to me ? and then, if death is to be regarded as so low in the catalogue of evils in my case, why not also in the case of the man who stands between me and the object of my desire ? '

This question must, I think, be considered by us in subordination to the existing feeling of mankind, whatever that may be in regard to human life.   It is, of course, easy to picture to ourselves a people who take so exaggerated a view of the evil of death ; who shrink with so morbid a sensitiveness from any risk to life for themselves or others, as to deprive them of all greatness or manliness of character and make them contemptible.   On such a people it would be safe and beneficial to inculcate Mr. Mill's lesson, without any qualification.   But we may picture to ourselves the opposite case, in which a general recklessness should prevail, making men ready to risk their own lives and the lives of others for very trifling objects, or for objects of very doubtful benefit, in which case it might be necessary to inculcate the exact opposite of Mr. Mill's lesson.   Neither of the supposed cases

corresponds, however, with the facts.   The
prevalent feeling of mankind in civilised countries at the present day cannot be said to come
under either of these descriptions, but I think it
approaches more nearly to the second of them
than to the first.   There is amongst civilised
men more of recklessness than of morbid sensitiveness in regard to human life.   Of the latter
there seems to me to be very little.   Where professional fame and advancement are concerned,
where the object may be represented as national,
where men have placed themselves at the disposal of a government—as in the military professions—in private life, where the feelings are
very strongly engaged, where the lives of others,
in immediate and palpable danger, are at stake,
or when the object in view is one with which
other men very warmly sympathise ; in all those
cases, those who would shrink from the risk of
death for themselves, form a rare exception.
To say nothing of our soldiers, our sailors, our
ministers of religion, our medical men, who are
always ready to put their lives in peril in the
performance of the regular duties of their respec-

tive professions, I believe that the men who (on occasions arising in private life similar to that which I have referred to in the case of the heroic miner) will unhesitatingly act as he acts may be reckoned up by tens of thousands in every rank of life. Unfortunately the prevalent disregard for human life, when the object is one which is great and noble, and commands the respect and sympathy of good men, is very apt to extend itself to cases in which the object is entirely wanting in those characteristics, to cases in which the sacrifice of life may be traced to stupidity or selfishness. The carelessness, want of skill, cupidity or culpable ambition of those to whom in large numbers the lives of their fellow-creatures are entrusted—railway companies, owners of passenger vessels, owners of mines, and, above all, governments—need to be strongly and constantly counteracted by the inculcation of a lesson on the value of human life. There is very little disposition in any quarter to take much trouble in the teaching and enforcing of that lesson. It is wonderful how disinclined men are—when there is no malice in the case

—to allow their judgments or feelings to press
with much weight on those who have sacrificed
hundreds or thousands of human lives to their
incapacity, negligence, or selfish ambition, and
with what inconsiderate ardour men will throw
themselves into any cause, however dangerous to
life, which their rulers may have dubbed with
the name of national, however little the honour
or interest of the nation may really be concerned
in the matter.   The misfortune is, that in this, as
in so many other matters, the faults of a government and the faults of the people act and react
upon each other, and give strength and per-
manency to the evil.   The indifference of the
people in regard to human life tempts rulers, by
the certainty of impunity, to embark in foolish
or unprincipled enterprises, such, for instance,
as the invasion of Russia in 1811–12, that of
Afghanistan in 1841, that of Mexico a few years
ago ; and the frequent exhibition of a lavish sacrifice of human life for objects which either they
cannot entirely approve or cannot clearly understand, confirms the people in that selfish and
dangerous indifference.   Heroic self-sacrifice to

save the lives of others in a case coming under
a man's own eyes is unfortunately quite compatible with great indifference to human life in
general, when the scene is laid at a distance and
is entirely outside the sphere of his individual
influence.   Daily experience proves this, and the
same man who in the morning may have put his
own life in the greatest jeopardy to save the lives
of others, will not in the afternoon be prevented,
by the news of a battle or a shipwreck a thousand miles off, in which hundreds of his countrymen have fallen victims to culpable neglect, or
still more culpable ambition, from eating his
dinner with his usual appetite.   The inculcation
of the great lesson of the sanctity of human life
is not likely, I think, to diminish the morning's
heroism of that man ; and if it should seriously
disturb the serenity of his afternoon, and make
him a little less tolerant of the mistakes or crimes
of those to whom human life on a great scale
has been entrusted, mankind could only be a
gainer by it.

As regards our own country, I confess I can
see no signs of a tendency to effeminacy in

regard to human life, and if the question of
retaining or abolishing the punishment of death
for murder were put to the vote, I greatly doubt
whether one-tenth part of the people would vote
for the abolition.   On the contrary, I believe
with Bentham that, for intentional, unprovoked
homicide, death is in England a popular punishment, and that the great bulk of the people
have, not only no present perception of the
objections to it, but that it would be a matter
of some difficulty to make them understand the
nature and force of those objections.   If the
abrogation of the death-punishment should be
postponed until juries show an indisposition to
convict undoubted murderers of the worst kind,
it may last for centuries.   Where the intention
to take life and the absence of strong provocation
are placed, by the evidence, beyond all possibility
of doubt—in such cases, for example, as those of
Thurtell, or Burke, or Palmer—juries have never
shown any unwillingness to convict.   When
there is hesitation, I believe it to arise from
one or other of two causes : either from a doubt
of the perfect conclusiveness of the evidence on

which the verdict of guilty rests, and the consequent reluctance to inflict an irreparable
punishment;[6] or from a dislike to inflict the

[6] That juries are much less easily convinced of the guilt of
the prisoner than they would be if the punishment fell short of
death, is not only undoubted as a matter of fact, but is very
honourable to juries.   Every right-thinking man will require a
stronger foundation of evidence for the infliction of a punishment which must be carried out at once in its entirety, than he
will for the infliction of one which, being spread over the whole
remainder of the convict's life, is not absolutely irreparable in
the event of his innocence being established before the termination of that life.   As a matter of fact, juries do not unfrequently
endeavour, in some indirect way, to escape from the responsibility of sending men to the scaffold, where the proofs of guilt
are not sufficient to exclude all possibility of doubt.   The case
of Wiggins, who was convicted, in 1867, of the murder of the
woman with whom he lived, is one amongst many which might
be cited in proof of this.   The case was one either of suicide or
of murder.   There was no evidence in support of the supposition of suicide, still less did it appear that the murder (supposing
it to have been a murder) might have been perpetrated by some
other hand.   The case against the prisoner was sufficiently
strong to make it indecent to acquit him, and yet not sufficiently
strong to make it tolerable to twelve men of good sense and
good feeling to take away a life which they could never restore.
Accordingly the jury endeavoured to save the prisoner's life by
suggesting that the fatal act might have been unpremeditated,
a most improbable supposition, in support of which there had
not been a particle of evidence.   Up to the very last moment
the man protested his innocence.   Within a few seconds of the
process which put an end to his life he exclaimed, ' I am innocent ; on my dying oath, I am innocent ; I never did it ; I am
innocent, innocent, innocent.'   So long as the smallest particle

same punishment, and one which stands so
completely apart in kind from all others, in cases

of doubt remains in the mind of the juryman, such protestations
of a dying man grate harshly on his ears.

It is natural that we should endeavour to persuade ourselves
that innocent men are never hanged, but the juryman who is in
the habit of attentively reading murder cases may be excused
for believing that weak points in the evidence on which executions for murder have rested are not the very rare exceptions
which they are represented to be. There have been cases of
erroneous conviction resting on circumstantial evidence of the
very strongest kind, and every intelligent man perceives that
if in such cases the error is not discovered in time to save the
prisoner's life, it is little likely ever to be discovered.

A good many years ago a man was convicted of the murder
of a clergyman in Huntingdonshire, whose name, if I remember
right, was Waterhouse. The evidence was entirely circumstantial. The prisoner, some days after sentence had been
passed upon him, having no doubt that he would be hanged,
confessed his guilt, and gave full particulars of the circumstances
attending the perpetration of his crime. Those particulars it
was possible to· verify. They were verified, and it was found
that they were entirely unconnected with the circumstances
deposed to on the trial on which the conviction rested. The
occurrence of such a case could not but produce upon the public
mind a painful impression that innocent men are not always
safe in our courts of justice. In this case, however, the judge
had not been free from doubt as to the conclusiveness of the
evidence, and the man, if he had not confessed, would certainly
not have been hanged. There is another and a much stronger
case of erroneous conviction on a much stronger case of circumstantial evidence, cited by Sir Fitzroy Kelly in his evidence
before the Capital Punishment Commission of 1864–5. Two
men (I will call them A. and B., for the names are not given
by Sir Fitzroy Kelly) were drinking with others in a public-

which stand at a considerable distance from each
other in the degree of moral depravity and of

house at night. A quarrel arose between them. A., after
having thrown a pint pot at B.'s head, ran out of the house,
pursued by B., who was heard to swear that he would be the
death of A. A. ran a considerable distance past sheds and
buildings towards a certain spot, and B. was seen by several
persons at different points between the public-house and that
spot. By one witness, who was in a shed very near that spot,
but who could not *see* what was going on there, blows were
heard, and cries and struggles ; shortly afterwards an appeal for
mercy and other blows and loud words were heard. A minute
after this, B. was seen running away in great agitation from that
spot at which, a few minutes later, A. was found stabbed in
three places and quite dead ; and when B. was seized he was
found with his hands and the front of his clothes covered with
blood. B. protested his innocence and told his story—just the
kind of story which a guilty man, having heard such a case
against him as that of which I have given the particulars, would
be likely to invent as a last chance of escape—which, resting on his unsupported assurance, could do little or nothing to
weaken the force of such overwhelming proofs of his guilt.
Fortunately for B. and for the cause of truth and justice,
another man, who lay under sentence of death for a highway
robbery with violence, committed in an adjoining county, confessed to the murder of A. just in time to save B.'s life and to
prove the truth of the highly improbable story which B. had
told in his own defence.

Other cases of erroneous convictions might be cited, but it
is unnecessary. One case, in fifty years, such as that narrated
by Sir Fitzroy Kelly is sufficient to throw doubt on the very
strongest cases of circumstantial evidence—and on that description of evidence, be it remembered, convictions for murder
chiefly rest—and to make good the argument against irreparable
punishments.

injury to the public.   If juries are influenced by
these feelings the fact is, I think, very much to
their credit and very much for the public good,
for it is more particularly necessary in the case
of great crimes, with a view to the formation of
a healthy public opinion, that rulers should not
be compelled by the state of the law to ignore
important and obvious moral distinctions.   There
are, for example, reasons conclusive to the
understanding of a juryman of average intelligence, reasons founded on moral grounds
universally recognised, and on obvious grounds
of public utility, why a punishment precisely
the same both in kind and degree, should not
be inflicted on the man between whom and his
victim there has been, with fault on both sides,
intense mutual irritation of long standing, and
the man who plans and executes the murder of
a stranger in order to possess himself of a sum
of money.

'It is not human life only,' says Mr. Mill,
'not human life as such that ought to be sacred
to us, but human feelings.   The human capacity
of suffering is what we should cause to be

respected, not the mere capacity of existing.'
This is true. It is impossible that moralists and
legislators should too frequently and strongly
impress upon mankind the duty of respecting
the feelings and the capacity of suffering of other
men, but not on this account ought they, I think,
to allow that sentiment of the sanctity of human
life by one iota to be lessened. If in no ex-
tremity of suffering are men justified in putting
an end to their own lives, how can they with
safety be allowed to pass judgment on the degree
of suffering which makes death desirable to
others ? Nothing can be more dangerous than
to encourage men to make comparisons between
the evil of death and the evil of given degrees
of pain, sorrow, or privation. Such comparisons
may easily be perverted to the very worst purposes, and produce effects the most lamentable.
Let the lesson that death is only one out of the
innumerable forms of human suffering be steadily
inculcated, and we might end by seeing a Hare
and a Burke bringing philanthropy to the aid
of their villany, and devoting themselves to the
task of searching out the lowest depths of human

misery, with a view to the promotion of medical
science by a supply of the bodies of those to
whom life was a burden and death, a relief from
torment.   Why, you will ask me, unfairly push
the maxims of an opponent to lengths to which
they were obviously not intended to be carried ?
But the question is not to what lengths Mr. Mill
carries his maxims ; for with him we know that
we are perfectly safe, but to what lengths ordinary
men might injuriously carry them, or wicked
men pervert them.   The question is whether
mankind can safely be trusted on this point, and
whether it is not more necessary, in the interest
of good government, pure morality, and social
improvement, to restrain existing recklessness
and indifference, than to stimulate the existing spirit of self-sacrifice in regard to human
life.

   Mr. Mill speaks with justice of the mania
which sometimes arises in this country for paring
down punishments.   The truth is, that in dealing with their criminals, as in some other
matters, mankind are apt to be capricious and
to fluctuate between mischievous extremes of

severity and mischievous extremes of mildness.
In England, in the course of the last fifty
years, we have seen offences against property,
by no means of the worst kind, punished with
death, and acts of atrocious cruelty to helpless
women and children punished by a few weeks of
imprisonment, commutable at the option of the
ruffian into the payment of a fine of a few pounds.
But we have improved and are still improving
in these matters, and there is now no longer
anything in our severity or our leniency absolutely shocking to humanity on the one hand, or
to common sense on the other.   There is some
ground, however, for the remark that, except
for very small offences, and offences against
property, our punishments are inadequate, and
that there is more need of strengthening than of
weakening them.   The death-punishment cannot be strengthened ; public opinion will not
allow of its being made either more painful or
more frequent.   The same may be said of all
punishments inflicting acute bodily pain.   What
needs strengthening, and may be strengthened,
is the punishment of imprisonment which,

applied—as we in practice apply it—for comparatively short terms, or for terms reducible
very much at the discretion of gaolers, chaplains,
or secretaries of state, is a most inadequate punishment for great crimes.   What is needed is that
we should fairly give our understandings to the
question whether imprisonment for long terms
of years, extended in the worst cases to the
entire remainder of life, and accompanied by
complete extinction of all intercouse with the
external world, may not be beneficially applied
to the prevention of great crimes.   Imprisonment for life is practically unknown to us ;
Mr. Mill would lead us to suppose that he is
shocked by its severity.   In this I think he is
mistaken, and that, in the long run, taking it
from its first day to its last, it would be less
severe than it seems ; but, be this as it may, if
punishments for crimes against the person are
to be strengthened, what other mode than this
is open to us of strengthening them ?   What
adequate punishment but imprisonment is possible for crimes against the person of a degree
of atrocity just falling short of the point at

which juries can be got to send men to the scaffold ?

[The following draft of a letter in Mr. Romilly's handwriting, found among his papers, and apparently addressed to a newspaper in reply to one published by Mr. Newman, appears to supply a fitting conclusion to the preceding letters, and is therefore here added.—EDITOR.]

April 1863.

May I be allowed a small space in your columns for the purpose of emphatically denying the truth of the proposition on which, in his letter to you of April 22, Mr. Newman rests his defence of capital punishment, viz. that all moral improvement is impossible in a prison life. I affirm, on the contrary, that there is no sphere so narrow, no situation so dead, as to afford no field for the exercise of Christian virtues. Within the walls of a prison there are always duties which may be performed, and passions which may be restrained, kindliness which may be fostered, past offences which may be mourned over, pain which may be·

courageously endured, words of persuasion or
of pity which may be spoken to make fellow
prisoners less wicked or less miserable. Mr.
Newman tells us that there is no possible
career within the walls of a prison. I say that
these things constitute a career, and one which,
if prolonged over a large part of a man's life,
may go far to atone for the crimes which may
have assigned their author to the narrow world
of a prison. Let a man be placed in any situation in which it is possible to place him ; let
him be confined for the remainder of his life in
a ship, in a mine, in a hospital, or even in a
prison, I say there are powers and faculties, implanted in him by the hand of God, which may
be freely used by him to make himself progressively better and wiser and less miserable as life
goes on, and that to affirm the contrary is to
affirm a doctrine which is as impious as it is
shallow.

If our prisons should ever become what
Mr. Newman would have us believe they now
are ; if life prisoners in England should, in
some terrible future, be subjected to treatment

of such a kind as to crush out of them all moral existence, and to make them more worthless and depraved at the close of their prison life than at its commencement; then the time will have come when she must relinquish all claim to be included in the list of civilised nations.

PUBLIC RESPONSIBILITY

AND

VOTE BY BALLOT.

TO WHICH ARE APPENDED

A LETTER FROM JOHN STUART MILL, M.P.

TO THE EDITOR OF 'THE READER,'
29TH APRIL, 1865.

AND OBSERVATIONS THEREON.

BY

HENRY ROMILLY, M.A.

REPRINTED FROM THE SECOND EDITION
PUBLISHED IN
1867.

THE writer thinks it necessary to say that he has used the word Ballot throughout the following pages in the sense of a method of voting at Elections of such a kind as to make it impossible that the Voter should give any proof of the vote he has given beyond his own unsupported assertion.

PUBLIC RESPONSIBILITY

AND

VOTE BY BALLOT.

———◦◦◦———

IN his speech of June 16, 1863, against the ballot, Lord Palmerston observed that its advocates 'placed the whole thing upon a wrong foundation; that they seemed to forget the vital principle, the breath of life of the British constitution, namely, public opinion and public responsibility.'

Nothing is more effective in the mouth of an orator than the confident announcement of some great principle as lying at the foundation of his own particular view of a subject, the absence of any such foundation being tacitly assumed as the weak point of the view taken by his adversary. The mere utterance by a great minister, in a certain tone of voice, and with a certain manner, of such phrases, as freedom of the press, necessity of military discipline, defences of the country, balance of power, public responsibility, often carries with it three-fourths of a well-disposed audience, whose cheers are apt to drown the voices of calm men, who might be disposed to call upon the orator to furnish his audience with some proof that his great principle was applicable to the particular question under discussion.

Lord Palmerston's great principle in the case of the ballot is public responsibility. His argument is that, if you divest a man of the responsibility to which he ought to be liable in respect of his public trust, you extinguish one of the essential principles of the British constitution, and substitute something which is unconstitutional and un-English. Nothing seems more clear and simple. The elector, according to this theory, is a trustee. When he goes up to the poll to give his vote, he is executing a trust, performing a duty to the public; and the public is entitled to call him to account for the proper execution of that trust, for the right performance of that duty; but how to call him to account, if he has dropped a card into a box, and if the secret of that card is to remain for ever buried within his own breast? How is the verdict of the public upon the quality of the vote to be pronounced, if the vote is to remain for ever unknown? How shall the voter receive his meed of praise for vote A., or of censure for vote B., when no man can tell whether his vote was A. or B.?

The friends of the ballot meet the argument with a question. If the argument is good for a voter at Marylebone, why not for a member of the Athenæum or the Carlton? To this, Lord Palmerston replies that clubs have nothing to do with the matter. 'These illustrations,' he says, 'are foreign to the purpose of the argument; for these private societies have no public duties and no public responsibilities. They are not responsible to the country for the election of their members. They are guided solely by the consideration of who are likely to be agreeable members of their societies and in the club-room.'

This argument is one of very ancient date. For fifty years past it has been the standing answer of the friend to open voting, who defends the ballot at his club, when he has been reproached with his inconsistency. 'Private societies have no public responsibility.' The proposition affords a not uninteresting field for discussion; a field, whose extent bears a certain direct proportion to the degree of latitude which a man may choose to give to that word public. But why discuss it? Suppose we grant it to be true. True or false, what bearing has it on the question of ballot or no ballot? The ballot is a device for the protection of men, not for the protection of societies. The question is this. Is there not the same reason for withholding the vote of a parliamentary elector, as for withholding the vote of a member of a club, from the knowledge of other men? What answer is it to that question to tell us that private societies have no public responsibility? No one wishes to make a secret of the acts of the general body, club or constituency. The acts of the Carlton and the Athenæum are known to any one who cares to know them; and what sane person would wish to make a secret of the fact that it was the borough of Queensville which returned John Brown to the House of Commons, or to protect the constituency of Queensville from the comments of the public and the press, on the merits or demerits of that act of theirs? It is the indi-

P

vidual elector, not the constituency, that needs protection.

These words public and publicity are, I believe,
chiefly responsible for the mist in which this question
of the ballot is enveloped.   Lord Palmerston speaks of
public responsibility as though there were no such
thing as a public short of the thirty millions of souls
which constitute the population of the British Isles.
Is there not a London public and an Edinburgh public;
a scientific public and a literary public; a public of
master-manufacturers and a public of operatives; a
military public and a naval public; a commercial public and a public of men of rank and fashion?   Every
considerable body of men constitutes a public to an
individual of that body.   A soldier is responsible to his
country and to the army, but he is still more closely
and directly responsible to his regiment.   The wider
responsibility does not destroy the narrower.   Lord
Palmerston says with truth that clubs are not responsible to the country for the election of their members.
With equal truth might he have said that the constituencies of Great Britain are not responsible to the
human race for the British House of Commons; or that
the Duke of Devonshire's butler was not responsible to
the inhabitants of Piccadilly for the safety of the plate
at Devonshire House.   It is quite true that the interests of the British empire are not likely to be much
affected by the result of the next ballot at Brooks's;
nor are the interests of mankind likely to be much
affected by the result of the next election for Middlesex.   The responsibility is so remote and indirect that
Lord Palmerston is perhaps justified in ignoring it

altogether.   But all this looks very much like trifling
with the subject. The remoteness or the entire absence of
responsibility towards the larger body does not disprove
responsibility towards the smaller.   The constituencies
of Great Britain are not perhaps responsible to the
civilised world or to Europe, but they are responsible
to Great Britain.   The great man's butler in Grosvenor
Square may not be responsible to the public of Grosvenor Square, but he is responsible to his master.   So
a London club may not be responsible to the country,
but an individual member of a club is responsible to
his club.   If the effect of his vote has been to admit an
unpleasant man into the club, the club is the sufferer.
If a parliamentary elector by his vote sends an incapable man into the House of Commons, the country
is the sufferer. In order to prevent incapable legislators
from getting into the House of Commons, Lord Palmerston thinks it right to subject the vote of the
elector to the criticism of the country; and yet he
denies that, in order to prevent unpleasant men from
getting into Brooks's Club, the votes of individual
members of Brooks's Club should be subjected to the
criticism of the club.   There seems to be some inconsistency in this.   Surely the comfort and respectability
of a club are as much dependent on the votes of its
members, as the good name of the constituency and the
welfare of England are dependent on the votes of parliamentary electors.

The analogy between the situation of a member of
a club when a candidate for admission is about to be
balloted for, and that of a voter at a parliamentary
election, is so close and perfect that it is difficult to

treat with becoming seriousness the assertion that there
is no analogy whatever between them ; and that the
purpose which by the ballot is successfully effected in
the one case, is unnecessary or unattainable in the
other.   Propose to a member of a club some question
which involves no personal considerations; such a
question, for example, as this : shall a valuable set of
the Latin classics be purchased for the library ? or
shall the members of the club be increased fron 600 to
800 ?   It will be a matter of perfect indifference to
him whether his vote is given openly or secretly.   But
propose to him the question whether A.'s application
to become a member of the club ought to be granted or
refused.   If you wish to get his real opinion on the
merits of that question, you must allow him to conceal
his vote from A. and A.'s supporters.   It may happen
that A., whom he considers a most unfit person to be a
member of the club, is connected with him in business,
or by relationship, or officially ; or that A. is an inti-
mate friend of persons to whom it would be most painful to him to give offence.   It might perhaps be best
if he had the moral courage to brave the anger of his
friends, and manfully do his duty by the club ; but
three gentlemen out of four have not the moral courage
o do this ; and if, by means of the ballot, it is possible
to get his real opinion, and to relieve him from all
unpleasant consequences, why should that not be done ?
Why call upon him for a painful effort of moral courage
which is wholly unnecessary ?   The case of the parliamentary elector is precisely similar.   Propose to him
some question which involves no personal consequences ;
such a question as this, for example : Which is the

most beneficial to a nation, agriculture or manufactures ? It will be indifferent to him whether he gives his vote upon it openly or secretly. But propose to him the question whether M. or N. shall be member for the borough or county of which he is an elector. If you wish to make sure of getting from him a vote corresponding with his real opinion of the comparative fitness of M. or N. for a seat in the House of Commons, you must enable him to conceal his vote from M. and N., and from their friends and supporters. M. may be his employer, or the near friend or relation of his employer, and it might be most painful to him to give offence to his employer, who has been a good friend to him and his family. And yet he may be intimately convinced that M. will make as bad a member of Parliament as N. will make a good one. It might be best if he also had the moral courage to brave the anger of his employer and the imputation of ingratitude, and do his duty by his country; but nine electors out of ten have no such courage, and if by giving him the protection of the ballot, you can get from him a vote corresponding with his real opinion of the comparative qualifications of the two candidates, without injurious consequences to himself, why should you not do so ? Why call upon him unnecessarily to sacrifice his feelings or his worldly interest in the discharge of his duty to his country ?

I am aware that Lord Palmerston is supported in this attempted distinction between a parliamentary elector and a member of a private society by very high authority, for I find in Mr. Mill's work on Representative Government the following passage :

' A member of a club is really what the elector
falsely believes himself to be, under no obligation to
consider the wishes or interests of any one else.   He
declares nothing by his vote but that he is or is not
willing to associate in a manner more or less close with
a particular person.   This is a matter on which, by
universal admission, his own pleasure or inclination is
entitled to decide.'

The admission, however, amounts merely to this,
viz. that no other person is entitled to interfere with
his discretion, which is equally true of the parliamentary
elector.   Surely, it does not go the length of maintaining that he is under no moral obligation to consider in
his vote what is likely to be agreeable, or the contrary,
to the other members of the society.   A member of a
club is surely as much morally obliged to consider the
comfort and respectability of the club as an elector is
obliged to consider the credit of the constituency to
which he belongs, and the welfare of the country.   The
degrees of importance in the two cases are different,
but the principle is the same.   There is a ballot at the
—— Club for A. B.   He is an ill-natured, quarrelsome
man, always seeking occasion to lead those in whose
society he finds himself into discussions, which he conducts with acrimony, want of candour, and personality.
I happen to be so constituted that to me this is an
agreeable excitement; but I am well aware that, to
some members of the club, the admission of this man
will be a serious calamity.   I vote for him, nevertheless,
on Mr. Mill's principle, that I am under no obligation
to consider any wishes or interests but my own.   Or take
a case of an opposite kind.   An accomplished man, of

unexceptionable conduct and agreeable manners, is proposed at the Oxford and Cambridge; I happen to have a dislike to him, of the same kind as that which some men have to Dr. Fell. According to Mr. Mill, I am morally justified in giving effect by a black ball to my selfish antipathy, in defiance to what 1 know to be the general wish of the club.[1] If a member of a club may do this, why may not a parliamentary elector vote for a personal friend, whom he knows to be quite unfit for the duties of a legislator? or withhold his vote from a virtuous and able statesman, of his own way of thinking in politics, on some petty ground of personal offence? The interests of the people of England are more important than those of a London club undoubtedly; but this seems to be the only difference between the cases. In both cases the individual man has a duty to perform towards the general body. If it is right in principle to protect the member of the club from the resentment of those to whose wishes he may find himself opposed in the performance of that duty, it is right so to protect the parliamentary elector. If it is right in principle to subject the vote of the parliamentary elector to the supervision of the public, it is right to subject the vote of the member of the club to the supervision of the club.

There are two kinds of motives by one or the other of which a parliamentary elector, when he gives his

---

[1] Practically, the member of the club, who might be tempted to conduct himself in this foolish and unprincipled way, would be stopped by a sense of responsibility and the suggestions of a more enlightened self-interest ; and the elector, under the ballot, would be restrained by similar considerations from any similar act of petty selfishness.

vote, must of necessity be actuated. His vote must either be given in subjection to the control of other men, or free from such control. Either his vote is determined by the fear of offending or the hope of conciliating some other man or men who happen to be friendly or to be hostile to the pretensions of a particular candidate, or it is the simple expression of his own conviction or inclination, free from all external pressure. Now, the purpose and the effect of the ballot is to withdraw the voter from that first class of motives, to relieve him from all external pressure, whether it take the more definite form of a bribe or a menace, or the less definite form of a disinclination on his part to give offence to other men. But then this question arises. If the elector be protected from external pressure, can he be trusted to carry his free judgment and inclination in the direction of the public good ? Granted that, by the ballot, you relieve him from an injurious influence —the seductive or coercive influence of rich and powerful men—but do you not, by that same ballot, withdraw him from a beneficial influence, the moral influence of an enlightened public ? The question is, in truth, two questions. First, when no longer liable to be tempted or frightened out of the path of duty, will not his inherent perverseness lead him to desert that path ? and, secondly, if that be so, would not public opinion—if, by the ballot, you had not rendered it powerless—have been effectual to keep him within it ? Mr. Mill, in the work from which I have already quoted, answers both questions in the affirmative; the advocate of the ballot answers them both in the negative.

To the second of these questions I will address myself hereafter. In reference to the first of them, the attempted distinction between the member of the club and the parliamentary elector seems to me to rest upon no intelligible foundation. Lord Palmerston and Mr. Mill would be the first to contend that, when a member of a club has been relieved by the ballot from all fear of giving personal offence, his individual interest is identical with the interest of the general body. The object of the club is to get well-conditioned, pleasant men into the club, and to keep ill-conditioned, unpleasant men out of it. The object of the individual member is and must be the same. But if this be affirmed of the member of the club, how can it be denied of the parliamentary elector, that, when protected by the ballot from the seductive or coercive influence of other men, his interest will be reduced to his interest as a citizen. The interest of the citizens, as a body, or, to use the equivalent but more common phrase, the interest of the country, is to send to Westminster the most honest and capable men that can be found. The interest of the individual citizen is and must be the same. If, when he is no longer liable to be corrupted or intimidated, the elector can be supposed to have some other interest, what is it? We can form no conception of any other, and Mr. Mill does not tell us of any other. He tells us, indeed, that an elector may be foolish or malicious, and have unworthy feelings within his breast; but the members of clubs are no more free from such defects of character than parliamentary electors; and the one is not much more likely than the other to sacrifice the permanent welfare of the body to which he belongs, to a morbid antipathy or an idle caprice. The responsibility theory of Lord Palmerston and Mr. Mill rests upon two propositions : first, that a parliamentary elector owes a duty to his country; and, second, that he cannot be got to perform that duty, except under public supervision. To the first, which is a truism, I have nothing to object; but to the second I demur. I maintain that if you place him by the ballot quite beyond the reach of the improper control of other men, you leave to the elector no intelligible interest, except that of the body of which he is a member—his interest as a citizen. In other words, you bring his interest into coincidence with his duty, in which case it is idle to say that he will not perform his duty unless the public eye is upon him. In other cases, when interest and duty coincide, we leave men to themselves. Why should we do otherwise in the case of an elector ?

For example, if there were any reasonable fear that farmers, manufacturers, and merchants would conduct their business for the purpose of reducing themselves to poverty, it would be necessary, under pain of ruin to the country, which would be the consequence of that particular mode of carrying on productive industry, to make them responsible to the public for the rational employment of their capitals. If physicians were likely to enter upon the practice of medicine with a view to the extension and aggravation of diseases, it would be necessary to make the medical profession responsible to the public for a legitimate use of its acquired skill and knowledge. Again, if there were any danger of Lord Palmerston and his colleagues conducting their delibe-rations with a view to the diminution of the dignity

and power of Great Britain, it might be necessary that
public reporters should be admitted to the meetings of
the Cabinet.   We do not in fact subject these persons
to any such supervision; we do not call upon the
merchant for his balance-sheet, the physician for his
prescriptions, or the minister for a report of the proceedings at Cabinet Councils, because we are satisfied
that they have no intelligible motive for exercising
their respective functions in a mode hurtful to the
public; indeed, that there is a motive of adequate
strength impelling them in the opposite direction.   We
are aware that the only thing we have to fear from
them is defective judgment, and that publicity is no
cure for that.   So, if there were any reasonable fear
that an elector, when protected from improper external
control, would deliberately choose a dishonest or foolish
man to make laws for him, it might be necessary to
make him responsible to the country for his vote.   But
the elector, when so protected, has no conceivable interest in voting for a dishonest or foolish man, and has
a certain obvious interest in voting for an honest and
wise man.   Indeed, if it could be made apparent to his
mind that candidate A. was, in one single particular,
however trifling, superior to candidate B., being equal
to him in everything else, we have no reason to doubt
that he would give a preference to candidate A.   He
might deceive himself in regard to the comparative
merits of A. and B., but, as I have already observed, to
make a man responsible to other men will not convert
a bad judgment into a good one.   The Palmerstonian
theory of electoral trusteeship seems, then, not to have
made its first step on very solid ground; for it is by no

means clear that it is necessary to make the elector a trustee at all.

If a man has a certain plain definite interest in acting for the public good, what do you gain by making him responsible to other men, some of whom have the same plain interest as himself, neither more nor less, the rest having, by your own admission, selfish interests which are *not* those of the public ? I do not deny that the plain interest of an elector to vote for the best man may be overruled by passion or caprice, but then the men to whom you would make him responsible are as subject as he is to those disturbing influences, often much more so. If you could pick out the 500 best and wisest men in the country, and erect them into a model public for the special use of your electoral body, well and good. Even then, however, it might be asked how this public of good and wise men are to bring their goodness and wisdom to bear upon the practical question, which has to be resolved upon the hustings. Grant that your model public is overflowing with wisdom and virtue ; but the elector is waiting to know, not whether he is to vote for wisdom and virtue against vice and folly, but whether he is to vote for A. or for B. How will your model public answer that question, except in the very rare cases in which an admirable Crichton stands opposed to a notorious knave or blockhead? They cannot answer it ; because in ninety-nine cases out of a hundred — wise and good as they are, they will not all be of one mind in regard to the comparative merits of A. and B. They will be reduced at last to say to the elector, what it would have been wiser to say at first : ' Judge for yourself. Vote for him whom you believe to be the best man, and, if all other electors do the same, there is nothing for *us* to do.'

This is no peculiarity of a parliamentary election ; your model public would have the same difficulty in all cases in which there is no certain criterion of right and wrong ; in all cases in which the question at issue is a matter of opinion. Poll the artists of Europe on the question, which is the greater landscape painter, Turner or Claude. What will you gain by talking to them of their responsibility to the world of art ? Take a vote upon the comparative merits of High Church and Low Church, or of the Federals and Confederates, or upon the question whether Smith, Jones, or Thompson is the fittest man to represent Warwickshire ; what good will you do by calling upon each individual voter to make public declaration of his opinion ? These are matters on which every man is entitled to use his own judgment, and on which, whether the votes be take openly or secretly, it is barely conceivable that, except from a desire to please, or a fear to offend other men, a man should vote one way when he thinks another.

The principle seems to be obvious. When you have some plain, infallible test of right and wrong in the matter, or some unerring insight into the motive, subject men to responsibility. If these things fail you —and in matters of opinion they always will fail you— leave a man to his own judgment. You can do nothing but mischief by meddling with him, except to protect his judgment from the interference of other men if such interference is threatened. If you have reason to think that he is capable of forming a sound judgment, do not interpose between him and his judgment. If you think

otherwise, do not call upon him for an opinion; in
the case of an electoral system, do not give him the
suffrage.

Sydney Smith, in his famous article against the
ballot, when he came to enforce by examples his doctrine of the responsibility of parliamentary electors, was
at once stopped short by the facts of the case. He was
reduced to the alternative of giving up his doctrine, or
of resorting, in support of it, to a supposition which has
no practical reality; which may perhaps be true once
in ten thousand times, or twice in two hundred years,
but not much oftener.

' Who,' says he, ' brought that mischievous profligate
villain into parliament ?   Let us see the names of his
real supporters.   Who stood out against the strong and
uplifted arm of power ?   Who discovered this excellent
and hitherto unknown person ?   Who opposed the man
whom we all know to be one of the first men in the
country ?   Are these fair and useful questions to be
veiled hereafter in impenetrable mystery ?   Is this sort
of publicity of no good as a restraint ?   Is it of no good
as an incitement to, and a reward for, exertions ?   Is
not public opinion formed by such feelings ? and is it
not a dark and demoralising system to draw this veil
over human actions; to say to the mass be base and
you will not be despised ; be virtuous and you will not
be honoured ? '

This is excellent declamation, and, if it did not rest
for its argumentative force upon an untrue description
of an English election, it would be excellent reasoning,
and would be a triumphant vindication of the principle
of responsibility as applied to parliamentary electors.

If, when a voter comes up to the poll, the question as between the candidates were a clear question between wisdom and folly, between integrity and profligacy, between patriotism and selfishness—so clear that no voter could possibly give his vote in ignorance that if he voted for A. he was betraying his country, and if he voted for B. he was discharging a plain, imperative duty, the sense of responsibility—however little it might be needed—could at all events operate only for good, that is, against the villain and in favour of the good man. The weak point of the argument is that it is founded on a fiction. The author carries us with him to a scene which is the creation of his fancy. He places us on what he is pleased to describe as an English hustings. There Vice stands opposed to Virtue, and there are infallible signs by which to distinguish them. Vice is elected, and carries his mischievous villany into Parliament. Higgins, the shoemaker who voted for the villain, is held up to the indignant reproof of England, and by that severe example the most beneficial effect is produced for all time coming on the conduct of parliamentary electors. Can anything be more unreasonable and unjust? Poor Higgins, who is a very respectable and sensible man and acted with the best intentions, was, when he gave his vote, entirely without suspicion of the real character of this monster of profligacy, which only developed itself at a later period; and although —as it turns out—a prodigy of wickedness was opposed to a paragon of virtue at this particular election, there are a thousand chances to one that a similar case will not recur for the next hundred years.

Continuing, for the purpose of this discussion, the

assumption of a public of wise and good men; still, in
what way, I would ask, can it exercise any useful influence over a particular class of acts, unless those acts
are of such a kind as to bear upon the face of them their
good or evil tendency, or the motive which dictated
them; unless, in short, it shall be easy to find, in
respect of them, ready and true answers to such questions as the following :—Has he acted honestly or dis-
honestly ?   Has he acted wisely or foolishly ?   Has he
performed the duties attaching to the office which he
holds—to the situation in which he has placed himself,
or to that in which accident has placed him—justly or
unjustly, efficiently or inefficiently, with firmness or with
weakness ?   There are cases innumerable of human conduct—but voting at a parliamentary election is *not* one
of them—in which such questions may be answered
without difficulty.   You may find examples of them at
every step.

For instance, a million of cotton operatives, in consequence of certain occurrences on the other side of the
Atlantic, over which neither they nor their employers
had any control, are suddenly deprived of their accustomed means of subsistence.   It is a clear case for a
national subscription to relieve their wants, and a subscription is set on foot.   Nine rich men out of ten at
once come forward with their contributions.   The tenth,
who happens to be so constituted that his feelings of
compassion do not very easily get the better of his love
of money, is tempted to hold back ; but there is something in that long subscription-list which will infallibly
appear next week in a conspicuous part of the county
paper, containing the names of all the rich men in the

neighbourhood except his own, which he has not the courage to face.   He yields to the force of public opinion, and sends his fifty guineas.

A member of Parliament, having won his election by an announcement of free-trade principles, goes up to Westminster, and on the first occasion which presents itself votes with the Protectionists.   His dishonesty is flagrant; public opinion cries out upon him; honest men cut him.   Slippery politicians are, by his example, for ever discouraged from seeking to obtain seats in Parliament on false pretences.

A foreign invasion is expected.   Volunteers collect from all quarters.   A. B., a young man, muscular but faint-hearted, is tempted to remain quietly at home; but the people of his village could not possibly be kept in ignorance of his absence from the place where his companions are about to risk their lives in defence of their country.   It is a greater trial to his courage to brave the comments of his neighbours than to face the enemy.   He bows to the force of public opinion, and hurries to the scene of action.

'England expects every man to do his duty,' said Nelson at Trafalgar.   No man in the fleet thought of asking, what is my duty?   Every man in the fleet knew that his duty was to brave every danger, to strain every muscle in doing what his commanding officer should order him to do.   He knew too that, when the battle should be over, those who had been by his side would be able to say whether he had done his duty or not.   His public was the fleet.   To him the difference between the admiration and contempt of the fleet was more than the difference between life and death.

Q

Here are four cases of human conduct which speak for themselves, on which all doubt as to what is right and what is wrong is as impossible in the mind of the actor as it is in the minds of those who will pass judgment on his conduct ; in which, therefore, the beneficial influence of public opinion is undoubted.

Take now the case of a juryman. The duty which his country calls upon him to perform is not less important than that of the seaman in Nelson's fleet. But what plain and certain criterion is there of the quality of the performance ? A man is tried for murder. Public feeling is strong against him. Eleven of the jurymen are for conviction. The twelfth, having applied such powers of mind as he possesses to a consideration of the evidence, concludes that there is no sufficient ground for a conviction, and finally brings round his eleven brethren to his way of thinking. The man is acquitted; the public is indignant, and wise men are of opinion that a murderer has escaped. Would it tend in the smallest degree to prevent the recurrence of similar failures of justice that his fellow-citizens should visit with their anger the mistaken juryman ? Would it increase the number of good verdicts and lessen the number of bad ones, to make the twelve men discuss in public the questions submitted to them ? Would a sensible judge take occasion, from such an occurrence, to lecture juries upon their public responsibilities ? To what purpose lecture them, when every man of the twelve knows perfectly well that the only point on which it is possible for him to go wrong is on the point of judgment, and that—publicity or no publicity—he is as anxious to be right on that point as the judge can

be, or as the public can be ? To remind a juryman of
his responsibility to public opinion will not give him
the power of weighing evidence, if he does not possess
it already ; and let the verdict on some particular occasion be what it may, neither judge nor public will be
able to prove conclusively that it was wrong.

If public opinion is to have any effect on human
conduct the public must be agreed what acts to approve
and what acts to condemn. There must be some principle of agreement, some plain criterion of right and
wrong. If the case be that of a contested parliamentary
election, it must be made apparent to the moral sense
of the country, that to vote yellow is a praiseworthy act,
and to vote blue a blamable one, or *vice versâ*. But if
one-half of the world believes blue to be wrong and
yellow to be right, and the other half believes yellow to
be wrong and blue to be right, how can the world give
a beneficial verdict in the matter, or any verdict at all ?
Public opinion in such a case may be aptly typified by
a jury, of whom six are for conviction and six for
acquittal. What moral authority has such a verdict ?
of what practical use is it ? An elector sets off for the
hustings to give his vote, the candidates being A. and
B. He is most anxious to secure the public approbation for his conduct. On the way he debates the matter
with himself, thus :—' If I vote for A. the Tories will
applaud vociferously. If I vote for B. the gentlemen
of the Whig committee will shake me by the hand, and
the rest of the Whigs will smile approvingly. My own
strong belief is that A. is all to nothing the best man ;
but A. is a Protectionist, and although my worldly
interest undoubtedly lies in the direction of Protection,

I am honest enough not to be led by worldly interest
to deviate from what I believe to be right. What shall
I do? If I vote for B. I shall be praised for my dis-
interestedness, but my conscience will tell me that I
have not voted according to my real belief of the merits
of the candidates. If I vote for A. my vote will be
branded for its selfishness, and yet it will have been the
true, honest vote. Will any one tell me what I am to
do to satisfy my conscience at the same time that I
satisfy public opinion?' No; nobody will tell him,
or can tell him; nor will anybody ever find in his vote
the groundwork for a correct moral judgment of his conduct. It is mere folly to interfere between him and his
conscience.

A holder of the responsibility theory, as applied to
parliamentary electors, may perhaps retort upon me in
this way :—'You do not deny that a member of the
House of Commons should be made responsible to
public opinion: and yet he may be called upon to vote
on questions just as incapable of being answered by a
reference to some plain, incontestable criterion of right
and wrong as the question of the elector between a blue
and a yellow vote.' True; but the act of the elector is
the one single act attaching to his office, which he is
called upon to perform on an average not more than
once in every two or three years; whereas the supposed
act of the member of Parliament is only one of a vast
number and variety of acts, taking place from day to
day, and extending over a considerable period of time;
and although, out of that long list of acts which make
up his parliamentary career, you might pick out single
acts from which it would be impossible to deduce any

accurate judgment of the skill or honesty with which he
has performed the duties of his office ; yet, if you passed
in review the whole of those acts, you would find no
such difficulty.   If members of the House of Commons
were sent up to Westminster for the purpose of voting
upon this one question, and no other :—' Shall A. or B.
be Prime Minister of England ?' there would—except
on one ground—be exactly the same reason for making
them vote secretly, and exactly the same absence of any
good reason for making them vote openly, that there is
in the case of the elector who has to choose between
M. and N. as member for Middlesex.   That one ground
is this, viz. that the member of the House of Commons
is a representative of other men.   The constitution of
the country intended that those who chose him should
have an opportunity, at certain recurring periods, of re-
considering their choice ; of re-electing him if they are
satisfied with his conduct, of substituting some other
person if they arc not.   His acts being the groundwork
of their choice, they must not be kept in ignorance of
those acts.   Their function would become a nullity, and
the intention of the constitution would be frustrated, if
he votes and proceedings in Parliament were kept
secret.   If an elector were also chosen by a more numerous body to represent them, the case of an elector would,
in this respect, be the same as that of a member of a
legislative assembly ; and under some Constitutions it
is so.   The fact that in England it is not so is proof
sufficient that, by the theory of the British Constitution,
parliamentary electors are supposed to possess within
themselves the capacity and the motives requisite for
the proper performance of their one single function.

It is a mistake to suppose that, in principle, the ballot would not operate in the same way and to the same beneficial end in a representative assembly as at a parliamentary election. The votes of electors are not the only votes that may be bought and sold; and the ballot would as effectually obstruct the corrupt practices of a minister as those of a rich candidate for a seat in Parliament. A century ago, before the virtuous example of the first William Pitt had made it dishonourable in members of Parliament to hold their votes at the disposal of the dispensers of the public money, it might almost have been a question whether the incontestable advantages of publicity were not too. dearly bought, at the cost of that mass of political turpitude, which it would have been possible, by means of the ballot, to sweep from within the walls of Parliament. But in the present condition of political morality in England, which, looking with undisturbed complacency at any number of corrupt bargains between candidates and electors, shrinks with horror from a corrupt bargain between a minister and a member of Parliament, the case is different. Within the walls of Parliament the evil of which secret voting is the specific remedy has, in the present day, shrunk to dimensions too small to detract in any sensible degree from the advantages of publicity; whereas, on the hustings, the case is exactly the reverse. There the advantages of publicity are, as they always must be, too small to lessen, in any sensible degree, the vast dimensions of that evil. It is as difficult to overrate the value of publicity in a representative assembly, as it is to underrate its value at the polling booth.

The first and greatest use of publicity is to give practical validity to the relation between elector and elected: and, inasmuch as in England no such relation exists between the general public and the parliamentary voter, no such use is in that case to be derived from publicity. To shut the doors of the House of Commons upon the public is in truth to place 656 men in a situation of high trust, and to refuse to those whose duty and privilege it is periodically either to continue them in the trust or to discharge them from the trust, all information as to the mode in which they have executed the trust. It is to restrict the choice of the constituencies to untried men. It is to call upon constituencies to choose, and to withhold from them the knowledge without which they can scarcaly choose well. It is to invest them with a political function, and to deprive them of the means of performing it beneficially. But if at the polling booth you should prohibit all intrusion into the secrets of the ballot box, you would not be withholding information necessary for the proper performance of a political function, for you have not conferred any such function. You have not given to those who might wish to penetrate that secret the power to retain the name of one single elector on the registration-list or to strike it off. At the point at which, in a representative system, the relation of elector to elected ceases, at that same point does the principal use of publicity cease. At some point or other in the system it must of necessity cease.

The second great use of publicity in a legislative assembly is, that the political education of a people depends upon it; and upon the political education of the

people—under which term I include both governors and
governed—depend the securities for the permanence of
the national welfare.   When the doors of the Legislative
Chambers are closed to a people, or when all legislative
and administrative power is in the hands of a single
ruler, that state of things—if it maintains itself un-
opposed as the normal condition of a country—presupposes, on the part of the people, an entire indifference
to their political institutions, and to the management
of the national concerns.   It presupposes that they
are satisfied to be governed in any way in which it may
please their rulers to govern them; and the virtues of
rulers can never be proof against such apathy on the
part of their natural and legitimate censors.   All experience has shown that permanent, good government is
incompatible with indifference, and its necessary accompaniment, ignorance on the part of the people.   The
people of Great Britain are perhaps the greatest politicians in Europe.   The far greater part of what is said,
or done, or proposed to be done by their rulers, is laid
open to them; and it is scarcely too much to say that
they are the best governed people in Europe.   The
Turks know least and care least about the acts of their
rulers, and they are the worst governed of all the
peoples who lay claim to the name of civilised.

When the acts and words of rulers are laid bare to
the criticism of the entire people, the moral effect is as
beneficial to the ruled as to the rulers.   The reports of
the proceedings of the British Parliament form the most
instructive work on practical politics in existence; and
no man, whether he be a philosopher or a mechanic at
weekly wages, can read them in a serious and truthful

spirit, without becoming a wiser man and a better
citizen.   The daily reading of those debates, in which
all opinions and interests find exponents, in which
everything that is noble and true, and every form even
of prejudice and selfishness, has its advocate and its
assailant, operates as a slow but sure check upon ignorance, narrow-mindedness, and intolerance.   Popular
estimates both of men and measures are brought nearer
and nearer to the truth by that continuous stream of
discussion outside the walls of Parliament, which is
created and stimulated by the publication of those
debates.   It is easy to find examples.   Take the case
of the laws which regulate the labour of women and
children in factories.   The attempt to legislate on that
subject was met at first by strong though unselfish
hostility : but it ended, under the influence of public
discussion, by being acquiesced in as beneficent and
necessary ; and of many of the greatest and best
measures of the present century—the Reform Bill for
instance, Catholic Emancipation, and the Repeal of the
Corn Laws—it has been the fate to be carried by de-
monstrations of opinion, which could never have acquired the necessary strength under any system but one
which threw open the doors of Parliament to the public.
The qualities in rulers which form the best securities
for good government, integrity, moral courage, disinter-
estedness, devotion to public duties, are precisely those
which are especially fostered by the rewards which an
approving people have it in their power to bestow ; but
a people can neither reward nor approve unless the acts
and words of their public men are laid open before
them.   Under that enduring ordeal of publicity the

more showy qualities of a legislator, the mere power of expression, dexterity in extempore reply, and the arts of the rl etorician slowly but as surely lose ground, as the higher qualities—truthfulness, candour, precision of mind, comprehensiveness—gain ground in the popular estimation.

Great and virtuous statesmen do, no doubt, like comets, appear from time to time in countries in which government is carried on under a veil; but the only possible rewards of statesmen in such countries—the pleasures, flatteries, and glitter of mere wealth and power—the material rewards, as contradistinguished from the moral rewards which publicity places at the disposal of a people—tend in no degree to foster the growth of such men. When they do appear, they appear in spite of the political system of the country, not, as in England, in consequence of it.

Whatever may be thought of the soundness of that principle of government which is expressed in the saying, ' *For the people but not by the people,*' it is quite certain that no government will long continue impartially to devote itself to the interests of all classes of the people, high and low, without favour or exception, if it is not carried on under the eye of the people. Of the England of the present day it may with truth be said that there is, within her shores, no class of persons, however humble, whose welfare is not a subject of frequent solicitude on the part of their rulers, and no class in whom a frequent observation of that fact has not produced a high degree of confidence in the excellence of their government. The same could certainly not have been said fifty years ago, and the change is

perhaps chiefly owing to the increased publicity of
parliamentary proceedings.   The tendency of that
publicity is twofold, and it is as constant as it is
beneficial ; it tends to strengthen the motives for exer-
tion and to raise the standard of excellence in the
minds of rulers, and it tends to diminish the incapacity
of the people to judge soundly of their qualities and
conduct.   It would be idle to waste words in proving
that no effects analogous to those I have described
have been produced, or are capable of being produced,
by making public the votes of parliamentary electors.
To follow step by step the public career of a statesman
or the history of a legislative measure is an instructive
process even to a stupid man ; but what instruction
will the cleverest man extract out of a knowledge of
the individual votes at a contested election ?

If, however, you insist upon telling an elector that
he is a trustee who cannot with safety be left to his
own discretion and virtue in the execution of the trust,
you must in common consistency furnish him with some
rule of conduct.   If you refer him to public opinion,
you must begin by telling him what you mean by the
public; of whom that body is composed, and what
steps he is to take in order to find out what they really
think about the rival candidates.   There are certain
persons, with Lord Palmerston at their head, who talk
of the elector's responsibility to the country as though
the word country were a mere synonym for a body of
men absolutely free from all the elements of internal
disagreement, bound together by one set of interests
and one set of principles, and possessed of one uniform
rule of conduct for the use of all applicants for informa-

tion or advice.   And yet these same persons will tell
you that the country is made up of a multiplicity of
different interests, each of which is entitled to its fair
share of representation.   Imagine the dreadful situation
of a strictly conscientious voter who goes up to the
poll at the Queensville election, burning with anxiety
to do his duty to his country.   His duty to his country!
What is his country?   The following are a few of its
component parts.   There is the shipping interest and
the colonial interest; the agricultural interest, the
manufacturing interest, and the railway interest.
There is the Church and the Dissenters; and there
are the Irish Catholics and the Irish Protestants; and
there is the old established Church of Scotland and the
Free Church of Scotland; and the Irish tenants and
the Irish landlords; and there are the direct-taxation
men and the indirect-taxation men, and half a hundred
other interests of less importance, which it would be
too long to enumerate.   Think of the problem submitted to the mind of this unhappy man.   His business
is to discover whether the most perfect adjustment of
all these discordant interests to the eternal principles
of truth, justice, and right will best be promoted by
voting for Sir Jasper Heaviside, the rich banker, or for
Mr. Plausible, the Under-Secretary of State for the
——— Department under Lord Paragon's administration.
When a right-minded man has such a problem as this
to resolve, is it not a refinement of cruelty to add to
his sufferings by talking to him, as Sydney Smith did,
about public responsibility and the obligation of doing
his duty to his country manfully and in the face of the
world?   Allow me to ask these gentlemen this ques-

tion: Why may not I, who am a simple man with my own opinions, be allowed to use my own understanding, and quietly vote for the man whom I believe to be the most likely to make a good member of Parliament, without control by, or responsibility to, other people, who may not be as competent judges as I am? 'No!' I am told, ' you are a trustee. The public must be allowed to judge of your conduct.' But what public? Is it the thirty millions of the census of 1861? or, if only a part of the thirty millions, what part? Is it the entire adult population of the kingdom which is to be my judge; or only the adult males, the women being thrown overboard? or is it that part only of the population called the manufacturing class—I being a member of that class?—or is it the class of non-electors, my brother electors being supposed to be able to take care of themselves? or, finally, is it merely my own little particular public of Queensville which is to be my judge? To that I should have no objection : but then, if I succeed in satisfying the public of Queensville, which happens to be the principal seat of the riband manufacture, how do I satisfy the men of enlarged economical views who would call this riband interest a narrow or selfish interest? In short, if I am to satisfy the general public, how am I to know their wishes? if the manufacturing interest, what will the agricultural interest say to it? if the riband interest of Queensville, what will political economy say to it?

Many thousands of English electors ask to be protected by the ballot from the pressure of certain corrupting and persecuting influences. No; we are told, your case is a hard one, but nothing can be done for

you ; for the remedy you propose would throw you
open to a still more injurious influence, that of your
own inherent folly and wickedness.   One thing you
must at all hazards be prevented from doing, and that
is to settle the question of your votes with your own
consciences and your own understandings.

' Thirty years ago,' says Mr. Mill in the same chapter
of his work on representative government, from which
I have already quoted—' thirty years ago it was still
true that in the election of members of Parliament, the
main evil to be guarded against was that which the
ballot would exclude—coercion by landlords, employers,
and customers.   At present, I conceive, a much greater
source of evil is the selfishness or the selfish partialities
of the voter himself.   A base and mischievous vote is
now, I am convinced, much oftener given from the
voter's personal interest, or class interest, or some mean
feeling in his own mind, than from any fear of consequences at the hands of others ; and to these influences
the ballot would enable him to yield himself up free
from all sense of shame or responsibility.'

Mr. Mill treats the matter as though it were a
simple question between two sets of injurious influences,
from one or the other of which there is no escape ; a
question between the evil of a vote dictated by another
man, and the evil of a vote emanating from mischievous
baseness or selfishness existing within the breast of the
voter.   The argument seems to say, that if, by secret
voting, you escape from one of these evils, by secret
voting you fall into the other ; that although the ballot
may give you the man's real vote, the real vote will be
good for nothing when you have got it.   But surely

the dictates of self-interest are not always mischievous. A man's interest may be bound up with that of other men. When the framers of a Constitution give the suffrage to a people, they do so in the hope that it will be exercised in accordance with an enlightened self-interest; that kind of self-interest which, when two or more candidates are set before me for election to an office of trust—involving duties in the efficient performance of which I, in common with my fellow-citizens, am personally interested—leads me to give my vote to the man whom I believe likely to perform them well, in preference to the man whom I believe to be likely to perform them less well. As an elector I have a perfectly clear intelligible interest in that preference; an interest which I understand myself and can explain to others. If the duties of that office are generally well-performed, I am a sharer with my fellow-citizens in the benefits which wise and impartial legislation confers upon a people; if they are generally ill-performed, I share in the injury which ill-considered or partial legislation inflicts upon a people; and I have a clear, definite, palpable interest in contributing by my vote to secure the first of these results and to prevent the second of them. This is no vain illusion, and it is as certain as anything in moral science can be that, in the absence of counteracting motives—and let Mr. Mill remember that to destroy such counteracting motives is the object and would be the effect of the ballot—that interest will determine my vote. It matters little what we call it; one man may call it patriotism, and another selfishness; but call it by what name we will, as the determining principle of the conduct of parliamentary

electors, such self-interest is that which all men who
really care for human progress will be anxious to foster,
it is that on which all rational theories of popular
representation are in reality founded.

I do not contend that all voters who give their
votes upon that sound and legitimate view of their interest will give them wisely; some will and some will
not. That depends upon the intelligence of the voter.
What I do contend for is this, viz. that, amongst the
various forms of self-interest which determine the votes
of an electoral body—supposing it not to be composed
of idiots—this beneficial form is one of those upon
which practically—if you will only protect the voter
from the selfish pressure of other people—you may
the most surely rely. Mr. Mill, however, in the passage I have quoted, passes it over as though it had no
existence.

Now a few words with respect to mischievous selfishness. Mr. Mill speaks of selfish partialities, baseness, personal interest, class interest, and mean feelings
in the voter's mind; but there is a good deal of vague-
ness in these phrases. The mischievous kinds of self-
interest are in truth all included under one or other of
the two following heads.

1st. The interest of the individual man, apart from
any interests which he has in common with other
men.

2nd. His interest as a member of a class; the
class having interests opposed to those of the public
at large.

Now as regards the first of these; will Mr. Mill tell
me what exclusive interest as an individual I can have

in voting for A. rather than B., except that I may hope
to secure the good will, or avert the ill will, of A. or
A.'s supporters, in return for my vote? But secret
voting makes it impossible that they should ever have
conclusive proof that I did vote for him. If I give my
vote openly, he has that proof, and I may reasonably
hope that he will show, in some practical form, his
grateful sense of the support I have given him. The
ballot will effectually crush any such hope. Mr. Mill
will surely not contend that it is possible for me to
extract exclusive personal benefit out of any possible line
of general parliamentary conduct which A. may pursue,
except in so far as I am one of a class of persons to
whose class interests A. is known to be favourable.

Now as regards mischievous *class* selfishness. How
is a vote dictated by a selfish class interest likely to be
prevented by open voting? Such vote, if it is unpopular with one portion of the public, will be just the
reverse with another. It will be applauded, not condemned, by that portion of the public with which I am
most directly and habitually brought into contact, and
to which I consider myself more particularly responsible. If I am a cotton spinner, I associate habitually
with cotton spinners; if a farmer, with farmers; if a
silk-weaver, with silk-weavers. The praise of my own
people will weigh a thousand times more with me than
the dispraise of the rest of the world; the more so that
the former will be near and clamorous, the latter distant and subdued. No one needs to be told what an
outcry a knot of men, great or small, will sometimes
make about the interests of their class; and how seldom
they receive, at the hands of the general public, even

R

the gentlest rebuke for their selfishness. The ballot, if it were good for nothing else, would be good for a great deal, if it weakened—as it would do—the power of selfish cliques, to convert all the rest of the world into mere props for the support of their separate class interests. Mr. Mill thinks that the sense of responsibility has the best effect upon voters, and yet speaks of base and mischievous votes given from class interests. But what is responsibility, if it be not the being accountable to a class; a class greater or smaller, more or less numerous? The little class interests are not more mischievously selfish than the large class interests. When the silk-weavers of Spitalfields clamoured for protection, were they one whit more mischievously selfish than the landlords, when they made their great stand against free trade in corn? The class interest of the British shipowner; is it less selfish than the class interest of the London needlewoman? What course of conduct, according to Mr. Mill, ought a small farmer, some twenty years ago, to have taken at the election of an agricultural county, as between the candidates on the protection-to-agriculture interest, and the candidates on the free-trade interest? To vote for the former was to vote for a mischievous class interest of the highest order of mischief; to vote for the latter was to set at defiance all sense of responsibility to the only public which to the voter was a practical reality.

I confess that under no system should I be much alarmed at the prospect of electors voting from a 'mean feeling in their own minds,' if by that phrase I may understand Mr. Mill to designate, not so much cases of selfish interest, as cases of irrational caprice or preju-

dice : such cases as that of an elector who should vote
for a candidate because he was six feet high and his opponent only five feet six, or—to give Sydney Smith's
examples—because his father knew the candidate's
grandfather, or because his second son is the candidate's
footman. Every one is entitled to have his own opinion
of the extent to which, in the serious business of life,
Englishmen are the slaves of such follies. If Sydney
Smith was right, and if no change for the better has
taken place, one can only lament the fruitlessness of all
that expensive machinery which has so long been at
work to promote the education of the people. But it
is useless to discuss the question. Without laying
open the breasts of some millions of people there is no
possibility of proving anything one way or the other ;
and in a country in which the upper class thinks itself
called upon to make a stand against the inroads of
democracy, it is idle to look for an impartial upper-
class estimate of lower-class virtue and good sense.
Let the irrational voters, however, be many or few, one
thing respecting them is certain, viz. that open voting
does not tend to diminish their numbers. The public
has no ground of judgment but the *vote*, and there is
nothing in the vote to indicate the irrationality of him
who gave the vote ; and, even if there were, you will
never shame a fool out of his foolishness. If you would
cure him you must educate him.

No one denies the existence amongst men of the
defects and vices enumerated by Sydney Smith and
Mr. Mill : selfishness, envy, servility, the spirit of
tyranny, the spirit of revenge, irrational caprice, simple
stupidity. I will even admit the possibility of one

R 2

man in ten thousand having within his breast that
passion to which Sydney Smith gave the name of the
Simious passion—the unprovoked desire to give pain
to others.   I will add religious bigotry and national
jealousy.   But what proof is there that these vices and
defects will in any important degree be restrained by
the publicity of the vote?   There is a preliminary
difficulty.   Possibly it may be more apparent than
real, but the [2] anti-ballotists have passed it over altogether.   The public sentiment of a country is the sentiment of the people of that country; and even the
anti-ballotists will not contend that the entire body of
a people will be less tainted with vice and folly than a
portion of that people selected for its presumed superior virtue and intelligence.   Is it then reasonable to
expect that the vices of the electoral body will be restrained by the sentiment of a public which is in a still
less degree exempt from those vices?   Possibly the
anti-ballotist may meet this objection with an arithmetical refutation after this fashion.   The public, he may
say, consists of a certain number of persons.   Let us
suppose one-tenth of them to be envious, one-tenth
foolish, one-tenth bigots, one-tenth 'simious,' and so
forth.   Now although there will be in that public a
taint, say of bigotry, yet as nine-tenths of the whole
will not be bigots, there will be a great preponderance
of opinion against religious persecution, and the bigoted
elector will thus be shamed out of his bigotry.   The

---

[2] The responsibility for the invention of the word ballotist
rests with Sydney Smith.   It is barbarous but convenient ; and
if one has the courage to print ballotist, one need of course not
boggle at anti-ballotist.

same of the other vices; each vice in succession being
compelled to hide its head on the hustings by an adverse
public sentiment of the arithmetical value of nine-
tenths of the whole. Or the anti-ballotist may get rid
of the difficulty in another way. He may say that he
attributes these defects to a small portion only of the
electoral body, and that, although the general public
may be tainted with similar defects in a certain proportion, to the extent, say, of one-fourth, the remaining
three-fourths will be pure; and that thus the comparatively small number of electors who might be disposed
to give way to their unworthy feelings or silliness on
the hustings will be kept right by fear of a public
opinion whose tone has been formed by the healthy
feelings of a majority of three to one.

I am not prepared to say that there may not be
some force in these supposed refutations of my preliminary objection, and I will therefore not insist upon it.
The other objections cannot, I think, be got rid of quite
so easily. For first, be it observed, these infirmities of
men are not all of one kind, some of them being moral
defects, and others defects of the understanding. Now
at a certain cost of time and trouble, men may be
educated out of defects of the understanding, but they
cannot, at a particular time and place, be shamed out
of them. The publicity of the vote will not only not
entirely neutralise irrational caprice, prejudice, incapability of reasoning, or silliness, but it will not do so in
any degree. The elector is wanting in intelligence.
Enlighten him, and you cure him; and you can enlighten him as easily under one system of voting as
under another. Out of the moral defects of electors,

their unworthy passions or feelings, more or less, you
may shame them, provided you can bring the sense of
shame to bear upon them at all.   I say '*more or less*,'
because some men are entirely unconscious that certain
of their feelings are unworthy.   On a man afflicted
with that description of moral blindness you can produce no effect whatever.   There are thousands of men
who, though the whole world should tell them they are
bigots or tyrants, will reply that their character is misunderstood; that what the world calls bigotry is in
truth only a laudable firmness in the maintenance of
what is right and just.   I need scarcely say that public
opinion will not move such men as these one inch from
their course.   Even thoroughly selfish men are often
stone blind to their own selfishness.   But let an anti-
ballotist, in proof of his theory of the virtue of public
opinion at elections, take the most favourable case that
it is possible for him to take, the case of a man who is
urged to a particular vote by a passion—let us say
Sydney Smith's simious passion—which he knows to be
utterly unworthy.   You will perhaps shame him out of
his unworthiness if you can bring the sense of shame to
bear upon him at all.   But how bring it to bear?   The
unworthy motive is his secret, which you have no power
to penetrate under any system of voting.   The vote
does not bear upon the face of it the unworthiness of
the motive.   If you could lay bare the man's breast,
and expose the unworthy motive to the indignant gaze
of his fellow-citizens, well and good; but you cannot do
so.   You suspect him of selfishness or malignity, and
you endeavour, on the strength of your suspicion, to
raise a cry against him; but you have no proof; no

man of good sense will join you in your cry. The
voter's reply to you will be this : I voted for A. because
I thought him the fittest man, and 471 other electors
have proved by their votes that they are of my way of
thinking. How will you answer that ? You may disbelieve him, but how will you refute him ? He cannot
prove that he was actuated by a laudable regard for the
public interest, but as little can you prove that he was
actuated by a contemptible feeling of spite, whim, or
passion.

If Parliamentary elections could be reduced to plain
unmistakable cases of vice *versus* virtue—as Sydney
Smith, in stress of argument, assumed them to be—the
vote would carry with it the worthiness or unworthiness
of the voter, and public opinion would have some hold
upon him. Three times only in the course of the present century a general election has mainly turned upon
questions which may be thought to make some slight
approach to such a case—Catholic Emancipation, the
Reform Bill, and the Corn Law question ; but I will
venture to say that neither Mr. Mill nor Sydney Smith
would have thought themselves justified, even in these
extreme cases, in holding up to the reprobation of the
country as an unworthy person the elector who should
have given his vote against the popular view of those
questions.

For the purpose of this discussion the electoral body
may be divided into two classes—the electors with a
conscience—a conscience, that is, in regard to the right
performance of the electoral duty—and the electors
without a conscience. With the latter class I have
already shown that the publicity of the vote will be in-

operative to check unworthy feelings. Now the elector
with a conscience, he who has no unworthy feelings
whose predominant feeling is an anxious desire to do
his duty by his country, finds himself in this position:
He has his own opinion of the comparative merits of the
candidates, and if he is to follow that, there can be no
possible objection to his voting secretly. If he is to
follow in the wake of public opinion, he must be made
to vote openly. But there are two publics differing
widely from each other. To which of them is he to
apply for advice or assistance? There is, first, the real
bonâ fide practical public which meets him wherever he
goes, and which consists of the people by whom he is
surrounded and with whom he habitually associates: a
manufacturing public, if he is a manufacturer; an
agricultural public, if he is a farmer or squire; the
Horse Guards and the army, if he is a military man; a
public represented by the ' Times ' and the London clubs,
if he is a member of the aristocracy. This is one kind
of public. The other is that intangible public which is
coextensive with the people of the British Isles, which
has no interest but the true interest of the entire people
high and low, and holds a perfectly even hand between
classes, cliques, and interests. Now the anti-ballotist
is in this dilemma. If he refers his conscientious
elector to the former of these, the practical public of
flesh and blood, he is placing him under the guidance
of what he himself denounces as a selfish class interest;
if to the latter, he is referring him to a mere abstrac-
tion, to a public whose verdicts are, in ninety-nine cases
out of a hundred, purely imaginary, and in the hundredth
almost as likely to be wrong as to be right. ·

In a question like this, which is one of practical politics, it is not enough arbitrarily to set up public opinion before us as a kind of Sibyl, with her doors open to the world, giving forth oracles of truth and wisdom to all comers. We must go back to the experiences of history, and look fairly in the face the acts and utterances of the people who in times past have acted the part of public, and not throw away the lessons of that experience. I say of the people who have 'acted the part of public,' because it has not unfrequently happened that a violent and clamorous minority, without understanding and without scruple, has been enabled, through the inaction of a majority whom fear has deprived of all power of speech and motion, falsely to set itself up as the embodiment of the opinion of a nation. What was public opinion in the State of Mississippi in the United States of America on a question of the repudiation of a State debt? What is the worth of public opinion in any country on questions affecting a rival nation? How did public opinion conduct itself in London in 1780 and in the county of Warwick in 1791 on questions of religious toleration? What is the value of public opinion in that not very rare condition of the public mind called a panic, political or commercial? It is precisely in cases like these, when public opinion is mischievously wrong, that it is difficult to resist its power. At periods of political excitement the practical sense to an elector of the phrase 'responsibility to public opinion' is too often this: 'Go up to that polling booth, and, at your peril, vote for any candidate but the popular candidate.' This may work very well in a period of a nation's history when the lower and middling

classes are struggling to obtain equal justice from a
monarch or from an oligarchy who have been rendered
selfish by a long continuance of power, and I have no
fault to find with the effect of popular dictation in the
case of the Reform Bill or the repeal of the Corn Laws.
But as a *permanent* element in an electoral system I do
object to popular dictation; and I ask how the matter
will stand at some future time, when, on questions of high
national honour and integrity—of justice, for instance,
to the public creditor; of equitable principles of taxation; of the fair and impartial adjustment of a quarrel
with a foreign State; of resistance to any tampering with
the sacred rights of property—a wise and far-seeing
upper class may perchance be struggling to maintain
great social principles against the clamour of an unthinking multitude. Read the history of France during
the last ten years of last century, and say whether
public opinion, on those rare occasions when it does
acquire an irresistible power, may not as easily excite
as restrain the dangerous passions of a people. The
truth is that in times of political quiescence public
opinion says nothing to the elector; in times of political
excitement it says too much, and too often says what is
wrong. In times of excitement the Sibyl is too apt to
lose her head; in ordinary times too apt to go to sleep.

There is one point upon which it is essential to a
right understanding of this subject, that the open-voting
men and the secret-voting men should understand one
another; and, strange to say, even Mr. Mill has done
nothing to clear up that point. How far does Mr. Mill
think that the function of public opinion should extend?
Does he desire that public opinion should merely assist

the judgment of the voter, or that it should supersede his judgment? If the former, the ballotists and he are of one mind; if the latter, they are at issue; for the publicity of the vote is as necessary for the latter purpose as it is unnecessary for the former. For example: Mr. Mill says that 'the opinions and wishes of the poorest and rudest class of labourers may be very useful as one influence among others on the minds of the voters as well as on those of the Legislature.' In one sense, and a very important sense, this is true. It is in the highest degree useful that the Legislature, and in a less degree that Parliamentary electors, should know what the wishes and opinions of all classes of the people really are, let those wishes and opinions be what they may, be they wise or be they foolish. The man who has the good of the people at heart, whether he be legislator or elector, will be materially assisted in his beneficent purpose by that knowledge. But the knowledge of another man's wishes, as an aid to your judgment in deciding what is best for him and his fellow-citizens, is a very different thing from the overruling influence of his wishes over your conduct impelling you, right or wrong, in the direction of those wishes or opinions. If the beneficial operation of public opinion is, in Mr. Mill's view of the matter, limited to the first of these things, the publicity of the vote at elections is not needed. An elector can use his eyes and ears and understanding as effectually in making himself acquainted with the prevalent feelings and opinions of the various classes of the community whether he gives his vote at the polling-booth openly or secretly. If Mr. Mill goes beyond this, and thinks that it is necessary

to influence the conduct of the voter independently of
his judgment, then, no doubt, the control of publicity
is necessary; but in that case it will also be necessary
to show that, in point of morality or intelligence, something will be gained by that control. Mr. Mill must be
able to say of his poor labourer what Madame Pernelle
said of Tartuffe :—

> Et tout ce qu'il contrôle est fort bien contrôlé.

But surely no one will seriously contend that—in any
country in which the representative system is not an
imposture—the average honesty and intelligence of the
electoral body is not superior to that of the community
at large, in other words, to that of a body made up of
electors and non-electors. Nor will any one seriously
maintain that it is desirable to set up an inferior intelligence for the purpose of overruling the decision of a
superior one, or a lower standard of morality to supersede the decision of a higher standard.

It is very desirable that the friends of the ballot
should make it clearly understood that the language
which they would put into the mouth of the electoral
body is this: ' We are most anxious to know what you
say, and think, and wish, and we are entirely opposed to
all systems which can impede free discussion between
us and you, whether you be landlords, or master manufacturers, or rich customers—whether you be operatives
or agricultural labourers—whether you come before us
as representing the non-electors, or in whatever capacity
you come before us, or be you what you may; but discussion is not compulsion, and we object in the
strongest way to be compelled, directly or indirectly,

morally or materially, whether by appeals to our
cupidity or appeals to our fears, whether by bribes of
worldly gain or threats of worldly loss, or threats of
moral censure, to act upon your opinion when it happens
to run counter to our own. We claim the right to
decide for ourselves after having heard all that is to be
said on all sides. If you can show, and more particularly if you, the non-electors, can show, that, on the
whole, your judgment is more to be relied upon than
ours, that may be a good reason for taking the suffrage
from us and giving it to you ; but it can be no reason
for depriving us of our free choice so long as the
suffrage is not withdrawn from us.'

According to Mr. Mill, there are two distinct political functions—a superior and an inferior. He speaks
of the indirect influence of those who have not the
suffrage over those who have, deriving its practical
efficacy from the publicity of the vote, as a minor
function which may beneficially be exercised by day
labourers whom it would not be safe to entrust with
the superior function, that of the suffrage. But, if by
this minor political function of day labourers is meant
something more than liberty to speak out what they
think, and feel, and wish so freely and openly, that the
rest of the world—electors included—cannot choose but
hear what they say; if Mr. Mill means something more
than this, and includes in this minor function a power
which, whether direct or indirect, virtually determines
the vote by some process other than that of convincing
the understanding of the voter, then I say that there is
no substantial difference between the two functions.
The day labourer, when he exercises his minor function,

is in truth exercising the power of a voter just as much
as if his name were on the register. Either the influence
of which Mr. Mill approves is intended to operate simply
and exclusively on the judgment of the elector, in which
case it will not be affected by this or that mode of
voting; or it is intended to operate on his vote independently of his judgment, in which case the possession
of that influence is equivalent to the possession of the
vote, and it would be better to give in name what is
possessed in substance. One thing only can make it
desirable that the non-elector should exercise over the
elector an influence greater than that which arises from
obtaining a fair hearing for all that he may have to say
for himself and his class, and that thing is his being
wiser and better than the elector; and surely this gives
him an undeniable claim to the suffrage.

I quite admit with Mr. Mill, that it is undesirable to
give to the least educated class in the community an influence in the Legislature to which the superior numbers
of that class would give dangerous predominance; but
this in no way detracts from the force of the argument,
that labouring men, if they are capable of exercising a
useful control over the actual possessors of the suffrage,
are themselves worthy of the suffrage. The danger
arising from their superior numbers may be a good
ground for giving them political power in limited
quantity, but it cannot be a good ground for withholding it altogether, if they are fit to exercise it well.
It might be wrong, for instance, to give to every labouring man a vote, but it might not be wrong to give to
every six labouring men the right to constitute one of
the six an elector.

But Mr. Mill contends that there is another advantage in open voting.[3] He thinks that the publicity of the vote will operate as an aid to truth; that fear of censure by those whose opinions are opposed to his will lead a man to take extraordinary pains to make sure of the soundness of his own views. With a thoroughly conscientious man, whose sole object is the truth, *a knowledge of the fact* that other men disagree with him will have that effect undoubtedly; but it is not so clear that the cause of truth will be promoted by the necessity—which publicity will impose upon him—of defending his opinion against their censure. He reasons thus with himself: ' Nine men out of ten seem to be against my view of this matter; I cannot reasonably assume that they are not as capable of judging as I am; the presumption, therefore, is that I am wrong, and I must carefully reconsider the grounds of my opinion.' Accordingly, he sits down and works out the question once more from beginning to end. Now, in the pro-

[3] ' It is a very superficial view of the utility of public opinion to suppose that it does good only when it succeeds in enforcing a servile conformity to itself. To be under the eyes of others —to have to defend oneself to others—is never more important than to those who act in opposition to the opinion of others, for it obliges them to have sure ground of their own. Nothing has so steadying an influence as working against pressure. Unless when under the temporary sway of passionate excitement, no one will do that which he expects to be greatly blamed for, unless from a preconceived and fixed purpose of his own, which is always evidence of a thoughtful and deliberate character, and, except in radically bad men, generally proceeds from sincere and strong personal convictions.'—*Considerations on Representative Government*, by John Stuart Mill, p. 200.

secution of this task of re-examination, one understands
perfectly how the prospect of having to defend his
opinion against that of other men—if that is painful to
him—should give him a bias in favour of their conclusions, and a wish to discover arguments which may
justify him in abandoning his own; but this is an effect
unfavourable, not favourable, to the discovery of the
truth. If that prospect is *not* painful to him, it will
have no effect upon his mind one way or the other.
The conscientiousness of the conscientious man will no
doubt go far to counteract any bias unfavourable to
truth, arising from fear of public censure. But nine
men out of ten—especially in the political world—are not
so perfectly conscientious as to be proof against all considerations except the pure love of truth. The men are
not few in number whose conscientiousness will make
but a poor struggle against the disinclination which
they feel to be put upon their defence in matters of
opinion. A man in a minority is always subject to
more or less of persecution on the part of the majority;
and many a man, in the investigation of a question of
morals or politics, will give a little innocent twist to his
understanding, just sufficient to turn it into a direction
likely to lead to conclusions which will secure him
against what is painful to him. I do not deny that
there are in the world both pure lovers of truth and
men with a passion for contradiction, but they are the
exception. In general, if you tell a man that the public
is against him, you will make him rather seek for arguments to justify him in a change of views, than make
him sit down to re-examine the subject in a perfectly
impartial spirit.

Mr. Mill admits the evil of bribery and of coercion, whether by landlords, employers, rich customers, trades unions, or mobs; but he thinks there is a greater evil still, the inherent folly and selfishness of the voter. But let me ask these questions : Granting the existence of the folly and selfishness, are they not in a great degree the product of bad political training? of evil habits created by the law? Are they not the natural fruit of those various baneful influences which I have enumerated? and is it not obvious that the first step to honesty and intelligence in the matter of vote-giving must be the independence of the voter? What we have been doing under our system of open voting is this, we have been creating and strengthening in a large proportion of our voters the habit of regulating their votes by a variety of considerations, which—differing from each other in certain respects—have yet all of them this one property in common, viz. that they are all entirely foreign to the one great consideration by which, on any intelligible principle of political morality as applied to the conduct of an electoral body, the voter ought to be guided. The practical questions which, by our system of open voting, we force upon many thousands of our electors are of this kind. Can it be necessary that, for the sake of one single vote, I should give offence to a good landlord? Can I afford, in a manner which occurs only once every two or three years, to lose a good customer? Is it reasonable to expect that I should, under any circumstances, run the risk of having to leave a comfortable home and to look out for a new master? Why, upon a view of a subject which after all may be mistaken, should I set at defiance a violent mob or a

S

pitiless trades union committee, which have it in
their power to persecute or annoy me ? Why may I
not give my family a number of little comforts which
will make them happy by accepting ten pounds from a
rich man who will not miss the money, who thinks himself obliged by my acceptance of it, and who, after all,
may make as good a member of Parliament as his opponent ? To leave the voter exposed to the influence of
such considerations as these is, in effect, to shut out
from him the one consideration which the law should
endeavour, by every means in its power, to force upon
him. It is practically to forbid him to ask himself the
one question which it is his duty to ask; this question,
namely, 'Which of these candidates, from what I know
of them or have heard of them, do I think most likely
to perform important public duties honestly, wisely, and
diligently ?'

There is no more superficial view of this subject
than that which overlooks the indirect effects of electoral
coercion; which assumes that no harm is done so long
as no tenant at will has received notice to quit, so long
as no steady workman has been dismissed from his employment. These are serious evils, but they are small
as compared with the great evil of all, habitual submission to degrading influences. Mr. Mill thinks that
the habit of voting at the bidding of an employer or a
landlord has diminished in the course of the last thirty
years. Perhaps so; possibly the act of bidding is no
longer necessary. There are many forms of coercion in
the world which, by long exercise on the one side and
submission on the other, have become so well established
that the announcement of the master's will is no longer

needed. Is it the fact that at elections in England tenants at will vote less universally than they did thirty years ago for their landlord's candidate ? If not, it is perhaps the habitual subserviency of the voters which conceals from us the reality of the landlord's power. None but a fool will command or even suggest degrading acts of obedience to his will, if experience has proved to him that the disposition to dispute his will no longer exists. If the voters are as subservient as ever, they are as much as ever the tools of other men ; as far removed as ever from the first step in the process of becoming honest and intelligent electors. No man who, in some particular matter, acts in habitual obedience to another man, will ever acquire the habit of forming a judgment of his own in that matter ; will ever acquire the self-respect and mental strengthening created by that habit. If he feels the obedience as a degradation, the subject becomes hateful to him ; if he does not so feel it, it is indifferent to him. In neither case will he ever arrive at that frame of mind which would lead him to look upon the act which he performs at the polling-booth as the discharge of an important public duty. We may talk as we will about an elector being a trustee, but, so long as he remains the contented mouthpiece of another man, the trust is a farce and the trustee an impostor. Having invested men with the privilege to choose their own rulers, having told them that they owe it to their country to make an honest and intelligent choice, can anything be imagined more unjust and irrational than to refuse to them that protection without which they are unable to act upon their own judgment ; and then, when they have sunk into a state of habitual

indifference, to argue from that condition of moral degradation, which is the work of our own hands, that they
are too base or stupid to be trusted with irresponsible
power? It is the reasoning of the slave owner. By
sheer violence he imposes upon his victims, generation
after generation, a system which consolidates their
moral and intellectual debasement, and then argues that
they are an inferior race, incapable of freedom.

' The Radicals,' says Sydney Smith, ' praise and
admit the lawful influence of wealth and power. They
are quite satisfied if a rich man of popular manners
gains the votes and affections of his dependants; but
why is not this as bad as intimidation?'[4] Whether
the lawful influence of wealth and power is as bad as
intimidation—which may with great propriety be
described as the *unlawful* influence of wealth and

---

[4] The passage continues as follows : ' The real object is to
vote for the good politician, not for the kind-hearted or agreeable man ; the mischief is just the same to the country, whether
I am smiled into a corrupt choice or frowned into a corrupt
choice ; what is it to me whether my landlord is the best of
landlords or the most agreeable of men ? I must vote for Joseph
Hume, if I think Joseph more honest than the Marquis. The
more mitigated Radical may pass over this, but the real carnivorous variety of the animal should declaim as loudly against
the fascinations as against the threats of the great.'

Whatever it may be reasonable to expect of the carnivorous
Radical, no one has a right to expect that the logical variety of
the animal should trample upon logic by repudiating his own
principles. The logical variety is a great friend to argument,
discussion, persuasion ; the more fascination the better, provided
the fascination, if it fails to fascinate, is not followed up by
something of greater practical efficacy.

power—is a question which I will discuss presently; but of this there can be no question, that the latter is an evil, and that you may prevent it; and that the former, whether an evil or a good, you cannot prevent. It may be as injurious to me that an artful scoundrel, taking advantage of my compassionate nature by some lying story of undeserved distress, should wheedle me out of ten pounds, as that a member of the swell mob should pick my pocket of the same sum; but that would be a very bad reason for not trying to put down pickpockets. It may be as hurtful to the country that my landlord should, by irresistible charm of manner, or by arguments of which I am not clever enough to detect the fallacy, induce me to vote for the least good of the three candidates at the county election, as that he should drive me so to vote, by threatening, in the event of my refusal, to turn me out of my farm; but that is a very bad reason for maintaining in the hands of landlords a power of punishment which it is admitted that they ought not to possess, and which the law may easily take from them.

But this phrase, ' the lawful influence of wealth and power,' suggests a topic the importance of which, in its bearing on the question of open or secret voting, it is difficult to overrate. Sydney Smith, in the passage I have quoted, in effect asks whether the mischief to the country is not just the same, whether the voter is smiled into a bad choice or frowned into a bad choice. My answer is, that the mischief lies neither in the smile nor in the frown, but in the power which open voting gives to the landlord—whether in the first instance his wishes have been urged by persuasion or by menace—

to enforce those wishes by the infliction of punishment. Take away the power of punishment and we object as little to the frowns as to the smiles. Indeed, his frowns he will not waste upon us ; and as for his smiles, they will always be welcome to us, as the fitting accompaniments of an appeal to our understanding or our good feelings. All we ask is to be placed by the law in a position to be able, with safety to ourselves, to disregard all attempts to drive us into a choice which is not ours.

In another passage [5] of his famous article, Sydney Smith argues on the opposite supposition, viz. that the

[5] ' But if landlords could be prevented from influencing their tenants in voting, by threatening them with the loss of farms ; if public opinion were too strong to allow of such threats, what would prevent a landlord from refusing to take as a tenant a man whose political opinion did not agree with his own ? What would prevent him from questioning, long before the election, and cross-examining his tenant, and demanding certificates of his behaviour and opinions, till he had, according to all human probability, found a man who felt as strongly as himself upon political subjects, and who would adhere to those opinions with as much firmness and tenacity ? What would prevent, for instance, an Orange landlord from filling his farms with Orange tenants, and from cautiously rejecting every Catholic tenant who presented himself plough in hand ? But if this practice were to obtain generally, of cautiously selecting tenants from their political opinion, what would become of the sevenfold shield of the ballot ? Not only this tenant is not continued in the farm he already holds, but he finds, from the severe inquisition into which men of property are driven by the invention of the ballot, that it is extremely difficult for a man whose principles are opposed to those of his landlord to get any farm at all.'—Works of Sydney Smith, vol. ii. p. 312.

ballotists are enemies, not friends, to the lawful influence of wealth and power. For he asks us, in a tone of triumph, ' What would become of the sevenfold shield of the ballot,' if the landlords were driven in self-defence to select tenants for their political opinions ; if Orange landlords were to fill their farms with Orange tenants, ' cautiously rejecting every Catholic who should present himself plough in hand' ? Our answer is, that the proceeding he describes would be a perfectly legitimate exercise of landlord power, and that we have not a word to say against it. We object to one thing, and to one thing only, viz. the coercion which practically deprives the voter of the right of private judgment. By all means let Orange landlords surround themselves with Orange tenants, and Catholic landlords with Catholic tenants, and when this has been done, so far from wishing to make the Orangeman vote for the Catholic, or the Catholic for the Orangeman, this is precisely the kind of dishonesty which, by the ballot, we wish to prevent. If landlords would only take the trouble to surround themselves with dependants of their own way of thinking in politics, no sensible man could possibly object to it. They might not get their land very well farmed, but *politically* the arrangement would be neither immoral nor inconvenient. What we find fault with is that the landlord takes no trouble about the matter ; that he puts upon his estate the best farmer he can find, without any reference to his political opinions, and then avails himself of the power which he derives from the ownership of the land to make his new tenant the mere mouthpiece of his political opinions or tool of his political interests. If rich and powerful

men would only agree to surround themselves with
their own *bonâ fide* political friends, and never attempt
to coerce or corrupt those who are not so, the agitation
of the ballot would cease at once.

But we go further than this. Not only do we not
object to a Catholic landlord letting his farms to
Catholic tenants, but we give him full leave, *on one
condition*, to use all his powers of persuasion and argument to bring over his Protestant tenant, if he has one,
to his own way of thinking. That condition is that he
will take the trouble to make it clear to that Protestant
tenant, beyond all possibility of mistake, that persuasion
is not to be followed up by coercion—that, *on the day
of election, his vote is to be his own*. Persuasion, argument, free discussion are the main elements of that lawful influence of the upper class over the lower which
we would foster, not repress. But we must be allowed
to point out what we mean by lawful influence, and
what by unlawful; for by including them both under a
common name, and attributing to us, in this way, a
hatred of both, the views we really hold have not unfrequently been misrepresented.

There is an influence which may be properly described as the influence of a man over other men, who
happen to stand to him in some relation of life which
gives to him a power over their worldly condition; a
power of such a kind that it enables him to raise them
or to lower them in the scale of worldly prosperity,
sometimes in a degree which may, to the unfortunate
man so acted upon, make the difference between a comfortable subsistence and destitution; at other times in
a degree represented by the possession or non-possession

of ten pounds or ten shillings. This influence is the influence of a landlord over his tenant at will, whom he can, if he pleases, eject from his farm; of the employer over his workman, whom he can, if he pleases, send forth upon the world to seek a new master and a new home; of the rich or noble customer over the trades-man, from whom he or she can, if he or she pleases, withdraw custom, or patronage which brings custom. It is the influence of the trades union, which can enter upon a course of petty persecution against a dis-sentient from the views of the society. It is the influ-ence of the mob, which can persecute any man within its reach by any one or more of those weapons of per-sonal annoyance which are at the disposal of mobs. It is the influence of the tempter who comes to a man with gold, or some equivalent of gold, to filch from him his honesty and self-respect. The advocates of the ballot have over and over again explained that it is their object to protect the elector from such influences as these, and *from such as these only,* and they contend that the ballot will be effectual for that purpose.

There is another and a very different kind of influ-ence against which no true and intelligent friend of the ballot ever uttered a word. Every advocate of secret voting, who is not distressingly ignorant of the prin-ciples of representative government, looks with hope to the extension, and with fear to the diminution, of this kind of influence; for it is the natural, legitimate, bene-ficial influence of more educated over less educated men; of strong over weak minds; of earnestness and high principle over indifference and laxity. It is essentially a moral as contra-distinguished from a worldly influ-

ence; it addresses itself to the understandings and
moral principles of men, and not to their interests.   If
it did not exist already it would be necessary to create
it.   But it does exist under all systems ; only, under a
system of open voting it is counteracted by those other
noxious influences of which I have spoken.   It makes
itself felt through a variety of channels ; through the
press, by example, by free discussion and interchange
of thought.   Even if the press were confined to newspapers, the writer in a newspaper is often unconsciously
exercising, over three-fourths or more of his readers,
the influence of a superior over an inferior mind.   The
practical adherence to right principles by magistrates,
members of parliament, official men, professional men,
and private persons in the business of their respective
callings and in the every-day transactions of life, being
matter of observation to persons of all classes in life
who are not blind to what is passing around them, is a
very effective form of the moral influence, the influence
by way of example.   The most important of all, perhaps,
is that which arises from discussion and interchange of
thought between men of the same class or of different
classes in life ; for the vigorous and well-regulated will
in nine cases out of ten—unconsciously often to both—
carry with it the less vigorous and less well-regulated
mind.   Let the selfishness or perverseness of a man be
what it may, to a considerable extent it will be counteracted by these moral influences which will operate
within his breast unknown to others, sometimes almost
unknown to himself.   The making a man, when he
votes at an election, speak out his vote, will not increase
them, the making him put his vote into a box will not

diminish them. The most determined anti-ballotist will not tell me that the ballot will tend in any degree to destroy an effect, whether favourable or unfavourable to a particular man or a particular cause, which has been produced upon my mind by the representations of rival canvassers, by conversation with my landlord or my next-door neighbour, by leading articles in the county papers, by my knowledge of the estimation in which a candidate is held in the neighbourhood, or by my own observation of his qualities. No system of voting that man can devise will destroy the effect of these things, but it may be counteracted by a system which enables certain persons, who have interests of their own to serve, to drive me or to tempt me to act against my own judgment. My conduct is determined in a certain degree by these moral influences ; in what degree it shall be so determined must depend partly on the amount of protection which you will give me against the corrupting and persecuting influences.

In so far as rich and powerful men are better and wiser than their inferiors, their moral influence will be beneficial, and to this extent therefore we may properly apply to it Sydney Smith's designation of the *lawful influence of wealth and power*, as contra-distinguished from *the unlawful influence of wealth and power, bribery and intimidation*. In what exact degree and in what precise respects rich and powerful men are better or wiser than their inferiors is a question which I cannot undertake to answer, but there is a fair presumption that, on those important subjects which are connected with Government and the management of the national concerns, they are wiser than the average of their fellow-citizens, and, if so, quite capable of giving wholesome advice on such subjects to the electoral body. That presumption rests upon the fact that they have had more leisure than their inferiors to acquire knowledge, and a greater command of good instructors, whether in the shape of books or men, and that their attention has been more closely and particularly directed to subjects connected with a career in life to which their superior rank naturally leads them to aspire. But there are two things which must not be forgotten : first, that of the highly educated class a large proportion are neither wealthy nor powerful; and secondly, that the moral influence of educated men is, under the open voting system, weakened not strengthened by the possession of wealth and power. Take two men capable, in exactly equal degrees, of exercising a purely moral influence over the minds of electors, and assume the one to be a wealthy landowner and the other to be the occupant of an obscure lodging with an income of a couple of hundred pounds. Let them address the elector in similar language, the language of sound argument. The words of the rich landowner, who can command the vote, will fall dead upon the ear of the elector. The words of the poor educated gentleman, whose only power over the vote is that which is to be obtained by producing conviction in the mind of the voter, will be listened to with respect and attention. Take away from the former all possibility of bringing his wealth or power to bear upon the cupidity or the fears of the voter, and *his* arguments also will be listened to with respect and attention. The system of publicity which gives to the landlord power to control the vote, takes from him all power to convince the understanding. The dependent voter suspects with reason that the argument of a landlord is little more than a decent covering for what is substantially a command. He says to himself, ' Convinced or not convinced, I must do what is expected of me. To what purpose listen to arguments?' The elector who has in his pocket the five sovereigns for which he has sold his vote, or who has in his mind a picture of the family break-up which may be the consequence of any flagrant act of opposition to the landlord's will, is not exactly in a state of mind to weigh reasons. Having determined, right or wrong, that his vote is to be given in completion of his bargain, or to allay his fears, his mind is impervious to moral influences, whether proceeding from his corrupter, from his landlord, or from other men. Let the reasons in favour of candidate A. be irresistible, still he must vote for B. Let the reasons in favour of B. be worthless, still he must vote for B. To what good purpose listen to the reasons? As well might the colonel expect his soldiers to listen with patient attention to a discourse on the merits of the war, when they are only waiting for the word of command to charge the enemy.

Sydney Smith draws a lively picture of the immoralities of secret voting. If his powers of painting had been employed upon the opposite side of the canvas, he might have drawn a picture equally lively, but more true, of the immoralities of open voting. Take the tenants of a great landlord. Divide them, as regards their political opinions, into two classes. Take, first, the man who thinks with his landlord. Ballot or no ballot he will vote with his landlord. But under the open system he gets no credit for his vote. It is in truth

the expression of his real opinion, but his friends and
neighbours set it down to subserviency. It is the vote
of an honest man, but it is believed to be the vote of a
coward. Take next the men who do not think with
their landlord. Setting aside those who do their duty
manfully and brave the consequences, the remainder
either do the bit of dirty work expected of them and
bluster, or do the bit of dirty work and blush. The
first makes a parade of his dishonesty. In such words [6]
as those which Sydney Smith puts into the mouth of
the radical voter for the nominee of the Tory Duke,
he impudently proclaims himself the knave he really is.
The second, painfully conscious of his baseness, slinks
away with shame from his companions, and endeavours
to conceal his dishonesty under an affectation of indifference to politics, or by pretending to hold opinions
which are the opposite of those he really holds. This is
not a very edifying moral spectacle, and we shall certainly not improve it by turning our eyes from the
tenant to the landlord.

'Go in at the front door,' says Sydney Smith [7] to

---

[6] 'I am a professed Radical,' said the tenant of a great Duke
to a friend of mine, 'and the Duke knows it; but if I vote for
his candidates, he lets me talk as I please, live with whom I
please, and does not care if I dine at a Radical dinner every day
in the week. If there is a ballot, nothing could persuade the
Duke or the Duke's master, the steward, that I was not deceiv-
ing them, and I should lose my farm in a week.'—Sydney
Smith's Works, vol. ii. p. 312.

[7] 'An abominable tyranny exercised by the ballot is that it
compels those persons to conceal their votes who hate all concealment, and who glory in the cause they support. If you are
afraid to go in at the front door, and to say in a clear voice

the elector, and say in a clear voice what you have to say, or if you don't like to do so, let me do so. The

what you have to say, go in at the back door and say it in a whisper. But this is not enough for you, you make me, who am bold and honest, sneak in at the back door as well as yourself; because you are afraid of selling a dozen or two of gloves less than usual, you compel me, who have no gloves to sell, or who would dare and despise the loss if I had, to hide the best feelings of my heart and to lower myself down to your mean morals. It is as if a few cowards, who could only fight behind walls and houses, were to prevent the whole regiment from showing a bold front in the field. What right has the coward to degrade me, who am no coward, and put me in the same shameful predicament with himself !'—Sydney Smith's Works (*Ballot*), vol. ii. p. 308.

But surely the representative system was not devised for the purpose of providing a field for the exercise of the heroic virtues. To give an honest vote in disregard of the power of a landlord, an employer, or a rich customer, may be an act of heroism undoubtedly, but the occasions for the display of courage in resisting persecution are sufficiently numerous in this world, without seeking to increase them. Why force heroism upon a man who is not a hero ; and if he is a hero, with a taste for martyrdom, what is there in secret voting to prevent him from indulging his taste? Being the tenant of a Tory landlord he has voted for the Whig. Let him proclaim that act of virtue in the market place, if he is one of those to whom virtue without fame is valueless. No one will disbelieve him, unless he is found to be a spurious hero, who has taken up martyrdom as a matter of business. The ballot was not intended for heroes or gentlemen, but for poor dependent voters who have either not the courage to brave persecution, or not the virtue to resist temptation. If it affords protection to these latter it has effected its purpose. The heroes and gentlemen, if they cannot live in peace without the fame of their good actions, must be at the

anti-ballotists seem to think that all true English manliness is summed up in performing a part on a public
stage.   Unhappily, there is often as little in common
between the actor on the stage and the real man off the
stage, on the hustings as at the theatre.   When we
see some four-and-twenty electors from a neighbouring
estate, on the day of election, 'go in at the front door
and say in a clear voice' what they have been brought
to that place to say, we may in truth be witnessing as
sorry an imposture as any that could be played before
us on the stage of a second-rate theatre in a provincial
town.

A man may smile and smile and be a villain.

<hr>

trouble to blow their own trumpets.   If the world suspects the
notes of the trumpet to be false, so much the worse for them.
The ballot is not to be made responsible for their inability to
convince the world of their truthfulness.

Sydney Smith objects to the ballot, that it deprives us of a
test of the sincerity of patriotic fervour.

'If ballot be established,' he says, 'a zealous voter cannot
do justice to his cause ; there will be so many false Hampdens
and spurious Catos, that all men's actions and motives will be
mistrusted.   It is in the power of any man to tell me that my
colours are false, that I declaim with simulated warmth and
canvass with fallacious zeal ; that I am a Tory though I call
Russell for ever, or a Whig in spite of my obstreperous panegyrics
of Peel.'

Very true.   But then how does open voting mend the
matter ?   The knowledge of the vote will not enable us to distinguish between the real Cato and the sham Cato.   The vote
may be as false as the speeches.   The hope of a snug berth at
the Post Office or the Excise for one of the sons may be at the
bottom of the whole thing.

And so may a man speak loud, and hold up his head and walk with a firm step, and be a knave. These things can as little be accepted as the signs of true manliness as the regular utterance of the responses at morning service at St. George's can be taken to be undoubted proofs of true religious feeling.[7]

I know nothing which presents so repulsive, and I believe so untrue, a picture of our upper classes as Sydney Smith's description of the flood of immorality which, in his belief, would pour in upon us if secret voting were established. Nothing can be more flagrantly immoral than the conduct which he imputes to them. By their superior education and rank in life they are more especially bound to set to their inferiors an example of respect for the law; and yet—if we are to believe Sydney Smith—they would unhesitatingly bring to bear upon the law every form of hostility and evasion in support of a selfish power over other men which the law had condemned. Not satisfied with having demoralised their inferiors by the practice of bribery for the best part of a century, Sydney Smith affirms of them that they would shamelessly set at defiance a law enacted for the express purpose of putting an end to the demoralisation of bribery. 'If ballot

---

[7] A certain elector has met with treatment from A. B. (who is a candidate for the representation of the county) which he believes to be in the highest degree unjust and cruel. He is convinced, however, that A. B. is a fitter man to represent the county than his opponent. He goes to the polling booth and drops into the ballot box a vote in favour of the man who has injured him. Does the secrecy of the vote destroy the manliness of that conduct?

T

were established,' he says, ' it would be received by the
upper classes with the greatest possible suspicion, and
every effort would be made to counteract it and get rid
of it.' Again, he says, ' Bribery carried on in any town
now would probably be carried on with equal success
under the ballot. The attorney, if such a system prevailed, would say to the candidate, " There is my list
of promises; if you come in I will have 5,000*l.*, and
if you do not, you shall pay me nothing;"' and then
he proceeds to show what precautions would be taken
againt fraudulent demands on the bribery fund. ' There
must be honour among thieves; the mob regularly
inured to bribery under the canopy of the ballot would,
for their own sake, soon introduce rules for the distribution of the plunder, and infuse with their customary
energy the morality of not being sold more than once
at every election.'

The case is this. Under our present mode of
voting a demoralising system of bribery prevails, set on
foot by the rich candidate or his supporters to secure
his election. The law steps in with a remedy. It is
objected to the remedy that it will not stop the immorality. Not stop it? How so? ' Because,' say the
objectors, ' the rich candidate or his supporters will
devise means to keep up the immoral practice in the
teeth of the law!' So long as the existing system is
maintained, the rich candidate may perhaps be justified
in saying that the law cannot be supposed entirely to
disapprove what it makes no serious effort to prevent.
If the law were altered and ballot were established, that
salve to his conscience would be taken from him.
Thenceforward bribery would not only be what it has

always been, a defiance of the laws of morality, but it would be a plain defiance of the laws of England. Nevertheless, Sydney Smith believed that rich Englishmen, ambitious of a seat in Parliament, would have no more scruple in thrusting their consciences out of doors in the new state of things than in the old. I am not able to think quite so ill of the upper class of my countrymen.

Again of landlords, Sydney Smith expresses himself thus: 'The cardinal position of the radicals is that landlords, after the ballot is established, will give up in despair all hopes of commanding the votes of their tenants. I scarcely ever heard a more foolish and gratuitous assumption. Given up? Why should they be given up? I can give many reasons why landlords should never exercise this unreasonable power, but I can give no possible reason why a man determined to do so should be baffled by the ballot;' and he proceeds to show that, on the contrary, the landlords who now exercise the power which open voting gives them, would, if open voting were made illegal, become doubly vigilant, inquisitive, and severe. Now what is the case? So long as the law maintains, against all opposition, a system of open voting, which gives to the landlord a practical control of a very perfect kind over the votes of his tenants, he may, with some show of reason, put forward that fact as proof that the Legislature is not convinced of the injurious character of that control. If that system were abandoned, the landlord could by no possibility interpret that abandonment otherwise than as a declaration by the Legislature that it was just and necessary that such control should, by force of law, be

T 2

made to cease. What Sydney Smith in effect affirms is this : that English landlords, from whom as a class our lawmakers are in great part taken, so far from setting an example of scrupulous obedience to the unmistakable intention of that new law, would forthwith set themselves to weaken and undermine it, and that by the not very honourable method in use by inquisitors. His prediction is, that the landlord, hopeless of directly depriving the voter of his newly acquired independence, would set up against him a promise-exacting and cross-questioning persecution ; and thus seek to force him or to entrap him into a position of moral perplexity of such a kind as to render the practical enjoyment of that independence thenceforward contingent upon the maintenance of habitual falsehood. No one who knew Sydney Smith will believe him to have been capable of attributing conduct such as this, so cruel, and at the same time so little, to any class of his countrymen, much less to the class to which he himself belonged, if he had taken much trouble to understand the true character of that conduct. It is impossible to avoid the reflection that one who could make so false a moral estimate of the upper class of his countrymen was not to be trusted in his estimate of the lower ; and that he was probably as much mistaken in supposing that the ballot would fail in consequence of want of common honesty and intelligence on the part of the poor voter, as he certainly was mistaken in supposing that it would fail from a small revengeful spirit of persecution, having for its object to cheat the poor voter out of the law's intended protection on the part of the rich landlord. The truth is that, on the point of morality, the article of Sydney

Smith was utterly at variance with itself. His chief argument in favour of open voting was based upon the beneficial moral influence of public opinion, and yet he took infinite pains to lower our moral estimate of those who constitute the public ; of landlord and tenant, of high and low, of rich men and poor.

One of the main props of the anti-ballot theory is that the ballot would lead to lying. Now lying is of several kinds, and the determining motives of lies are not a bad measure of their wickedness. There is the lie of vanity, and the lie of malevolence, and the lie of cowardice, and the lie of selfishness, and the lie of legitimate self-defence. The wickedness is not exactly the same in all cases. For example : it was much less wicked—if, indeed, it was wicked in any degree—in the author of certain celebrated books to reply, to the impertinent question of a prince, that he was not the author of those books, than it would be in you or me, by giving a false character to obtain for one whom we knew to be a thief a situation in a respectable family. A rich man in contravention of the undoubted purpose of a law which says to him, ' You shall no longer be allowed to interpose your private interests or political leanings between this poor man's privilege and its free exercise,' endeavours to force from that poor man the secret which has been given to him as a shield, but which he can successfully defend from the moral violence by which it is threatened no otherwise than by a lie. Let any man of sense and honesty say which of these two is the greater moral delinquent, the educated inquisitor striving to wrest the law from its acknowledged purpose, or the uneducated voter who defends the law and his own privilege by a lie. Let him rack his brain and picture to himself, if he can, a more grotesque perversion of all moral consistency than this rich man and his apologists holding forth on the wickedness of lying.

There is one truth which no amount of hammering seems likely ever to drive into the head of a thorough-going ballot-hater; and that is, that there are other and worse infractions of the moral law than that of defending oneself from unjust persecution by a lie. Under the system of publicity you have the dishonest vote : the vote for A. from fear of worldly loss, or in exchange for worldly gain, when B. is believed to be the best man. If the world would only agree to call this by its right name, 'falsehood'— for substantially it is falsehood, and, when committed by a citizen in discharge of the most important perhaps of all the duties of citizenship, falsehood of a very bad kind—the anti-ballotist would be refuted out of his own mouth. But you never can get him to look upon it as anything more than a little bit of excusable moral weakness; a mere loosening of one of the strings of a code of political morals which have been screwed up a little too tight. Because it happens not to come within his definition of a lie, it is not worth talking about. What he understands by a lie is a deliberate affirmation of something as a fact which is not a fact. You cannot get him to look into motives. Whether it has been my object to slander my neighbour, to cheat my customer, to escape from a troublesome duty, or merely to protect myself from unauthorised impertinence is no concern of his— 'I have stated as a fact that which is not a fact.' That

is enough for your thoroughgoing anti-ballotist. If
England can only be saved from that one particular
form of falsehood, the rest of the moral law may be left
to take care of itself. This seems to me to be both a
superficial and a dangerous view of morality. I believe
the dishonest vote to be morally worse than the lie in
defence of the honest vote. Be this, however, as it may,
what are we to think of men who reject a proposed
cure for one form of immorality, on the ground that
their own selfish conduct is likely to make the efficacy
of that cure dependent upon the practice of another
form of immorality ? Why do they not clear away the
selfishness from their own breasts ? This would relieve
us from all difficulties. Let rich and powerful men
only, in good faith, take the necessary steps to dispossess themselves of a power over the poor voter which
the law never intended them to possess, and there need
be no further discussion on different forms of immorality
or different modes of voting.

'Take the necessary steps to dispossess themselves,'
I purposely use that phrase, because I admit that, as
regards the men of wealth and power, the principals in
the business of electoral bribery and intimidation, this
is something more than a simple question of abstaining
from the exercise of an injurious power. They, directly,
in their own persons, have rarely exercised that power.
The man of many acres has seldom or never been
brought into direct personal contact with a refractory
tenant ; nor has the moneyed candidate ever, with his
own hands, tendered the bribe to the ten-pounder
householder of the easy political conscience. Their
function in the business has been the simple one of

shutting their eyes. There *is* a machinery, but, although worked for their benefit, it is not worked by them. They know nothing of it except the result—the announcement of the successful candidate at the close of the poll. It is worked by friends, dependants, political adherents, paid and unpaid, who, knowing perfectly well what has to be done, have learned by long experience to apply to the doing of it a mechanism which is as silent as it is effective ; a mechanism which works so smoothly as very rarely to excite the public attention ; which compromises no one ; which enables him who reaps the reward to say, 'I know nothing of it ;' and enables him who moves the wheels to say, 'They are not moved for my benefit.' In this world of skilful appliances of all kinds, material and moral, abounding with cloaks in which the ugliest things may be decently wrapped up, nothing is more easy than for a great man to enjoy in substance a power injurious to other men, which in name he repudiates. A great landowner in Britain may retain substantial possession of the votes of his tenants, and yet be able to say truly that he never asked a question in his life about the vote of a single man among them ; and it is perhaps too much to expect that our landed aristocracy, for no more direct and immediate benefit than the political welfare of England—in so far as that welfare depends upon the creation and maintenance of a broad popular constituency, thoroughly independent, earnest and true—should undertake to deprive themselves for all time coming of a power which they may continue to enjoy with little personal unpopularity, and with a notable increase of personal consequence. The difficulty of the case is that, unless the great men, for whose benefit the machinery exists, are virtuous enough, for the public good, to break up the machinery—and that is not always a very simple task—there is no way left but for the injured parties—to wit, the great bulk of the general public—to take the matter into their own hands. In the case before us, the object in view being an independent electoral body, there seems to be no alternative but this—the ballot; or a virtuous effort of self-denial on the part of those who profit by the existing corruption and subserviency of the electors, of which, as coming from the whole of a numerous class of persons, there are, I fear, but few examples in the history of the world.[8]

[8] To secure the votes of his tenants against all interference, direct or indirect, so completely as to give them the reality and the feeling of independence, cannot be a very easy task for a great landowner, surrounded as he is by friends and dependants filled with zeal for his interests ; but the thing may, no doubt, be done. That it seldom or never *is* done can, however, excite no surprise. It is scarcely reasonable to expect that a man who has strong political opinions should refrain from using the power he possesses to advance those opinions. Even though it should be apparent to him that it is wrong to use the power of a landlord to control the votes of tenants, yet if he sees that power used without scruple by his neighbours for the advancement of doctrines which he believes to be false and mischievous, he is perhaps entitled to say that he is acting from a sense of duty when he employs similar weapons for the support of what he believes to be the cause of truth and right. The current of public opinion is not likely ever to set very strongly against a practice which may be defended by so plausible an argument, and it is idle, therefore, to look forward to a general voluntary abandonment of electoral intimidation. If it should ever come to an end it will be by the pressure of an Act of Parliament.

In one passage of his work on Representative
Government Mr. Mill imputes to the ballot a moral
mischief of a kind which he describes as follows : After
saying truly that 'the spirit of an institution, the impression it makes on the mind of the citizen, is one of
the most important parts of its operation,' he goes on to
observe that ' the spirit of vote by ballot—the interpretation likely to be put on it in the mind of an elector—
is that the suffrage is given to him for himself, for his
particular use and benefit, and not as a trust for the
public;' and that 'this one idea taking root in the
general mind, does a moral mischief outweighing all
the good that the ballot could do, at the highest possible
estimate of it;' and he adds, that Mr. Bright and his
school of democrats have given currency to this mischievous idea by maintaining that the franchise is a
right and not a trust.   But the advocates of the ballot
do not all belong to Mr. Bright's school of democrats;
and many of them, except in a legal sense, acknowledge
no rights except such as can be proved to be for the
general advantage.   Mr. Grote is or was the leader of
the ballot movement, and *he* held it out as one of the
principal advantages of his proposed measure that it
would make it impossible for the elector to use the
franchise for his own particular use and benefit.   Any
such false idea of the suffrage may at all events be
easily corrected.   When a man's name is placed upon
the register, let it be required of him that he shall make
before a public officer the following declaration: ' I
hereby engage to the best of my ability to use for the
public benefit a privilege which the constitution of my
country has given me for the public benefit, and for that

only.' If there is risk of misapprehension in the mind of the elector, this is an easy cure for it; but there is really no such risk. Mr. Mill's estimate of the stupidity of common men passes all bounds of belief. After observing that 'an ordinary citizen, on whom there devolves any social function, is certain to think and feel, respecting the obligations it imposes on him, exactly what society appears to think and feel in conferring it' —a proposition no one will dispute—Mr. Mill proceeds to say that 'the interpretation which such citizen is almost sure to put upon secret voting is, that he is not bound to give his vote with any reference to those who are not allowed to know how he gives it, but may bestow it simply as he feels inclined.' But surely society will not *appear* to think and feel one thing when in fact it thinks and feels another and a very different thing, and makes no secret of that fact. The question of the ballot having been publicly discussed in and out of Parliament at frequent intervals for the last fifty years, the grounds upon which it rests must by this time be pretty familiar to the public mind; and the interpretation which the public puts upon it can scarcely be other than that which its advocates put upon it. Now its advocates have explained themselves with unmistakable clearness. Their position has been this: ' We recommend that the public be excluded from the direct knowledge of individual votes, because experience has proved that a powerful section of the public cannot be trusted not to abuse the power which that knowledge gives them.' That is the Alpha and Omega of the advocacy of the ballot. If society should ever adopt the ballot, it will be because it has become convinced of the soundness of that position. To suppose that any class of citizens will understand the ballot to be given to them as a free licence to caprice and selfishness, and a full discharge from all regard to public interests, when for fifty years its advocates have been urging its adoption on a plain simple ground of a totally different kind, is really a most gratuitous and unwarranted imputation of stupidity. An Englishman of sane mind can no more suppose that the election of members of Parliament is not intended for the furtherance of the public good, than a juryman, when he discusses with his eleven brethren the evidence on a trial for burglary, can suppose that such discussion is not entered upon in the interest of public justice. The case of the elector may be aptly illustrated by that of the juryman. If it had been the practice for juries to discuss the question of the verdict aloud in open court, and if that practice had been found to open a door to persecution in cases where individual jurymen happened to take a view of a case displeasing to persons thus becoming cognizant of the particulars of that discussion, could any one misunderstand the purpose of society if it should determine to alter the law, and thenceforward to send the jury out of court to discuss their verdict in a private room? Is there one man in a thousand so stupid as to look upon that change from publicity to secrecy as meaning that jurymen were thenceforth to be under no obligation to society, and were to be free to convict or acquit *as they felt inclined?*

But Mr. Mill's excellent observation as to the effect of the spirit of an institution on the mind of the citizen is capable of another application. Mr. Mill observes that ' the effect of a doctrine on the mind is best shown, not in those who form it, but in those who are formed by it.' Now, apply these words to the doctrine of shaming electors out of unworthy votes by the pressure of public opinion. That doctrine rests upon the assumption, as a matter of fact, that English electors are for the most part morally incapable of overcoming prejudice, passion, or caprice in a degree sufficient to bring their votes under the control of a sense of public duty, and of their own interest in good government. In Mr. Mill's words :—' A man's own particular share of the public interest, even though he may have no private interest drawing him in the opposite direction, is not, as a general rule, found sufficient to make him do his duty to the public without other external inducements.' In other parts of the same chapter Mr. Mill enumerates the unworthy feelings which will lead men to give base or mischievous votes. Sydney Smith gave still more particular expression to his unfavourable opinion of the moral condition of a large class of English electors. ' If a man,' said he, ' be sheltered from intimidation, is it at all clear that he would vote from any better motive than intimidation ? . . . . The landlord has perhaps said a cross word to the tenant; the candidate for whom the tenant votes in opposition to his landlord has taken his second son for a footman, or his father knew the candidate's grandfather. How many thousand votes sheltered—as the ballotists suppose—from intimidation, would be given from such silly motives as these? How many would be given from the mere discontent of inferiority ? or from that strange simious schoolboy passion of giving pain to others, even when the author

cannot be found out? motives as pernicious as any
which could proceed from intimidation.'

Now, I would ask, what impression is likely to be
made upon the minds of electors by an institution which
is founded and defended upon such a view as this of their
moral condition?   Mr. Mill and Sydney Smith are virtually addressing them in such language as the following : ' You have an important public duty to perform ;
you are yourselves sharers in the advantages which will
be derived to the public from the right performance of
that duty ; you have no substantial private interests
running counter to that duty.   Nevertheless, we cannot
trust you ; we dare not leave you to yourselves ; for,
being men, you are capricious, ignorant, prejudiced,
selfish, or malignant ; regardless of worthy objects in the
desire to gratify some contemptible whim or passion ;
ready to serve any fancied petty interest of your own,
in preference to that of the public.   To keep you in a
path which is at once the path of duty, and that of an
enlightened self-interest, the public must keep its eyes
constantly upon you.   We can trust nothing to your
own intelligence, public spirit, and honesty ; our trust
must be in your fear, lest your baseness or folly should
expose you to the anger or contempt of your fellow-
citizens.'   ' The effect of a doctrine,' says Mr. Mill, ' is
best shown in those who are formed by it.'   What sort
of electoral body, I would ask, is likely to be formed by
addressing to them such language as this?   Are we
likely to make men honest, intelligent, and public-
spirited by telling them that it is necessary to take
against them precautions required by dishonesty,
stupidity, and selfishness ?   What would be thought of

the wisdom of the master of one of our public schools, who should announce to the school that no boy was to be trusted out of the sight of a master or a monitor? When the United States of America find themselves, as they soon will, with four millions of negroes upon their hands, will they render the task of raising those negroes to the condition of intelligent, honest, industrious freemen easier, by applying to them a system of treatment fitted only for the incurably indolent, stupid, or vicious? No man had a deeper knowledge of human nature than Dr. Arnold. This was not his method of raising the moral standard of human beings entrusted to his care. His language to his boys was in a very different spirit. The following is an example of it. He said to them, 'If you say so, that is quite enough; of course I believe your word.' The self-respect of the boys was raised, and in Arnold's school, a boy who told a lie disgraced himself as much in the eyes of his schoolfellows, as in those of the master. Dr. Arnold thought that it was, on the whole, both more politic and more true, to treat boys in a spirit of blind confidence, than in a spirit of blind distrust; to look upon an offence as the exception rather than the rule. He believed that he would more surely enlist the feelings of his boys in favour of what is good and true, by treating every unworthy act as a falling below the existing standard, than by treating every worthy act as a rising above it. The elector, nay, the minister of state, is but a graver and more knowing schoolboy. Might it not then be worth the experiment to treat our electoral body in Dr. Arnold's spirit, and address them in language such as his; to say to them, 'The suffrage is given to citizens in the belief that they are honest and intelligent enough to exercise it properly. We do not choose to believe otherwise of you. We will not lower you in your own eyes, and in those of your fellow-citizens, by the supposition that your conduct at the poll stands in need of public supervision.'

I believe that Mr. Mill greatly overrates the difficulty of making an elector understand the position in which the constitution of his country has placed him. I see no necessity for talking to him either of rights or trusts, and I see no objection to telling him that he is to consult his own interest. He knows perfectly well that the only substantial interest which he can have in the matter of voting, when once the law has made it impossible that other men should bribe him out of his vote, or frighten him out of his vote, is that interest which he has, in common with the rest of his fellow-citizens, in being governed by the best and wisest men. It is a very superficial view of the matter to suppose that a man never acts upon an enlightened view of his interest, unless he sits down at a table to construct a chain of causes and effects. When he debates the matter with himself, his reasoning may be perfectly sound, although he does not know what it is to reason; and although, if you called upon him to explain his conduct, his explanation might be unintelligible. The fact may be that he has voted against Squire A. because the squire is known to him as a man whose only serious occupation in life is the preservation of game, and who was never able, at a public meeting, to utter three consecutive sentences which were intelligible; and that he has voted in favour of the second son of Squire B., because every one he meets on market day at Queensville tells him that young B. was a great man at college, that he is a rising lawyer, and is running away with all the business at assizes ; and that in the House of Commons, up in · London, they always listen to what he says. This is not the less voting from an enlightened view of his interest, because, if asked to explain his interest in the vote he has given, he may stammer and look like a fool. With the most stupid agricultural tenant in all England, considerations of this kind will, I believe, have more weight than Sydney Smith's simious passion ; all men, even small agricultural tenants, feel a pride in seeing their native place represented by a man who is respected and looked up to.

Before taking leave of the subject, I wish to guard against being understood to contend that secret voting is better than open voting in all supposable states of society. Indeed, it is evident that, in a country of which the people should universally respect each other's right of private judgment in the choice of representatives, the concealment of the vote would not only be useless but would universally be so considered. There is one plain and great advantage in secret voting, and only one, viz. that all encroachments on the right of private judgment would be paralysed by it, all influences which —whether exercised by landlords, rich men, or mobs— act upon the will of the elector otherwise than through his understanding. If such influences had no existence, or if, existing, they could be rooted out by some more direct and simple method than the ballot, a discussion on the comparative merits of open and secret voting would be a very idle occupation. If in England, for

U

instance, the public sentiment on the suffrage were universally of such a kind, that no elector could have any
reasonable hope of particular advantage or fear of particular injury as a consequence of his vote, there would
be an absence of all motive for concealment in the
matter of voting; and it would be immaterial whether,
at the polling booth, votes were given *vivâ voce* in the
presence of other men, or were silently dropped into a
box. In either case, practically, the votes would be
known. In that supposed condition of the public feeling, you would no more think of doubting the veracity
of your neighbour when he told you that he had voted,
or was about to vote, for Johnson in preference to
Thomson, than you would doubt his veracity if he told
you that he was sowing one of his fields with oats and
another with barley; and your neighbour would no
more think of making a mystery of the one matter than
of the other. There can be no greater mistake than
that of supposing that, by the ballot, all confidence in
the good faith and veracity of electors would be destroyed. It would be destroyed only, where it is the
object of the ballot to destroy it; that is, where there
is injustice or immorality to be counteracted; in all
other cases it would remain unimpaired. It would be
destroyed in all cases in which an immoral bargain had
been entered into, or an unconstitutional power was
assumed; and to destroy it in such cases is to destroy
one necessary condition to the successful carrying out
of the corrupt bargain, or to the maintenance of the unjust power. The mode in which the ballot would operate is plain enough. The vote, under the ballot, would
be the voter's secret, which he might reveal or not,

as he pleased. The secret, if revealed, would rest upon his unsupported testimony. He would have no proof to offer but his own assurance. Now the case is this: that no rational man would be satisfied with that assurance if it came from one who had been dishonest enough to sell his vote, or if it came from one whose situation in life was such as to make it necessary that he should defend himself from the attempted coercion of a landlord, a patron, or a mob; whilst, on the other hand, no rational man could fail to be satisfied with that assurance, if it came from one who, being neither dishonest nor dependent on other men, had no conceivable motive for concealment. When the honesty and independence of an elector are universally respected by his fellow-citizens, no man of sense will doubt his good faith in regard to the vote of to-morrow, or his veracity in regard to the vote of yesterday.

The operation of the ballot in an electoral system bears a certain analogy to that of a safety-valve in a steam engine. The function of both is to get rid of excessive or irregular power. If you could go on generating steam in the exact quantity required for the work to be done by the engine, the safety-valve would have nothing to do. If, in the election of representatives, no man desired to arrogate to himself a power which the constitution has not conferred upon him, the ballot would have nothing to do. But so long as men refuse to see anything dishonourable in attempting to get possession of other men's votes by appeals to their cupidity or their fears, the ballot has its appropriate work to do and would continue to do it.

Those attempts would be baffled by the impossibility of penetrating the secret of the ballot box.

If the public sentiment should change, and such attempts should be abandoned as dishonourable, then vote by ballot would become a useless form. I say useless, because a machinery which has been devised to restrain an injurious power has lost its use when men have been brought voluntarily to relinquish that power. I say *useless* but not *hurtful*. Hurtful it never could be ; for the mere *form* of secrecy cannot be injurious, if the absence of all motive for concealment has made the reality of secrecy morally impossible. There would, however, be as little wisdom in giving up the ballot because an improved state of the public feeling had rendered it for the time needless, as there would be in fastening down the safety-valve because the engine had gone on for a certain time generating steam in the exact quantity required. When men have relinquished the exercise of an injurious power, why, if it can be avoided, expose them to the temptation of resuming it ? You may have no reason to doubt the sincerity of their newly acquired virtue, but after all the best security for the continuance of the virtue is the continued impossibility of sinning. The law is a wonderful help to public morality. Without taking a very low view of human nature, one may be allowed to doubt whether, if, in England, the law making the slave trade illegal were repealed, English opinion might not, in the course of time, come to lose a few degrees of the intensity of its horror for slavery ; and whether—to give another instance—if the Government of Lord Palmerston had succeeded in enforcing the penalties of the Foreign

Enlistment Act, that infliction might not have had the effect of infusing serious doubts into the minds of British ship-builders in regard to the morality of furnishing ships of war to be used in violation of the international duties of their sovereign. So a law whose special object it should be to make electoral bribery and intimidation impossible, would give wonderful stability to the opinion that they were dishonourable.

I should wish to recapitulate in a few words the leading points of the controversy between the friends of the ballot and the enemies of the ballot. One fundamental point is beyond dispute, viz. that the injurious influences which can affect the electoral body are all comprised under the two following heads. First, corrupting or coercive influences brought to bear upon the elector by other men; secondly, selfishness, stupidity, or malevolence, in all their various forms, which may be supposed to operate within his own breast. If it can be proved that open voting does more, on the whole, than secret voting to extirpate these two classes of evil influences, the agitation for the ballot ought to cease; if the contrary can be proved, that agitation ought to be kept up until it is brought to a successful issue.

Now the ballotists and the anti-ballotists stand opposed to each other in the following relative positions. The ballotist offers a specific remedy for the evil influences of the first class. To that remedy the anti-ballotist makes one objection, which is something more than a vague expression of dislike, and only one; and that objection simply amounts to an allegation that those who profit by the evil—landlords and others—may be expected, if that specific remedy should receive the sanction of the law, to enter upon a course of conduct which would render that law a dead letter. The ballotist maintains that, even on the supposition that the upper class of Englishmen—whose superior station imposes it upon them as an imperative duty to set an example of respect for the law—are capable of the flagrant immorality of a systematic attempt to defeat or elude the law; the ballotist, I say, maintains that, even on this extreme supposition, the law would possess within itself an efficacy which would render all such attempts unavailing.[9] The anti-ballotist has no remedy of his own to propose for the evil influences of the first class, for corruption and coercion. He cannot of course deny that, under the existing régime of publicity, one portion of the public—rich, educated, and powerful—gives its support to those evil influences; but he may, if he pleases, without any à priori absurdity, contend that the remaining portion of the public possesses

---

[9] The writer has not entered into any formal proof of this point, because that work has been much better done than he could do it by others, and by one person in particular, whose name carries with it a great weight of authority. It is easy to refer to the admirable speeches of Mr. Grote. No one will ever put the argument on which that proof rests more clearly and forcibly than he did. By Mr. Mill and other distinguished advocates of open voting it has not been denied that the ballot would be effectual, in spite of all opposition or evasion, to prevent bribery at elections, and to secure the independence of the elector. That denial rests principally on the authority of Sydney Smith, who, in the article from which I have so often quoted, refers, in words of deep lamentation, to the reported fact that 'Lord John Russell, and some important men as well as he,' had said, 'We hate ballot, but if these practices continue we shall be compelled to vote for it.'

enough of virtue and moral strength to shame the rich and powerful men out of that support. No anti-ballotist has ever, I believe, taken up that view of the case, because direct experience has conclusively disproved it. The fact that, in the course of the last century, corruption which has disappeared from within the walls of Parliament, under the régime of publicity, still maintains itself at the polling booth, proves clearly that the sense of shame, although sufficient to keep statesmen in the path of political virtue in their relations with each other, is not sufficient to do so in their relations with the constituencies.

Now, as regards the evil influences of the second class: selfishness, stupidity, or malevolence inherent in the breast of the voter. The anti-ballotists, with Mr. Mill at their head, maintain that public opinion, having, under the system of publicity, the opportunity of passing judgment on the merits or demerits of each individual vote, will shame the voter out of his unworthy feelings, and thus make room in his breast for the admission of a sense of public duty. The ballotist contends that public opinion will have no such power; that some of those unworthy feelings, being mere defects of the understanding, are not accessible to the sense of shame, but only to the influence of education ; and that with respect to all of them—whether defects of the understanding or moral defects—public opinion, having nothing to guide it but the vote—which does not bear upon its face the feelings or motives which determined the vote—can no more bring its shaming or enlightening power to bear upon the elector under one system of voting than under another.

Then if the anti-ballotist, laying aside his theory of inherent electoral baseness and of public opinion as its appropriate antidote, should reduce his argument to this; viz. that practically —and without entering into nice distinctions between acts and motives—an elector may be expected, on the whole, to make a better choice between rival candidates if he votes under the inspiration of public opinion than if he simply votes upon his own judgment ; the ballotist, in refutation of that view of the matter, has to urge what follows. First, that the public which practically most influences a man, is that which, from the accident of his rank in life, occupation, family connections, or place of residence, comes into more direct and frequent contact with him than any other ; that this is generally but a small fraction of the general public; and has so frequently interests and opinions at variance with those of the general public, that nothing—even in Mr. Mill's view of the matter—could be gained by subjecting him to its influence. Secondly, that, even if this were otherwise, and that the elector were always ready to follow the inspiration of the general public, it would be found that, in times of political quiescence, the general public is in so hopeless a condition of internal disagreement in regard to the comparative merits of contending candidates as to be incapable, at such times, of assisting him in his choice ; and so easily led astray from the path of good sense, prudence, and high principle, in times of political excitement, as to be, at these latter times, a most unsafe guide.

Finally, the ballotist contends that one great object to be aimed at is the progressive improvement of the electoral body ; that the independence of the voter must be the first step to his becoming intelligent, earnest, and true in the performance of the great duty to society which the possession of the suffrage imposes upon him ; that the destruction of the corrupting and coercive powers is a necessary condition of that independence ; and the ballot a necessary condition of that destruction.

POSTSCRIPT.

It may seem strange that no attempt should have been made in the preceding pages to disprove an allegation which has been so frequently made by opponents of the ballot as the following :—viz. that in France, America, and other countries, vote by ballot, having been tried, has proved a failure.

The question between secret voting and open voting in Great Britain might undoubtedly be decided by an appeal to the experience of other countries, provided the following points were first established. First, that, in the country in which it is alleged that the experiment has been tried, vote by ballot is so practised as to give the reality and not the mere name of secrecy ; and, secondly, that the specific evils, for which secret voting is in England proposed as the specific remedy, have, in that other country, any substantial existence; for it is obvious that vote by ballot—so called— may exist without secrecy, and secrecy without anything for secrecy to cure. If, for instance, that were the case in America, the example of America could prove nothing against the ballot in Great Britain, where there *is* something to cure, and where it *is* possible so to take the votes as to ensure secrecy. When the opponent of the ballot has established these preliminary points, but not before, it will be possible and useful to discuss with him the question whether secret voting has or has not been tried and failed.

Under the name of vote by ballot a plan has sometimes been put forward for leaving to the elector a free choice between an open vote and a secret vote. If that plan were adopted, bribery and intimidation would be very much what they are under the existing system of compulsory open voting. It seems almost needless to say that a power which is effectual to force a man's will against his judgment when the question at the polling booth is this, ' *For whom do you vote ?* ' would not be materially weakened by the preliminary question, ' *Do you choose to vote openly or secretly ?* ' By the dependent or corrupt voter that preliminary question could of course be answered only in one way. A secret vote— when the alternative of an open vote had been offered— would as surely be looked upon as a breach of faith with the purchaser, or a defiance of the power of the landlord, as an adverse vote given openly.

LETTER FROM JOHN STUART MILL, M.P.

To the Editor of 'THE READER,' *April* 29, 1865.

THIS pamphlet is a defence of the ballot, or rather an answer to the objections to it. The writer is evidently a man of intelligence and knowledge, and accustomed to discussion. It is always fortunate when disputed questions are treated, not in a rhetorical, but in a dialectical, spirit. The pamphlet contains incidentally many true and useful thoughts, and some others which excite surprise that the writer can have gone through the process of putting them on paper without perceiving their untenableness. To the present reviewer—who must be understood as speaking for himself only—the discussion appears, as to its main object, a failure.

The arguments for and against the ballot are so trite and familiar, that the world is excusably tired of them. But in the answers to them there is still room for novelty, and it is in these that the main stress of the practical controversy lies. The author of the pamphlet directs his principal efforts against one of the anti-ballot arguments, which he is quite right in regarding as the strongest—namely, that the franchise is a trust for the public, and the voter should be responsible to the public for the use made of it.

There are two ways in which a writer might meet this argument. He might admit the moral responsibility of the elector, and the beneficial effect on his mind of fulfilling his trust under the eye and criticism of those who are interested in its right fulfilment ; but, he might say, the voters are in such a state of helpless dependence—each of them, so to speak, has a tyrant with eyes so fiercely glaring on him—that since his vote, i known to his friends and family, will be known to his master, the salutary influences of honour and shame cannot be admitted without letting in, along with them, the more powerful ones of terror. Darkness is the only element in which the voter can be free to do his duty ; and we must trust, for a good vote, to such spontaneous feelings of conscience and patriotism as may

not need the support of publicity. This would reduce
the question to one of fact, on which every one would
form his own opinion. He who thinks that the electors,
or a large proportion of them, are in this state of compulsory subjection, will probably be a supporter of the ballot;
though even then he ought to ask himself whether this
slavish dependence is likely to last, whether the whole
of the changes now taking place in society do not tend
to its diminution and even extinction. There might be
a good case against its being yet time to abolish the
ballot, if we had always had it, and yet no case in favour
of introducing, for a temporary purpose, a novelty which
when the time comes, for which we ought to be looking,
will be mischievous, and which has a decided tendency
to unfit men for that coming time.

This, however, in our judgment, is the only line of
defence for the ballot which can ever be, to a certain
extent, tenable. The author of the pamphlet has not
chosen this mode. He prefers to reject the principle of
electoral responsibility altogether. He does not deny
the voter to be discharging a duty, for which he is accountable to conscience; on the contrary, a high sense
of duty to the public is always present to the author's
mind. But he thinks that responsibility to public
opinion will seldom operate with much force; that,
when it does, it will as often operate on the wrong
side as on the right; and that the voter is more likely
to vote well if left to his personal promptings, uninfluenced by praise or blame from any one. For, 'if
you place him by the ballot quite beyond the reach of
the improper control of other men, you leave to the
elector no intelligible interest except that of the body

of which he is a member—his interest as a citizen.'
(P. 218.)   It would hardly be fair to hold the author to
this dictum, to which, we are sure, he could not, on consideration, adhere.   Has no elector any private interest
but what other people's bribes or threats create for him?
We will not take advantage, against the author, of his
own exaggerations.   We will give his argument a
liberal construction.   He means, and in many places
says, that, in the absence of other motives to an honest
vote, we may safely rely on the voter's interest as a
citizen ; his share of the public interest.

Now, we venture to say that this motive, in the
common course of things, does not operate at all, or
only in the slightest possible degree, on the mind either
of an elector or of a member of Parliament.   When he
votes honestly, he is thinking of voting honestly, not
of the fraction of a fraction of an interest which he,
as an individual, may have in what is beneficial to the
public.   That minute benefit is not only too insignificant
in amount, but too uncertain, too distant, and too hazy,
to have any real effect on his mind.   His motive, when
it is an honourable one, is the desire to do right.   We
will not term it patriotism or moral principle, in order
not to ascribe to the voter's state of mind a solemnity
that does not belong to it.   But he votes for a particular
man or measure because he thinks it the right thing to
do, the proper thing for the good of the country.   Once
in a thousand times, as in a case of peace and war, or
of taking off taxes, the thought may cross him that he
shall save a few pounds or shillings in his year's expenditure if the side he votes for prevails. ·But these
cases are few, and, even in them, the interested motive

is not the prevailing one.   It is possible, indeed, that
he or his class may have a private interest acting in
the same direction with the public interest, as a man
who has speculated for a fall in corn has an interest in
a good harvest; and this may determine his conduct.
But, in that case, it is the private interest that actuates
him, not his share of the public interest.

Since, then, the real motive which induces a man to
vote honestly is, for the most part, not an interested
motive in any form, but a social one, the point to be
decided is, whether the social feelings connected with
an act, and the sense of social duty in performing it,
can be expected to be as powerful when the act is done
in secret, and he can neither be admired for disinterested, nor blamed for mean and selfish, conduct. But
this question is answered as soon as stated.   When, in
every other act of a man's life which concerns his duties
to others, publicity and criticism ordinarily improve his
conduct, it cannot be that voting for a member of Parliament is the single case in which he will act better
for being sheltered against all comment.

The author, indeed, says with truth, and it is his
strongest point, that public opinion is itself one of the
misleading influences.   In the first place, the public
opinion nearest to the voter may be that of his own
class, and may side with, instead of counteracting, the
class interest.   Besides, the opinion of the general
public has its aberrations, too, and its most violent
action is apt to be its worst.   'At periods of political
excitement, the practical sense to an elector of the
phrase, "Responsibility to public opinion," is too often
this: Go up to that polling-booth, and at your peril,

vote for any candidate, but the popular candidate.'
(P. 249.) Such cases of physical violence are not what
we have here to consider. If voters are liable to be
mobbed, and if the state of society, as at Rome in the
time of Cicero, is so lawless that the public authorities
cannot protect them, *cadit quæstio*, the ballot is indispensable: though, in that case, even the ballot is a
feeble protection. We are for leaving the voter open
to the penalties of opinion, but not to those of brute
force. The author overlooks what, under this limitation, is the most important feature of the case; he supposes that, if public opinion acts on the elector at all,
it must act by dictating his vote. When it is violently
exerted, it does so; but its more ordinary operation
consists in making the voter more careful to act up to
his own sincere opinion. It operates through the quiet
comments of relatives, neighbours, and companions;
noting instances of variance .between professions and
conduct, or in which a selfish private purpose or a personal grudge prevails over public duty. In countries
used to free discussion, it is only in times of fierce
public contention that a man is really disliked for voting
in conformity to the opinion he is known to hold. If
he is reproached even by opponents, it is for something
paltry in the motive; and, if there is a paltry motive,
it is generally no recondite one, but such as the opinion
of those who know him can easily detect, and therefore
may be able to restrain.

   The author deems it a fallacy to distinguish between
the election of members of a club and that of members
of Parliament on the ground that the voters in a club
have no public duty. They have a duty, he says, to

the members of the club. This we altogether dispute.
A club is a voluntary association, into which people
enter for their individual pleasure, and are not accountable to one another. What is there wanted is, that
each should declare by his vote what is agreeable to
himself; whatever has then a majority is proved to be
agreeable to the majority, and whoever dislikes it can
leave the association. But if we were all born members
of a club, and had no means, except emigration, of
exchanging our club for any other, then, indeed, the
voter would really be bound to consult the interests of
the other members, the case would be assimilated to
that of an election to Parliament, and the ballot, accordingly, would be objectionable.

There is no room to follow the writer through all his
arguments, but we cannot leave unnoticed the answer
he makes to the objection that the ballot would lead to
lying. To this he replies, that lies are of very different
degrees of criminality; that there are many greater
moral delinquencies than 'the lie of legitimate self-
defence;' that a dishonest vote, given from a selfish
motive, is worse; that such a vote ought to be called a
falsehood; and that to think so rigorously of the mere
breach of verbal truth, and so gently of a grave violation of public duty, is shallow and false morality. In
all this we heartily concur; but the fact remains, that
the majority of mankind do feel the lie an offence and a
degradation, and do not so feel respecting the breach
of public duty. We would gladly make them think a
dishonest vote as bad as a lie, but it is to be feared
we should only succeed in making them think a lie no
worse than a dishonest vote. When people have only a

few of the moral feelings they ought to have, there is the more danger in weakening those few. This is a truth which many moral saws in general circulation overlook. We are often told, for example, that an equivocation is as bad as a lie. It is well for mankind that everybody is not of this opinion, and that not all who will equivocate will lie. For the temptation to equivocate is often almost irresistible; indeed, the proposition that everything which can be termed an equivocation is necessarily condemnable, is only true in those cases and those relations in life in which it is a duty to be absolutely open and unreserved. But to confine ourselves to what is really culpable: a person may be a habitual equivocator of a bad kind, he may have no scruple at all in implying what is not true, and yet, if when categorically questioned he shrinks from an express falsehood, this ultimate hold on him makes it still possible for his fellow-creatures to trust his word. Let no one underrate the importance of what mankind would gain if the precise literal meaning of men's assertions could be kept conformable to fact. There may be much unworthy cunning and treachery notwithstanding, but the difference for all human purposes is immense between him who respects that final barrier and those who overleap it.

Did space permit, we might point out some cases in which the author, though habitually candid, yields to the temptation of caricaturing an opponent's argument; as in charging a writer (pp. 238 and 257) with arguing as if all votes, given under the shelter of the ballot, would be base or selfish, when the only thing asserted, or needed, was that some would. But we prefer to quote

X

a passage which tells strongly against the writer, and in favour of our own case : ' A century ago, before the virtuous example of the first William Pitt had made it dishonourable in members of Parliament to hold their votes at the disposal of the dispensers of the public money, it might almost have been a question whether the incontestable advantages of publicity were not too dearly bought at the cost of that mass of political turpitude which it would have been possible, by means of the ballot, to sweep from within the walls of Parliament' (p. 230). If, at the time spoken of, our ancestors, to get rid of this mass of turpitude, had introduced the ballot into the House of Commons, they would have done the exact parallel of what we should do if we adopted it in parliamentary elections. And ought not the fact that all this profligacy has been got rid of without the ballot to be a lesson to us for the other case ? We see that the progress of the public conscience could and did, in the space of a single generation, correct political immoralities more gross and mischievous than those which now remain, and apparently harder to remove, because affecting the *élite*, socially speaking, of the nation. Such an example in times when the public conscience was much less alive, and its improvement far less rapid than now, ought to reassure us, to say the least, as to the necessity of the ballot, and should deter us from putting on the badge of slavery at the very time when a few more steps and a very little additional effort will land us in complete freedom.

J. S. M.

REPLY TO THE ABOVE LETTER.

Reprinted from 'THE READER' *of May 27, 1865.*

SIR,—I ask your permission to be allowed to make a few observations in reply to an article on a pamphlet written by me entitled 'Public Responsibility and Vote by Ballot, by an Elector.' The article in question appeared in 'The Reader' of April 29, and as it was signed with the initials 'J. S. M.,' I presume I may take it for granted that it was from the pen of Mr. John Stuart Mill. The object of my pamphlet was to defend the practice of secret voting, and Mr. Mill has prefaced his strictures upon it by the following short summary of the line of defence which I had adopted :—

'The author rejects the principle of electoral responsibility altogether. He does not deny the voter to be discharging a duty for which he is accountable to conscience; on the contrary, a high sense of duty to the public is always present to the author's mind. But he thinks that responsibility to public opinion will seldom operate with much force; that, when it does, it will as often operate on the wrong side as on the right; and that the voter is more likely to vote well if left to his personal promptings, uninfluenced by praise or blame from any one. For, "if you place him by the ballot quite beyond the reach of the improper control of other men, you leave to the elector no intelligible interest except that of the body of which he is a member—his interest as a citizen."'

Now, I must begin by saying that I prefer to describe in my own words the line of defence which I have

X 2

adopted; not that Mr. Mill's description of it is incorrect, but that it is wanting in that completeness and precision which is required to enable a reader, who takes an interest in the subject, to enter upon the question with a clear perception of the points on which the controversy turns. My description, then, would be this :—

I reject the principle of electoral responsibility altogether. I do not deny that the voter is discharging a duty for which he is accountable to conscience ; on the contrary, a high sense of duty to the public is always present to my mind. But I believe that, if you place the elector, by the ballot, quite beyond the reach of the improper control of other men, you leave to him no intelligible interest except that of the body of which he is a member, his interest as a citizen. That when interest and duty do not run counter to each other, you may safely rely upon a man's doing his duty to the best of his ability. That nothing will be gained, but rather the contrary, by making him responsible to public opinion. That such responsibility, at periods of political excitement—when it is very difficult to resist its power, and when the consequences of a mistake may be very mischievous—will as often operate on the wrong side as on the right. That at *no* period will it operate as a check on unworthy motives, because the vote does not furnish any sure ground on which to judge of the motive. That the public cannot be trusted to pass sound moral verdicts on the intrinsic goodness or badness of the vote considered apart from the motive ; and that if it could be so trusted, those verdicts would be as extensively and usefully impressed upon the electoral mind whether the votes of *individual* electors were known or remained

unknown to the public. I think that, if this view of
the case be correct (that if the public cannot be trusted
to pronounce rightly upon the honest vote, and has no
sure method of detecting the dishonest one), then there
is absolutely no advantage in making *individual* electors
responsible to public opinion, to be set against those
disadvantages of open voting which are admitted on all
hands; that the evil of making known *individual* votes
to persons—whether landlords, employers, moneyed men,
or mobs—who have not the virtue to abstain from making
a bad use of the power that knowledge gives them, is,
in that case, an uncompensated evil.

I may, perhaps, be told that the important point is,
not what I *proposed* to prove, but what I *succeeded* in
proving. But I think both points are important. Possibly not one in fifty of those who have read Mr. Mill's
article may have read the pamphlet which it criticizes;
and not one of the forty-nine who have not read it can
reasonably be expected to read it, if they are led to
believe that the author aims only at proving something
which, when proved, does not dispose of the question at
issue. But, in a controversy, it is essential to a fair
judgment that both sides should be heard.

Mr. Mill, having quoted from the pamphlet the
following sentence—'If you place him by the ballot
quite beyond the reach of the improper control of other
men, you leave to the elector no intelligible interest
except that of the body of which he is a member, his
interest as a citizen'—makes this remark upon it: 'It
would hardly be fair to hold the author to this dictum,
to which, we are sure, he could not, on consideration,
adhere. Has no elector any private interest but what

other people's bribes or threats create for him? We
will not take advantage, against the author, of his own
exaggeration—we will give his argument a liberal construction. He means, and in many places says, that,
in the absence of other motives to an honest vote, we
may safely rely on the voter's interest as a citizen—his
share of the public interest.' Now, I neither plead
guilty to Mr. Mill's charge of exaggeration, nor do I
altogether accept his liberal construction of my meaning. The sentence he quotes seems to me to be one of
two things, either a denial of plain facts or a truism.
If you separate the sentence from the context, and
ignore the fact that it occurs in the course of a discussion on modes of voting at elections, it is plainly
false; if you take it in subordination to that fact, it is
plainly true. To place the elector quite beyond the
improper influence of other men, will not, if he is a
shopkeeper, make it less his private interest to increase
the number of his customers; but it will make it quite
impossible for him to make his vote subservient to that
end, or to any other purely private end. In one way,
the votes of parliamentary electors are made, in every
variety of form and degree, subservient to purely private
ends; that is, through the operation, on the minds of
other men, of a desire to reward a favourable, and to
punish an adverse, vote. The history of elections in
England furnishes us, year by year, with a constant
supply of examples of that deplorable fact. But I know
of no other way in which an elector's vote can be made
to promote his purely private interest. I can conceive
no other way, and Mr. Mill tells us of none. Mr. Mill,
indeed, tells us that an elector may give his vote from

private pique, or from irrational caprice or prejudice ; but he can scarcely mean to include such feelings as those under the term *private interests*. He is not, at all events, entitled to call upon me to do so, because I carefully distinguished between the two, and specifically and separately considered the operation of irrational or unworthy feelings existing in the breast of an elector, showing that open voting in no degree tended to check them. I dealt in the same way with what are called class interests, carefully distinguishing between the elector's purely private interest (his interest, that is, as an individual, apart from any interest he may have in common with other men) from his interest as a member of a class. I admitted that, in so far as the class has interests opposed to those of the community at large, an individual member of the class may be said to have selfish private interests. I admitted that his share in those private class interests might influence his vote, even though the law should have placed him quite beyond the improper control of other men. But then I showed—what is sufficiently evident—that selfish class interests are rather strengthened than weakened by responsibility to public opinion; the public which has practically most influence on a man being that of the persons with whom he habitually associates. It follows from what precedes that, without denying the accuracy, as far as it goes, of Mr. Mill's liberal construction of my meaning, I cannot be altogether satisfied with it ; for, whereas it supposes me to contend for no more than this—viz. that, in the absence of other motives to an honest vote, reliance may be placed on a voter's interest as a citizen—I do in fact contend for much more than this, endeavouring to show that this interest—which is inseparable from that of his fellow-citizens—not only affords to the elector a *sufficient*, but that it affords the *only* motive to an honest vote; and that the influence on which Mr. Mill relies to give additional force to that motive—viz. the sense of responsibility to public opinion — must, of necessity, fail to perform what he expects from it.[1]

When an elector has been protected by the ballot from all improper external control, the question as to what passes or does not pass through his mind when he gives his vote seems to me to be a very unimportant one. I agree with Mr. Mill, that probably not one man in a hundred will make a calculation of his own par-

---

[1] There are four distinct kinds of interests or feelings, and only four, which can operate on the vote of an elector :—

1st. His private interest, apart from any interest he has in common with other men—such, for example, as the interest of a shopkeeper in securing the custom of a wealthy candidate; the interest of a tenant-at-will in standing well with his landlord, or the interest of a voter in obtaining money for his vote.

2nd. The interest he has, in common with other men belonging to the same class as himself, such as was—years ago—the interest of a landowner in the Corn Law; or the interest of a cotton manufacturer in the prohibition of the exportation of machinery.

3rd. His irrational prejudices, caprices, and stupidities.

4th. His interest as a citizen in the good government of the country in which he lives.

What I affirm is this—viz. that, by secret voting, you produce no change, one way or the other, in the No. 3, weaken the No. 2, and altogether extinguish the No. 1 ; thereby, in a very material degree, strengthening the No. 4—the interest leading to the honest vote—which open voting does not strengthen in any way, or in any degree, great or small.

ticular thirty-millionth part of the interest of the nation in good government, and that ninety-nine out of a hundred will vote for a particular man, because they think it is for the good of the country and the right thing to do. This, I dare say, is the account a respectable ten-pound householder would give of the matter, if you were to question him about it. But when a man talks of a thing as being the right thing to do, his words are not necessarily the words of a parrot, nor his mind a blank sheet of paper. He has probably thought over the matter many times in his life, and has a general idea, deviating in substance very little from the truth, of the House of Commons, of the duties of its members, of the kind of men who are most likely to perform the duties well—viz. men who are reputed to be wise, honest, diligent—of it being a right thing to vote for such men, and of his—the elector's—particular interest in the matter being the same as that of his fellow-citizens. What calculation he may make when he goes up to the poll is a matter of indifference. The important thing is that, under the ballot, he has, *in fact*, no interest in the matter but the *general* interest, and will give his vote—consciously or unconsciously—*under the influence of that fact*. Mr. Mill says that the motive is a social motive, and I have no objection so to consider it. But when he goes on to ask whether the sense of social duty in performing an act can be expected to be as powerful when the act is done in secret, and he, the actor, can neither be admired for disinterested, nor blamed for mean and selfish, conduct, I meet his question by another, and maintain that *my* question must be answered before it is possible to give any answer to *his*.

Will the knowledge of the vote enable the dispensers of
the admiration and the blame—to wit, the public—to distinguish between the disinterested votes and the selfish
votes ?   In other words, does the vote of an elector bear
upon its face the good or bad motive which dictated it ?

On the question whether the principle which has
led to the adoption of secret voting at clubs is applicable
to the case of parliamentary elections Mr. Mill makes
the following observations : ' The author deems it a
fallacy to distinguish between the election of members
of a club and that of members of Parliament on the
ground that the voters in a club have no public duty.
They have a duty, he says, to the members of the club.
This we altogether dispute.   A club is a voluntary
association, into which people enter for their individual
pleasure, and are not accountable to one another.
What is there wanted is, that each should declare by
his vote what is agreeable to himself.'   Let us test Mr.
Mill's view of the matter by examples.   I will take the
Political Economy Club, which is a voluntary association.
A and B are proposed as members.   S has to choose
between them.   A is a distinguished professor of the
science, whose writings are read with admiration all
over Europe.   B is an amiable and entertaining man,
with very slender pretensions to the title of political
economist.   The acknowledged purpose of the club
being the promotion of truth in political economy, is
not S morally bound to vote for A in preference to B,
on precisely the same principle on which, as a parliamentary elector, he is bound to vote for the candidate
whom he thinks most competent to the discharge of the
duties of a legislature ?   I would ask a similar question

in the case of a political club, a literary club, a military or naval club, a chess club, a club of merchants and bankers, &c. Every voluntary association has some common object of greater or lesser importance. Even though the object should not go beyond agreeable social intercourse between educated men, that object would scarcely be promoted by laying it down that each member was expected to make himself happy and comfortable in his own way. Vote by ballot in clubs does not mean that there is no common object to be promoted, and consequently no duty to be performed; it means that the common object will be better promoted and the duty will be better performed by secret than by open voting. The practice of ballot in clubs does not affirm that the members are under no obligations; but that there is no serious temptation to ignore the obligations, except from a cause which secret voting will remove; that cause being the dislike to give offence to particular members of the club who happen to take a personal interest in the success of particular candidates. . Vote by ballot at parliamentary elections means something precisely analogous to this. The common object may be more important in the one case than in the other. The good government of England is more important than chess, perhaps more important than political economy or literature; but there is, in every case, a common object of some kind or other, and a duty arising out of it. Mr. Mill argues that a citizen who should suffer by the misgovernment brought about by the bad votes of electors would have no remedy, or no remedy but to abandon his country; whereas the man whose enjoyment of his club has been destroyed by the introduction of members who are displeasing to him, has his remedy, and may exchange his club for another; and that this affords a reason for making parliamentary electors responsible, which does not apply to members of clubs. The distinction, however, seems to me to be more apparent than real; and a member of the Athenæum—if that club should receive a very large infusion of fox-hunters and members of the turf—would scarcely consider the proposed remedy sufficient. He would seek in vain for a second Athenæum to console him for the loss of the first. I may be told, perhaps, that it is trifling with the subject to talk of the members of the Athenæum, under the ballot, bringing fox-hunters into the club; but I, on my side, think it is trifling with the subject to suppose that parliamentary electors, under the ballot, would send uneducated or disreputable men to Westminster. I admit that there is a phenomenon affording a presumption against my view of this matter, which Mr. Mill may properly call upon me to explain. ' If,' he may say, ' the principle is the same in both cases, if the ballot would operate to the same beneficial end at the polling booth as it does in the club room, how comes it that Englishmen of the highly accomplished class—of the class which gives the tone to political opinion—universally adopt the ballot in clubs, and that nine out of ten of them reject the proposal to introduce it at parliamentary elections, with a good deal of-indignation and contempt?' I tender my explanation with some reluctance, for I have no desire to fly in the face of good society; but I cannot, of course, allow a presumption which has no real weight to tell heavily against me in this discussion.

The truth, then, is, that the class in question has a strong personal interest in the matter, and their judgment, being, of course, biassed by their interest, is not to be trusted. This again requires explanation. When a ballot takes place at a club, all that happens is, that a new member is added to the *general body*; but the result of a parliamentary election is very different; it adds one—or more than one, as the case may be—to a *small body governing the general body*, invested for that purpose with political power and patronage, and holding in its hands the purse-strings of the nation. To be one of that chosen band is of course an object of intense desire, and it seems to follow, in accordance with the well-known principles of human nature, that the class from whose ranks that chosen band is chiefly recruited, and which obtains the largest share of the good things which governing bodies always have at their disposal, should be hostile to any proposal which has for its object to render electors more independent than they now are of the control of the more wealthy and powerful sections of that class. The position of the territorial aristocracy of England in relation, first to the large class of tenants at will—for whom the protection of the ballot is chiefly sought—and in relation, secondly, to the large class of educated aspirants for employment in the various departments of the State, is too well understood, and affords too obvious an explanation of fashionable opinion on the subject of the ballot, to make it necessary that I should pursue the subject into its details.

In his remarks upon that passage of my pamphlet which replied to the charge that the ballot would lead to lying, Mr. Mill raises more than one important ques-

tion of practical morality. But they open too wide a
field of discussion to be entered upon within the compass of a letter like the present. I will make only one
observation on this part of the subject. When Mr. Mill
contends that open voting ought to be maintained, lest
the popular reverence for the truth should be weakened
by the practice of verbal lying, he seems to forget that
the verbal lie of the elector, in defence of his independence, would not be a *necessary*, but only a *contingent*
consequence of the ballot; contingent upon conduct
by other men making defence necessary. Is Mr. Mill
satisfied that the contingency would arise? Take the
case of the great landowner. If vote by ballot became
the law of the land, two courses would be open to him :
one, to accept that new law in its spirit, and scrupulously to abstain from all encroachments, direct or indirect, on the newly acquired electoral independence of
his tenants ; the other, to enter upon a course of proceeding having for its object to retain his control over
their votes, in contravention of the spirit of that new
law. Mr. Mill's argument virtually assumes that he
will take the latter of these courses, and that assumption seems to me tc be altogether unwarranted. There
are different degrees and different kinds of immorality.
A man may be capable of one degree or one kind, and
not of another. A landlord may be morally capable of
the neglect of duty—if it can be so called—which is
involved in not taking active steps to secure the electoral
independence of his tenantry against a system which
substantially transfers their votes to himself—especially
if he can, with truth, allege that the law, by refusing
to meddle with the system, seems to give a sort of

indirect sanction to it—and yet be utterly incapable of
attempting, by a miserable process of inquisitorial persecution, repugnant to the feelings of a gentleman, to
cheat his tenants out of the intended protection of a law
enacted for the express purpose of securing their independence.

Mr. Mill thinks that a certain historical fact, to
which I advert in my pamphlet—that of political corruption having disappeared from within the walls of
Parliament in the course of a single generation, without
any assistance from the ballot—ought to reassure us in
regard to the corruptions of our electoral system. In so
far as bribery is concerned, this hope may not, perhaps,
be altogether futile. Public opinion has happily become
so much less lenient to pecuniary immorality at elections
than it was forty years ago, that another forty years
may possibly see the end of it. Still, if it be possible
to put an end to a practice which is both a national
calamity and a national disgrace, thoroughly, at once,
and for ever, why wait forty years, or twenty years, or
one? The disappearance of corruption from within the
walls of Parliament is not, however, an example pertinent to the case of electoral *intimidation*; and there
the prospect is less reassuring. Granting that the tendency of upper-class opinion is favourable to a gradual
relaxation in the pressure of territorial influence against
the independence of agricultural tenants—of which I am
unable to see any signs—yet unfortunately the remedy
comes too late. Immense mischief has already been
done, which can with difficulty be undone. The coercion
of fifty years has produced its natural fruit, has, to a
great extent, rooted out rebellious tendencies; and the

existing condition is much less one of unavailing resistance to the power than one of contented submission to it. The submission is, no doubt, an evil of a different kind; but, in the long run, and viewed in relation to its permanent effect on national character, it is perhaps the more injurious of the two. Even under the ballot the recovery would probably be slow from that state of degrading insensibility to public duties; but under the open-voting system, recovery seems hopeless. The liberation of the voter from external control is the first and necessary step to his perception of a political duty and his appreciation of a political privilege.

Mr. Mill says that 'he is for leaving the voter open to the penalties of opinion, but not to those of brute force.' But why leave him open to any penalties? Why punish a man, or why reward him, for answering a plain question according to the best of his knowledge? He is called upon by his country to exercise, in conjunction with some hundreds or thousands of his fellow-citizens, an act of the judgment—to choose freely between A and B; and thereupon Mr. Mill says to him: We will protect your decision from physical violence, but not from moral violence; from blows, but not from persecution; from the coercion of the strong arm, but not from the coercion of the bitter tongue. We will shield you from the mob, but we will not shield you from invective, or ridicule, or the imputation of unworthy motives. This seems to me to be not only in the highest degree cruel and unjust, but to be in entire contradiction to those principles of liberty which Mr. Mill has, in other works, enforced by unanswerable arguments.

Mr. Mill thinks that 'the more ordinary operation of public opinion consists in making the voter more careful to act up to his own sincere opinion; that it operates through the quiet comments of relatives, neighbours, and companions noting instances of variance between professions and conduct, or in which a selfish private purpose or a personal grudge prevails over public duty.' I reply, that the friends and relatives are likely to fall into great mistakes and exercise a very mischievous influence by commenting on these things. They are not competent judges of another person's motives. The *argumentum ad hominem* is altogether unsuited to the case. Let them argue A's claim to the support of the constituency as much as they like. I, as an elector, will listen to them patiently, will consider all they have said, and will then decide for myself; but I beg they will not meddle with my motives, of which they can know nothing. Such interference is simply impertinent. I am more interested in the preservation of my political consistency than they can be. Take the strongest case, that of a personal grudge. Does Mr. Mill mean to lay it down that I am deserving of reproof if I vote against a candidate who has injured or offended me ?. Suppose I sincerely believe him to be the least good of the three candidates. Am I to vote for him in order to show that I am superior to the passion of revenge ? Is this a fit mode of discharging my duty to the State ? Mr. Mill is the last person who would maintain such a doctrine.

Allow me to say, in conclusion, that Mr. Mill is mistaken in supposing that I have in any instance ' yielded to the temptation of caricaturing the argu-

Y

ments of my opponents.' If I have misrepresented
any passage on which I have commented, it has been
unintentionally. I have either misunderstood his meaning, or not clearly expressed my own. If I were immoral enough to play tricks with an opponent's arguments, I am not rash enough to make the attempt with
such a writer as Mr. Mill. Something must be left to
the intelligence of readers. It might be said, for
example, that, in the present letter, I am misleading
my reader by not adverting to the fact that there are
large landowners whose tenants are holders of long leases.
But precautions against misconception may be carried
too far. No reader of ordinary intelligence requires to
be told that, when large landowners are spoken of in
connection with the subject of undue influence at
elections, the term is not meant to extend to those
whose tenantry hold their farms on conditions which
exempt them from the possibility of undue influence.

I am, &c.,

HENRY ROMILLY.

FURTHER OBSERVATIONS ON MR MILL'S LETTER.

An advocate of open voting has one great advantage
over his opponent, which is this, that one of his arguments being the necessity of giving to the public an
opportunity of commenting on the elector's vote, he
seems to be in a special way the friend of free discussion ; whereas his opponent, who denies that it is either
necessary or desirable to give the public any such opportunity, is presumed to be an enemy of free discussion.

So far, however, from admitting the accuracy of this presumption, I profess myself both an advocate of secret voting, and as firm a friend as Mr. Mill himself to freedom of discussion, perfect freedom of discussion, on all topics of public interest. In a State which enjoys the benefit of Constitutional Government, there are no two topics of greater public interest than the comparative merits of candidates for the national representation, and the rules by which, either generally or on particular occasions, electors should be guided in their preference of one candidate to others. The more discussion there is on these points in books, pamphlets, newspapers, at public meetings, in private society, even in the family circle, the better. The more people think, and talk, and argue on such subjects the more likely is it that sound views of them will prevail. Neither the amount nor the freedom of such discussion is directly affected by the mode of taking the votes. A man's being compelled by law to give his vote in such a way that no other man shall know how he has given it, will not deprive him of eyes, or ears, or understanding. He may read, and listen, and reflect, and ask questions, under the one system as much as under the other. Secret voting will neither stop discussion, nor make any class of electors less capable of profiting by it.[1]

---

[1] In England, more or less, *open* voting *does* stop discussion ; or—to speak more exactly—it does, in a somewhat numerous class of cases, render the mind of the elector inaccessible to discussion on the one question on which it is important that discussion should not be stopped by a foregone conclusion. I mean the question of the elector's duty to the public. I have gone fully into that matter at page 59 of the pamphlet, and it

Why then, I shall be asked, if you are such a friend of
discussion, do you object to your vote being discussed?
I will tell you why. I object to your discussing a
private question under pretence of discussing a *public*
one. ' *Which is the fitter man to represent the country,*
A or B?' That is an important public question which
cannot be discussed too fully and freely. ' *Is John
Thompson to be praised or to be blamed for having given
his vote to A?*' That is a private question, the discussion of which may, in various ways, be hurtful to John
Thompson, and can be beneficial to no one, because the
facts which are necessary to a fair discussion of it cannot, under any system of voting, be certainly and completely ascertained. To discuss it is, at the best, a
piece of useless impertinence, and at the worst a piece
of cruel tyranny. The merits or the demerits of the
vote for A may be discussed in perfect freedom, and
with all possible benefit, without connecting it with the
name of John Thompson. If you insist upon connecting it with his name, it can only be because, under
pretence of passing judgment on his motives, of which
you can have no certain knowledge, you wish to control
his choice; to take away from him the right of private
judgment, which you conferred, or professed to confer
upon him when you invited him to give an opinion; in

would therefore be waste of time to go into it again. It may,
however, be summed up in a very few words. When an elector
has sold his vote for money, or when he holds it at the disposal
of some person on whom his worldly prosperity depends—the
publicity of the vote holding him fast to his wretched bargain—
arguments founded on public interests are too plainly inappli-
cable to his case, and remind him too painfully of the degrading
position in which he stands, to be listened to with patience.

other words, when you gave him the suffrage. John
Thompson may be a man with a good deal of moral
courage and in an independent position in life; in which
case he will treat your comments on his vote with indifference, perhaps with a little wholesome contempt.
Or he may be independent in position, without having
the moral courage; in which case he will perhaps be
worried or ridiculed out of his real opinion. Or his
position in life may be such as to place him substantially
in your power; in which case—unless he is one of the
small band of men who are ready for opinion's sake to
brave persecution—he will of course, right or wrong,
vote as he knows you expect him to vote.[2]   The
holders of the ' electoral-responsibility-theory' call this
' *the wholesome influence of public opinion.*'   It seems
to me to be tyranny; the tyranny of powerful men over
dependants; or the tyranny of society over dissentients

---

[2] ' But surely,' it may be said, ' comment on John Thompson's vote for A may be made in the spirit of a fair candid
appeal to his understanding, an appeal dictated by a pure love
of truth and regard to the public interest.'   True; but what I
contend for is, that his understanding will not be less open to
such an appeal, nor will the appeal itself be less convincing,
because its author (let me call him Verax), having been shut out
by law from all knowledge of individual votes, has been unable
to give to his arguments any personal application to John
Thompson; and although it may not be in the nature of Verax
to deal with such a subject otherwise than in a spirit of truth
and candour, there are those—too numerous, unhappily—who,
when such personal application is open to them, are led by their
prejudices, their party spirit, their love of power, or their
private interests, to carry their treatment of the subject out of
the domain of argument into that of persecution, more or less
irritating or cruel.

from prevailing opinions. No writer in Europe has raised his voice against it so powerfully as Mr. Mill has done in his admirable treatise ' On Liberty.' I will quote one out of many passages, all breathing the same spirit. ' Like other tyrannies, the tyranny of the majority was at first, and is still vulgarly held in dread, chiefly as operating through the acts of the public authorities. But reflecting persons perceived that when society is itself the tyrant—society collectively, over the separate individuals who compose it—its means of tyrannising are not restricted to the acts which it may do by the hands of its political functionaries. Society can and does execute its own mandates ; and if it issues wrong mandates instead of right, or any mandates at all in things with which it ought not to meddle, it practises a social tyranny more formidable than many kinds of political oppression, since, though not usually upheld by such extreme penalties, it leaves fewer means of escape, penetrating much more deeply into the details of life, and enslaving the soul itself. Protection, therefore, against the tyranny of the magistrate is not enough : there needs protection also against the tyranny of the prevailing opinion and feeling ; against the tendency of society to impose, by other means than civil penalties, its own ideas and practices as rules of conduct on those who dissent from them ; to fetter the development, and, if possible, prevent the formation of any individuality not in harmony with its ways, and compel all characters to fashion themselves upon the model of its own. There is a limit to the legitimate interference of collective opinion with individual independence ; and to find that limit, and maintain it against encroachment, is as indispensable to a good condition of human affairs, as protection against political despotism.' [3]

I am aware that these words of Mr. Mill were meant to apply only to the interference of society with the private concerns of men; but I say that they do in truth apply quite as strongly, perhaps more strongly, to the case of the man who is invited by his country to give an opinion on a public question, and is told to do so in perfect freedom. There is no freedom, if society is allowed to step in and say to him, '*Decide so as to please us and we will commend you, decide so as to offend us and we will censure you.*' Who are the people that set up this pretension? They call themselves '*the public,*' and their judgments '*public opinion*;' but, in nine cases out of ten, they are a knot of men, more or less numerous, falsely investing themselves with an imposing name, in order, under the authority of that name, to tyrannise the more securely. In a manufacturing town they are perhaps the Trades Union Committee with its tools and supporters; who, without any breach of the peace, or of the law, will contrive, nevertheless, to make their neighbour's life miserable if he insists upon thinking for himself on the wages question. In the country they are, perhaps, the tradesmen, dependants, and hangers-on of the great territorial magnate. In the metropolis they are, perhaps, what is called *good society*, backed up by the fashionable newspapers. When an elector is told that he is responsible to the world for his vote, this is generally the kind of world to which he is responsible. 'The world, to each individual,' says Mr. Mill in the same treatise from which I have already

[3] Pp. 13 and 14 of Mr. Mill's treatise *On Liberty*, 2nd edit.

quoted, 'means the part of it with which he comes in contact; his party, his sect, his church, his class of society: the man may be called, by comparison, almost liberal and large-minded to whom it means anything so comprehensive as his own country or his own age.' [4] The misfortune is that the *influential* world is that with which he comes into close daily contact; and it is not so easy for the liberal and large-minded elector, under the open-vote system, to induce his *narrow* world to waive its claim upon him, in favour of that *broader* world which represents the spirit of the age and country, and which, on many occasions, he would prefer to take for his guide. So long as he can go conscientiously with his *narrow* world, all is well; but the moment he thinks that they are taking a mistaken or illiberal view, and shows signs of dissent, the party, the sect, the church, or the class of society, as the case may be, is down upon him, each with its appropriate weapon, which is very seldom physical force, but very often something nearly as effective.

More or less, on some point or another, and with different forms of coercion, the interference of '*collective opinion with individual independence*' has existed in all ages. In the present day, an Englishman may with impunity sign his name to a refutation of witchcraft, or give his vote to a dissentient from that doctrine; which is more than he could have done three hundred years ago; but he cannot, with impunity, either at the polling-booth or on the platform, make himself known as an advocate of a highly popular suffrage, on the special ground that it tends to a more equal distribution of

[4] P. 35 of Mr. Mill's treatise *On Liberty*, 2nd edit.

landed property. This is almost as great an outrage on
English upper-class opinion in the nineteenth, as the
denial of witchcraft was on European opinion in the
sixteenth century; and, although the penalty in the
present day is not bodily torture, recent experience has
proved that it may be something very difficult to bear;
misrepresentation, the imputation of unworthy motives,
and a very general indisposition, amongst persons of
the same class in life as the victim, to put a fair and
candid construction on his language and conduct.[5]
There are other instruments at the command of the
holders of prevailing opinions, not so effective, perhaps,
as misrepresentation and unfair criticism, but which
are not without their power; ridicule, for instance,
which, with a certain class of minds, and when unsparingly employed in the service of the same class of
society as that to which the victim belongs, is by no
means an ineffective weapon.   There is no question on
which it has been used so unsparingly and with greater
success than on this very question of the ballot.   When
a noble writer of authority, in an elaborate treatise on
parliamentary government, pronounces it to be needless
to enter into a question which has been completely ex-
hausted; when a great parliamentary leader speaks of
the annual discussion of that question, in the House of
Commons, as of the performance of an annual comedy;
or when the wittiest man of the age speaks of the
greatest advocate of the ballot as of a man who 'would

---

[5] This was written not very long after the appearance of the
celebrated letter of Mr. Cobden to the principal editor of the
Times newspaper, in defence of Mr. Bright.

be an important politician if the world were a chess-
board,' not one in a dozen, of the ordinary run of
educated men, especially of the young, has the courage
to abstain from joining in the laugh, or to avow the
desire which perhaps, to his honour, he really feels, to
weigh the arguments and verify the facts for himself.
The false shame generally gets the better of the desire
for more knowledge; and many a man, who is not
entirely insensible to the love of truth, will yet allow
his mind to settle down into a state of comfortable
acquiescence in doctrines which happen to be convenient, and which are enforced by methods which it is
so troublesome and painful to resist.

If the great majority of prevailing opinions were
well-considered opinions, on which any reasonable
amount of thought had ever been bestowed, there would
be less mischief in this tyranny; but, unfortunately, an
opinion, even in a country like England, will often
become a prevailing opinion from causes which are, in
a very trifling degree, connected with any fair discussion
of its merits. It will have been taken up, perhaps, on
very inadequate grounds, by a favourite statesman or
by a newspaper which happens to be very much in
vogue; at one time it will originate in a panic, at another in some sudden paroxysm of national pride or
jealousy. Once established as a fashionable opinion,
it will derive new strength from the adhesion of those
who habitually take their opinions on trust. Thenceforward it will be invested with all the power and
dignity of a great truth, and not one man in fifty will
have the courage to open his lips against it. Dissentients will be talked down, or sneered down, or

smiled down.[6] Any one who ventures to oppose the
stream will be spoken of as a dealer in paradox, a man
of crochets, one whose vanity it is to be thought original,
&c. &c. Society, strong in superior numbers, will be
always addressing dissentients in the kind of language
which Célimène addressed to Alceste—

> 'Et ne faut-il pas bien que Monsieur contredise ?
> À la commune voix veut-on qu'il se réduise ?
> Et qu'il ne fasse pas éclater en tous lieux
> L'esprit contrariant qu'il a reçu des cieux ?
> Le sentiment d'autrui n'est jamais pour lui plaire ;
> Il prend toujours en main l'opinion contraire ;
> Et penserait paraître un homme du commun,
> Si l'on voyait qu'il fût de l'avis de quelqu'un.'

The man of the minority, if he happens to be en-
dowed with great moral courage, will return laugh for
laugh and sneer for sneer, and manfully stand up for
his opinion; but nine men out of ten, painfully conscious (like Alceste) 'que les rieurs sont contr'eux,'
will bow their heads to the storm and will each make
his little contribution to the apparent unanimity of
public opinion.

Even though it were otherwise—though prevailing
opinions were always on the side of high principle and
good sense—yet no one has so well shown as Mr. Mill
has done, the importance of cultivating in the great
body of the people the habit of thinking for themselves;
of acting or of choosing on reasons conclusive to their
own understandings. It would be difficult to overrate

[6] Let any one who believes this to be an exaggeration call to
mind the treatment which any person, sympathising with the
cause of the North, received at the hands of good society in
England during the early period of the late war in America.

the wisdom of the following observations extracted from the treatise ' On Liberty.'

' The human faculties of perception, judgment, discriminative feeling, mental activity, and even moral preference are exercised only in making a choice. He who does anything because it is the custom, makes no choice. He gains no practice either in discerning or in desiring what is best. The mental and moral, like the muscular powers, are improved only by being used. The faculties are called into no exercise by doing a thing merely because others do it, no more than by believing a thing only because others believe it. If the grounds of an opinion are not conclusive to the person's own reason, his reason cannot be strengthened, but is likely to be weakened by his adopting it : and if the inducements to an act are not such as are consentaneous to his own feelings and character (where affection or the rights of others are not concerned), it is so much done towards rendering his feelings and character inert and torpid, instead, of active and energetic.' [7]

I may perhaps again be reminded that the exercise of the suffrage is a matter which *does* concern the rights or interests of others, and that, throughout his treatise 'On Liberty,' Mr. Mill makes a broad distinction between conduct which does, and conduct which does not, concern other persons. I admit the distinction ; but, although Mr. Mill lays it down that, for the latter kind of conduct, a man *is not* amenable to society, he nowhere lays it down that there are no exceptions to the rule that for the former he *is* amenable to society.[8] On the

[7] Pp. 105 and 106.

[8] Indeed, at page 25 of his treatise, Mr. Mill admits that

contrary, his essay is full of such exceptions.   One
whole chapter is devoted to a most important class of
cases, which do, in fact, form an exception to that rule ;
I mean the chapter on the Liberty of Thought and Discussion.   An article in a newspaper or a review concerns
other people as much as a vote at an election.   In the
opinion of society the vote may have been given for the

'there are often good reasons for not holding him to this responsibility.' He goes on to say that 'these reasons must arise
from the special expediencies of the case ; either because it is a
kind of case in which' the individual 'is on the whole likely to
act better when left to his own discretion than when controlled
in any way in which society have it in their power to control
him, or because the attempt to exercise control would produce
other evils, greater than those which it would prevent.'
    The case of the individual elector seems to me to be precisely
a case of this kind.   He is called upon for a judgment on a
simple matter of opinion (the comparative fitness of two or more
persons for the discharge of certain public duties).   Society has
no power of controlling him in any way which shall, with any
certainty, influence that judgment beneficially.   The *moral
coercion of public opinion*' can be applied to him in no possible
way which shall not weaken his powers of discrimination and
independence of character, and which shall not let in upon him
a coercion of quite another kind—that of individuals or bodies
of men who have passions and private interests very different
from those of society at large.
    I do not deny that, if the parliamentary electors of Great
Britain were a *representative* body, subject, at certain recurring
periods, to re-election by the bulk of the people, one of ' *the
special expediencies of the case*' might be to give to the people,
through the publicity of the vote, the opportunity of reconsider-
ing the fitness of each individual elector to be continued in his
responsible office.   But, inasmuch as this is no part of the
British Constitution, there is no such special reason for maintaining the publicity of the vote in Great Britain.

wrong man, and the article may contain doctrines which are false or dangerous. One principal purpose of that chapter of Mr. Mill's book is to deny the right of society to carry their resistance to doctrines which they deem false or dangerous, out of the domain of free discussion, into that of personal penalty. How, without inconsistency, will he maintain that right in the case of the elector's vote? How will he call upon the voter for his name on the plea that it is necessary to protect society from foolish or dishonest votes, and yet refuse to call upon the journalist for his name, as a protection to society from false or dangerous doctrines? How support the right of private judgment, against the tyranny of prevailing opinions, in favour of the man who thrusts his doctrines uninvited on the world, and yet refuse to support that right in favour of the man who has been called upon by his country for a free judgment, which, without neglect of a public duty, he cannot withhold?

The spirit of that admirable chapter on the Liberty of Thought and Discussion may be expressed in a single sentence; *Attack the opinion, but do not punish the man*; and when society drags forth one man or a hundred men from a list of voters, and holds them up to obloquy or ridicule for some vote which it believes to be wrong or ridiculous, society is, in truth, following up dissent by punishment, just as much as when a Government meets the argument in favour of some doctrine which it believes to be politically immoral or dangerous, by a public prosecution. I grant that ridicule is not so hard to bear as imprisonment; but I deny, and, if I understand him right, Mr. Mill denies that punishment,

of any kind, in any degree, direct or indirect, whether
at the hands of a Government or at the hands of society,
can be justly or beneficially applied to an expression of
opinion.

If this is admitted in the case of the unsolicited
opinion of the writer in a newspaper, how can it be
denied in the case of the solicited opinion of a parliamentary elector? If society will not allow of anony-
mous voting, lest the elector should cease to be personally
responsible, on what principle does it allow of anony-
mous writing? The risk to society is at least as great
from false doctrines as from bad votes; and the doctrines
are at least as likely as the votes to be influenced by the
dread of what society has it in its power to inflict.

In conclusion, let me implore the honest enemies of
the ballot[9] to disabuse their minds of the notion, that
the question between open and secret voting is a very
simple one, which may be settled off-hand, in a few well-
turned sentences, affirmatory of the value of public
responsibility. The responsibility which attaches to
the performance of public duties is not always the
same either in degree or in kind. It is always such
as should be binding on the conscience, but it is not

---

[9] By *honest* enemies of the ballot, I mean both those persons
who do not allow themselves to be influenced in the consideration of this subject, by their knowledge of the fact that the
power and worldly interest of themselves, or of the class to
which they belong, is promoted by the practice of open voting;
and those persons who, having no interest in the matter but
that of the community at large, have no temptation to consider
the question otherwise than on its real merits. It is of course
useless to address arguments to any one who is not honest in
one or other of these senses.

always such as to make publicity necessary or even desirable. The duties of a member of the House of Commons, for example, are such as may be safely and beneficially performed in the presence of the public; but it does not follow that the same thing is true of the duties of an elector. A more important consideration is this, viz. that the responsibility, be it of what kind it may, is reciprocal. Society may charge me with a duty of such a kind, that she may be morally bound to protect me in the performance of it. It may be beset with grave dangers, material and moral; and society cannot, with any regard to decency, call upon me to brave persecution, or to show myself superior to very strong pecuniary temptations, in the discharge of my obligation to her, when she is all the time ignoring her obligations to me.

On the question of the kind and degree of responsibility which attaches to the elector, and of the duty, in the way of protection and forbearance, which society owes to him, there is no work which can be studied with more advantage than that essay 'On Liberty' to which I have so often referred in the course of these observations. Not that, in that essay, Mr. Mill treats directly of those questions; but he lays down, with admirable force and clearness, principles, which must be thoroughly understood and fairly applied, if those questions are to be rightly decided.

One distinction there is, which has been very generally lost sight of, and which lies at the bottom of the whole question; the distinction—if I may be allowed, for shortness, so to call it—between votes and voters; between the intrinsic merits of the vote *per se*, and its merits in particular relation to the particular man who gives it. I am sure that it is as unfit to discuss the second of these questions as it is fit and necessary to discuss the first of them; and that the first may be discussed, in perfect freedom and with great benefit to all parties, without discussing the second. It must, I am sure, be plain to any one who will bestow a moderate amount of thought upon the subject, that the comment on the vote of the individual voter is necessarily either one or the other or both of the two things following; either a superfluous repetition of the discussion of the general question—the comparative claims of the candidates—or a discussion of the voter's motives; and that, on the question of motives, it is impossible that the public should ever possess any such accurate knowledge as is needed to ensure a just sentence.

H. R.

PRINTED BY
SPOTTISWOODE AND CO., NEW-STREET SQUARE
LONDON

Z

MR. MURRAY'S LIST.

LORD BEACONSFIELD'S CORRESPONDENCE WITH HIS SISTER. 1832–1852. This work is a continuation of Lord Beaconsfield's Home Letters, written in 1830–31, which were published in 1885. With Portrait. Cr. 8vo. 10s. 6d.

TIRYNS: A PREHISTORIC PALACE OF THE KINGS OF TIRYNS. Disclosed by Excavations in 1884–85. By HENRY SCHLIEMANN, D.C.L., &c. With Preface and Notes by Professors ADLER and DÖRPFELD. With 188 Lithographs, 24 Coloured Plates, 5 Maps and Plans, and numerous Woodcuts. Crown 4to. 42s.

POPULAR GOVERNMENT: FOUR ESSAYS. I.—PROSPECTS OF POPULAR GOVERNMENT. II.—NATURE OF DEMOCRACY. III.—AGE OF PROGRESS. IV.—CONSTITUTION OF THE UNITED STATES. By Sir HENRY MAINE, K.C.S.I., Author of 'Ancient Law' &c. *Second Edition*. 8vo. 12s.

THE ENDOWMENTS AND ESTABLISHMENT OF THE CHURCH OF ENGLAND. By the late Professor J. S. BREWER, M.A. *Third Edition*. Revised and Edited by LEWIS T. DIBDIN, M.A., Barrister-at-Law. Post 8vo. 6s.

LECTURES ON ECCLESIASTICAL HISTORY, including the ORIGIN AND PROGRESS OF THE ENGLISH REFORMATION FROM WYCLIFFE TO THE GREAT REBELLION. Delivered in the University of Dublin by the late BISHOP FITZGERALD. Edited by WM. FITZGERALD, A.M., and JOHN QUARRY, D.D. With Memoir. 2 vols. 8vo. 21s.

ACROSS THE BRITISH EMPIRE: SOUTH AFRICA, AUSTRALIA, NEW ZEALAND, THE STRAITS SETTLEMENTS, INDIA, THE SOUTH SEA ISLANDS, CALIFORNIA, OREGON, CANADA, &c. By Baron HÜBNER, Membre Associé de l'Institut de France. 2 vols. Crown 8vo.

THE STUDENT'S HISTORY OF MODERN EUROPE; FROM THE FALL OF CONSTANTINOPLE TO THE TREATY OF BERLIN, 1878. By RICHARD LODGE, M.A., Fellow and Tutor of Brazenose College, Oxford. Post 8vo. 7s. 6d.

₊ Forming a New Volume of MURRAY'S STUDENT'S MANUALS.

THE VEGETABLE GARDEN; OR THE EDIBLE VEGETABLES, SALADS, AND HERBS, CULTIVATED IN EUROPE AND AMERICA. By MM. VILMORIN and ANDRIEUX of Paris. An English Edition. With 750 Illustrations. 8vo. 15s. (Uniform with ROBINSON'S 'English Flower Garden.')

A NEW, REVISED, AND POPULAR EDITION OF THE AUTOBIOGRAPHY OF JAMES NASMYTH, Inventor of the Steam Hammer. Edited by SAMUEL SMILES, LL.D. With Portrait and Woodcuts. Small 8vo. 6s. (Uniform with 'Self Help.')

JOHN MURRAY, Albemarle Street.

SYMBOLS AND EMBLEMS OF EARLY AND MEDIÆVAL CHRISTIAN ART. By LOUISA TWINING. With 500 Illustrations from Paintings, Miniatures, Sculptures, &c. Crown 8vo. 12s.

HANDBOOK TO POLITICAL QUESTIONS, WITH THE ARGUMENTS ON EITHER SIDE. By SYDNEY BUXTON. *Sixth Edition.* Enlarged 8vo. 7s. 6d.

THE MOON: CONSIDERED AS A PLANET, A WORLD, AND A SATELLITE. By JAMES NASMYTH, C.E., and JAMES CARPENTER, F.R.A.S. With 26 Plates and numerous Woodcuts. *New and Cheaper Edition.* Medium 8vo. 21s.

A GLOSSARY OF PECULIARLY ANGLO-INDIAN COLLOQUIAL WORDS AND PHRASES; ETYMOLOGICAL, HISTORICAL, AND GEOGRAPHICAL. By Col. YULE, C.B., and ARTHUR BURNELL, Ph.D. Medium 8vo.

POPULAR EDITION; LETTERS OF THE PRINCESS ALICE TO THE QUEEN. With a Memoir by H.R.H. PRINCESS CHRISTIAN. Portrait. Crown 8vo. 7s. 6d.

GLENAVERIL; OR THE METAMORPHOSES: A POEM IN SIX BOOKS. By the EARL OF LYTTON. 2 vols. Fcap. 8vo. 12s.

LIFE OF GENERAL SIR CHARLES NAPIER, G.C.B. By the Hon. WM. NAPIER BRUCE. With Portrait and Maps. Crown 8vo. 12s.

SKETCHES OF THE HISTORY OF CHRISTIAN ART. By the late LORD LINDSAY (Earl of Crawford and Balcarres). *New Edition.* 2 vols. Crown 8vo. 24s.

THE LIBERAL MOVEMENT IN ENGLISH LITERA-TURE. A SERIES OF ESSAYS. By W. J. COURTHOPE, M.A., Editor of 'Pope's Works.' Post 8vo. 6s.

LIFE OF WILLIAM CAREY, D.D., Shoemaker and Missionary, Professor at the College of Fort William, Calcutta. By GEORGE SMITH, LL.D. Portrait and Illustrations. 8vo. 16s.

HOME LETTERS; WRITTEN IN 1830–31. By the late EARL OF BEACONSFIELD. *Second Edition.* Post 8vo. 5s.

LETTERS AND JOURNALS OF THE LATE RIGHT HON. JOHN WILSON CROKER, RELATING TO THE CHIEF POLITICAL AND SOCIAL EVENTS OF THE PRESENT CENTURY. Edited by LOUIS J. JENNINGS. *Second Edition, revised.* Portrait. 3 vols. 8vo. 45s.

LANDSCAPE IN ART, before the Days of CLAUDE and SALVATOR. By JOSIAH GILBERT, Author of 'Cadore; or, Titian's Country' &c. Illustrations. Medium 8vo. 30s.

THE COUNTRY BANKER: HIS CLIENTS, CARES, AND WORK. From the Experience of Forty Years. By GEORGE RAE. *Fifth Edition.* Crown 8vo. 7s. 6d.

JOHN MURRAY, Albemarle Street.

www.ingramcontent.com/pod-product-compliance
Lightning Source LLC
Chambersburg PA
CBHW021757110726
47902CB00006B/1557